Ninety-Nine Ashes

BOOK 2 OF THE NINETY-NINE SERIES

ELISHEBA HAXBY

JESSE VINCENT

ABOVE THE
SUN

Contents

Print ISBN-13: 978-1-7336006-4-4
eBook ISBN: 978-1-7336006-5-1
Cover by: Get Covers

Published by Above The Sun LLC,
Eugene, Oregon

Scripture quotations or paraphrases are taken from the HOLY BIBLE, NEW
INTERNATIONAL VERSION®. ©1973, 1978, 1984, by Biblica, Inc.™ Used
by permission. All rights reserved worldwide

For my dad who passed on to glory during the writing of this book.

Thank you for giving me your dreamer's heart.
With it, I've had the courage to press though the pain
and believe for a better day.

CHAPTER 1

November 29, 9:00 a.m.

TAMARA

Return to Sender

The line blurred as moisture pooled in my eyes, and I pressed the envelope hard against my chest.

Another dead end.

I took a long breath of the frigid morning air before closing the mailbox and heading back inside.

What now?

I kicked off my flip-flops and drug my feet across the cold linoleum floor into the kitchenette, mind spinning. My parent's old phone number was dead. An internet search of social media platforms had yielded zilch and now this. I set most of the mail on the table, but the letter I had sent to my mother a little over a month ago was still firmly clutched in my hand. Heart heavy, I stared at the red words stamped at the top of the envelope. What had I expected anyway? That finding them six years later would be easy? That they'd be exactly where I had left them, frozen in time and waiting to reunite?

I tossed the letter aside, crossed the studio to the bathroom and opened the medicine cabinet. Sighing, I reached for the bottle of antidepressants the doctor had prescribed a little over a month ago for postpartum depression. I didn't like the idea of taking medication, but they seemed to help as I walked through the grieving process. Having the symptoms of giving birth to a baby without actually bringing one home had seriously messed with my head. The first week was the worst with my hormones shifting constantly and my body swollen from the baby weight. Each time I'd look down at my empty, stretched marked stomach, I cried from the hollowness I'd felt. As the weeks dragged on, a foggy numbness had settled over my brain, muting life and its colors. I opened the bottle, tapped a pill into my hand and swallowed it with a glass of water.

I set the container back on the shelf, closed the cabinet and examined myself in the mirror. Wild hair framed my oval face, and bemused green eyes stared back at me. Would I ever be back to who I was before the pregnancy? Outwardly, I was almost there. Only six pounds to go until I was my original weight and most of my clothes fit. Inside, though, was a different story. Since the adoption, there had been a vacant part of me that couldn't be comforted no matter what I did. Was that why I'd been so set on finding my family lately? Was it some way to fill the void Hope had created?

Shaking off the thoughts, I threw my hair into a loose ponytail and went back to the kitchen. Truth was, I had wrestled with the idea of finding them for months. Lately, though, the need had intensified. I grabbed a blue mug from the cabinet, filled it three-quarters full with coffee and added an ample amount of cream and sugar before taking a sip of what had become my only vice. Leaning against the counter, I picked up the envelope once more. What was the connection between Hope and my family? They were both part of me, but neither were in my life.

It would be years until I'd be able to see Hope without it killing me emotionally, but after hours of therapy and prayer, I thought I was ready to reunite with my family. Before I'd been terrified to face them with the hurt that had been between us, but in one moment that had changed. The day I gave up Hope

—the instant I placed her in Levi's arms and said goodbye—I realized what I'd done to my parents by staying away for so long. Letting her go made me see how awful it could be for a parent to lose their child. As I let her go, it felt as though a part of my heart had been ripped out, leaving a hole I wasn't sure would ever mend.

But as painful as it was, I had the peace of knowing Hope was in a good place, being raised by wonderful people, given the love and care she deserved. My parents—specifically my mother, who had never laid a hand on me—had no idea where I was. I could be dead for all they knew. And even though my dad had an angry side to him that had twisted me up on the inside, a part of me still loved him.

A light tapping at the door drew me from my thoughts. "Who is it?"

"It's me, sweetie."

Joe? Why wasn't he using his key?

I set my coffee down and hurried across the small room before swinging the door open.

Joe stood in front of me, holding two cups, a warm smile on his handsome face. "Good morning, beautiful." He offered me one of the drinks. "White chocolate mocha, extra whip."

I mirrored his expression and took the cup from him. In many ways, Joe was my own personal star, illuminating my darkest nights. "You brought me coffee before going to work? You're the best."

He slowly shook his head, his grin growing wider. "I went in early and took care of some things. Claire's covering everything else."

"We get the whole day together?" With us working opposite shifts managing the diner, that never happened.

"Yup." Joe put his free arm around me and leaned in.

I tried to duck away from him, but he held me tight. "Give me a minute. I still need to brush my teeth."

3

"A little morning breath isn't enough to stop me." He chuckled and kissed my cheek instead.

"Ewwww." I giggled and squirmed out of his embrace. "So, what's the plan for today? Want to grab brunch and then hit a matinee?"

"Actually, I had something a bit different in mind." A hint of mischief sparkled in his eyes.

My curiosity was piqued. A romantic adventure with Joe could be just the distraction I needed. I glanced at the stack of mail on the kitchen table. Should I tell him about the returned letter? Not now. It would only spoil his mood. "What should I wear?"

"Think a little nicer than casual."

I scanned him from head to toe, noticing for the first time the way he was dressed. He wore dark jeans and a black sweater that hugged his muscles. And here I stood in front of him with my messy ponytail and morning breath. The thing was, I didn't even feel self-conscious. This wonderful man loved me and had proved it time and again.

I set my cup on the dresser and found a burgundy sweater dress and leggings before excusing myself to the bathroom. After a quick shower, I threw on the outfit, brushed my teeth, and put on a light smattering of makeup. When I stepped out of the bathroom, Joe was sitting at the table sipping his coffee, staring dreamily out of the window.

"Nickel for your thoughts."

His perfect lips arched into a crooked grin. "Isn't it supposed to be a penny?"

I gave a half-shrug. "Inflation."

"Nothing, really." The chair creaked as he pushed away from the table. Then he crossed the room and put his arms around me, bringing his hand to my face, tracing the outline of my cheek. "Today is about you, Tamara. I'm so proud of you."

His words washed over me, warming the center of my being. "Really? For what?" I snuggled into him.

"For what you accomplished over the last six months. Most recently, your GED."

"That's no big deal. I should have done that years ago."

He put his finger under my chin. "It *is* a big deal. Especially with everything you've been through."

Sadness trickled into my stomach as the last few months played through my head again. The nights had been the hardest when I was alone in the quiet of my apartment without the busyness of work or Joe there to hold me. There were times I cried so hard from the grief I wasn't sure I'd ever stop. The months of counseling with David, processing the trauma of what Kyle had done, hadn't been a picnic either. Working on my GED had been a mental vacation from it all.

Joe kissed the tip of my nose as he stepped away. "Stay right here. Don't move. I'll be back." He grabbed my car keys off the hook on the way outside.

Why would he take my keys? We never drove my car. I almost followed him, but he seemed adamant about me staying put. Instead, I cleaned the coffee mess, then grabbed the mocha he'd brought me and sipped as I paced the room.

Tap, tap, tap. What now? I dashed back across the room and flung the door open.

Joe leaned on the doorway, holding a single long-stemmed red rose in one hand and a muffin in the other.

I laughed out loud. "What are you doing?"

He handed me the rose, lips twitching. "That's for me to know and for you to wonder about."

"Ohhhh. Man of mystery."

"Yeah, baby." He wiggled his eyebrows.

I laughed again. He was too adorable. "Oh, behave," I said in my best British accent.

"I knew our Austin Powers marathon was going to come back to haunt me." He chuckled, took hold of my hand, and tugged me forward. "We need to get this show on the road."

The weather was crisp, but sunny with a few cotton-candy

clouds floating in the sky—the kind I'd always found animal shapes in. My gaze landed on my Cabriolet, which already had the top down.

I stopped mid-step and turned to Joe, arching an eyebrow. "What's this?"

A playful grin lit his warm hazel eyes. "I thought we could take your car for a change. And you love driving with the top down."

I threw him a disbelieving look. "You can't be serious."

"Oh, I'm serious."

I smacked him on the arm. "It's freezing out."

"What happened to your sense of adventure? What happened to the girl who loved the wind in her hair?"

"That was before I met Jesus," I joked.

"Just get in the car. It'll be okay. Promise." He opened the passenger door with a wink and handed me the muffin.

I climbed in and watched him circle the front of the car. "Why do you always get to drive?"

"Because, frankly, my dear, you have no clue where we're going," he said as he settled into his seat.

"So, tell me and then I can drive." I took a bite of the blueberry muffin. Mmmm. So good. A perfect mixture of moist and sweet.

"Not a chance, darlin'." That adorable mischievous grin was back. He reached into his back pocket and took out a handkerchief. "Everything's a surprise today."

I eyed the hankie. "A blindfold. Seriously?"

He nodded, his eyes dancing. "Trust is the building block to any good relationship."

"No way." I leaned away from him, raising a hand in protest.

"Come on, T. Just go with it."

"Fine." I turned my head in surrender.

He secured the blindfold around my head. "Now, no peeking."

"I make no promises." My world was dark, but my heart felt light.

The car started, and there was motion as Joe backed out of the parking spot. Cold wind blew against my face as the vehicle accelerated. "How about some music?" I yelled over the sound of the airstream.

He shouted back, "I thought you'd never ask! I made us a mixed tape. A compilation that reminds me of us."

"Don't you mean a playlist, Gramps?"

"No, I mean a mixtape. I'm not the one still driving a car from the eighties."

"Seriously? You made an actual *tape* tape?" Cute.

"Yes. Do you want me to put it on or not?"

"Abso-freaking-lutely!" Seconds later, the country twangs of Merle Haggard filled the car. Oh. My. Goodness. He had to be joking. I flung my hand against his chest. "Joe! Put on some real music."

He let out a cough and a deep inhale as if I'd hit him harder than I had. "What? You don't like good ole' Merle? I had no idea!" He teased and then forwarded it to the next song.

Harmonious beats and rhythmic percussion thrummed out of the speakers, and I instantly recognized the tune. "Crazy" by Seal. The wind whipped the hair around my neck, sending icy chills through my body. I unbuckled my seatbelt and leaned into the current. If only I could rip off the blindfold. This moment would be so much better if I could see.

"What are you doing?" Joe's elevated voice had a hint of concern in it.

"Just getting a little crazy!" I stood and yelled at the top of my voice. In that moment, the sadness of the last few months evaporated into the wind. Giving up my baby, my missing family, the pain of what Kyle had done flew off my back and into the horizon. A burst of freedom pulsed through my veins. "Wooooooohooooooo!"

Joe joined in on the yelling and honked the horn.

A few moments later, I sat back down, laughing through chattering teeth.

"Oh my goodness, baby. You're freezing."

"N—n—no. I'm o—okay." I forced out, my body shaking.

The wind slowed as the car came to a stop. "Hold on a sec." His door opened and closed. There was rummaging around, followed by the scraping sound of the top going up.

Within minutes, the air around me was much warmer. Joe returned, wrapped what felt like his leather jacket around me and cupped his hands over mine.

I shivered. He was just as cold as I was. We were two icicles trying to heat each other up.

"This was probably not my most brilliant plan." A tinge of chagrin laced his tone.

"You can't be serious. That was the most alive I've felt in months."

He was quiet for a beat, and I could imagine the look in his deep eyes. "You're insane. You know that?"

"We won't survive," I said through a shiver, "unless we get crazy."

He chuckled and blew on our hands. "You're my kind of crazy, woman."

His arm came around me, and I curled into him. Hot air from the vents blew on us. The whole thing reminded me of our first date, except for the blindfold. Joe's finger traced the line of my neck and slid through my hair, sending shivers down my spine. Then his lips were on mine so tenderly I felt as though I could melt into him. Heat pooled in my stomach and spread through my body. *Almost Paradise* played in the background, and a little chuckle escaped my lips.

"What?" A hint of a smile lightened Joe's voice.

"I feel like I'm inside a cheesy eighties movie all of a sudden."

"Exactly what I was going for."

"Mission one-hundred-percent accomplished." I adjusted the blindfold.

"Hey, no peeking," Joe scolded. "We better get back on the road. Otherwise, you'll be blind the whole day."

If he would have just allowed me to take the darn blindfold off, I would've been content to stay right there for the rest of the day—nuzzled into him, stealing as many kisses as I could. He pulled away, and a few seconds later, gravel crunched under the tires. The vehicle rolled forward then accelerated, and the music grew louder. Joe laced his fingers through mine, and I leaned my head on his shoulder. It was a strange sensation not being able to see. But it seemed to make me more aware of my other senses, like the smell of Joe's spiced cologne and leather jacket. The music was hitting my soul like freshly squeezed lemonade on a hot summer day—sweet and refreshing. Joe had done a great job on the mix. If I were to label the tape, it would have been called *Best of the Eighties, Nineties, and Deep Worship*. A little bit of Journey, Lifehouse, Water Deep, and Hillsong United, to name a few. Twelve and a half songs later, the car rolled to a stop, and the engine died. Were those raindrops hitting the windshield?

Joe's hands came to the back of my head, untying the blindfold. Massive waves were crashing against the shore with a dark-gray backdrop. The blue skies had vanished, replaced by huge rain clouds bursting at the seams.

We were at Cannon Beach—the place Joe had taken me on our first date. I looked over at him, my heart swelling. Was that sadness in his expression?

"What's wrong?"

He shrugged and averted his gaze. "I wanted this day to be perfect, but the weather is not cooperating."

"Are you kidding me? There's nothing better than watching a storm gathering over the ocean. Talk about raw power." I crawled over the center console and wedged myself onto his lap.

He swept a lock of hair behind my ear and ran his hand

softly down my arm, causing a tingling sensation to open inside my core. Through the window, a streak of lightning lit the sky. He kissed me then, deep and slow, his hands cradling the back of my head, fingers threading through my hair. "Tamara," he whispered my name as he drew away from the kiss.

I let out a quiet moan and rested my forehead on his. Another lightning bolt flashed, followed by a thunderclap. I jumped a bit at the noise and settled back into him.

Gently, he traced my fingers, caressing them in the sweetest way. "The last time I brought you here was the day I realized that I was, without a doubt, hopelessly in love with you."

I smiled at the memory. "What exactly was it? My running off into the freezing cold water or me coming out looking like a drowned rat?"

"Both." He slowly lifted my hand and laced his fingers through mine. "I knew that day we fit together perfectly."

A wonderful feeling of euphoria swept through my body, followed by a strange moment of clarity. Every broken path of my life had actually led me to Joe. I'd wondered many times how I could survive so much, but ending up here, being so deeply loved, almost made it all worth it.

For a long time, we were quiet as we watched the waves crash against the shore and lightning streak across the sky. I was so relaxed I could have fallen asleep, but then Joe jumped. "Oh. We gotta go."

Confusion interrupted my bliss. Moving was the last thing I wanted to do, but I followed Joe's nudging and climbed back into my seat. He reversed the car, peeled out of the parking lot and sped north on Highway 101.

What was the rush about? "You going to tell me why you're speed-racing my car?"

He pushed the accelerator. "Oh please, this thing can barely hit seventy."

"Exactly."

"The old beater will be fine."

"Hey, lay off my car. This baby has treated me well over the years."

He rolled his eyes and slowed down a tad.

"Are you at least going to tell me where we're heading in such a hurry?"

Joe pressed his lips together in a thin line and made a zipping motion with one hand.

Another surprise? I supposed I could live with that. I leaned back in my seat and watched the changing scenery as the ocean came in and out of view. At least Joe hadn't blindfolded me again.

Ten minutes later, we reached Seaside, and he slowed a bit. Daydreams swirled around my mind as I took in the shops and restaurants lining the road. Maybe someday Joe and I could live in a town like this. The car came to a stop in front of the restaurant he'd taken me to the last time we were here. Joe parked, grabbed an umbrella with a small black plastic bag from the back, and exited the car. He held the umbrella over my head as we ran toward the building.

The maître d' opened the door for us and gave us a once over as we entered.

"Reservation for Phillips," Joe said.

Reservations? How long had Joe been planning this?

The gentleman scanned the large black book in front of him. "Oh yes, right this way." He picked up two menus and led us into the dining room.

Joe took my cold hand in his, and we followed him to the exact same table we had sat last time, right next to the fireplace. After setting menus in front of us, he filled our glasses with water and explained the day's special. Filet mignon with a lobster bisque. Joe and I exchanged a glance. Another wave of déjà vu hit me. Last time I had ordered almost the exact same thing, but back then I was scared to let him spend so much on me. Now I felt safe. Secure.

"We'll take two cups of hot tea to start off with," Joe told the man.

"Yes, sir. The server will be here soon to take the rest of your order," he said before walking away.

As I gazed at the fireplace, orange flames danced against the wood, and tenderness filled my insides. "Do you know how wonderful you are?" I turned my attention to Joe and stretched my hand across the table.

His hand spread over mine, a half-smile on his lips. "Just trying to give you the life you deserve."

For a long moment, I lost myself in his gaze, taking in his kind words. So much had changed between us since the last time we'd been here. Over the last few months, he'd been my rock, my safe place when the storms of life raged around me. I couldn't count how many times he'd held me together when I was falling apart.

The waitress brought us our tea and took our orders. I decided on the special, and Joe ordered a New York steak topped with mushrooms and onions with a loaded baked potato on the side.

Joe traced circles on the top of my hand. "How are you really doing over there?" His eyes held a deep concern that I was infinitely grateful for.

I thought about the returned letter sitting on the kitchen counter. A part of me wanted to tell him, but with the effort Joe had put into this date, it would be wrong for me to overshadow it with my problems. Besides, I was enjoying this day being about us and us alone. "I feel good today. I mean, even before you came over and took me on this romantic extravaganza." I gave a cheesy grin and took a sip of my tea. It wasn't a total lie. Before I'd received the letter, I had felt a little better.

"I'm glad to hear that." Joe squeezed, then let go of my hand and grabbed the plastic bag he'd brought in with him. "I got something for you." He brought out a rectangular present, wrapped in red paper, tied together with a black ribbon.

My mouth dropped open in surprise. What was this? The whole day had already been a gift.

He pushed the present across the table with his signature room brightening smile.

I stared at the perfectly wrapped package, a bit overwhelmed. "You're really pushing the romance thing to a whole new level."

"Like Hugh Grant level?" He raised an eyebrow and pursed his lips in a hilarious mock-smoldering expression.

I laughed and threw a wink. "Close."

"Open it." The anticipation radiating off him was palpable.

I let out a pleasant sigh and lifted the gift. I untied the black ribbon, tugged the tape at the corner of the red paper, and glanced up. Joe tapped the table, staring at me with a look that said, *Hurry now, you're killing me.* I ripped away the rest of the paper. Underneath was a chestnut-brown, leather-bound journal with my name engraved at the bottom. My heart expanded, filling with gratitude. What a beautiful gift. I ran my fingers over the engraving. "This is perfect. Thank you." I held it against my chest. "I love it."

"Do you remember the last time we were here we talked about our dreams?"

I nodded as I flipped through the pages of the journal. They were a rich cream color and thick, like cardstock.

"You said your dream was to write, and you shared that poem with me. It was really good, Tamara."

"I remember." The poem, based on a recurring dream I'd been having, was written out of a painful place but was never finished.

"I haven't seen you write for a while, and I wanted to encourage you to start again."

I set the journal down and flipped through the blank pages. The fresh paper aroma danced across my nose. I leaned in close and took in a long sniff, imagining I was in a bookstore, standing in front of books *I* had written. Would that ever be a possibility? Seemed farfetched, but something came alive in me at the thought. "That's very thoughtful, Joe." Would I ever be worthy of this man in front of me?

"What's wrong?" Joe's hand rested on mine again.

"Sometimes I don't understand what I did to deserve you."

"Tamara, sweetie. You are such an amazing, kind, and strong person. If you saw half of what I see, you would realize that I'm the lucky one."

"How can you say that? I've been a puddle of tears for the last few months."

"You've been through a lot, but your strength and resilience through the hard times is one of your greatest qualities. But you're so much more than that. You're smart, funny, beautiful. You're my best friend, T. My other half."

Tears rolled down my face at his words. "You see me better than I really am."

"I see you as you are." He brought his hand to my cheek, caressing away the tears. His gaze held enough emotion to knock me over. One day, I hoped I'd be the woman he thought I was.

The waitress came to our table with our steaming plates of food. The smell of flame-broiled meat, onions, and garlic wafted in the air, and my stomach growled. I set aside the gift to make room for my plate.

Joe reached for his knife. "This looks amazing." He cut into the New York Strip, popped a piece in his mouth, and let out a quiet moan.

The moment the cooked-to-perfection steak hit my mouth, I understood Joe's reaction. The meat was so tender it almost melted in my mouth. "Mmmm. I don't remember it being this good last time."

"Me either," Joe said around a mouthful.

"Then there's the fact that I don't have pregnancy hormones messing with my taste buds." My heart constricted at the words, but I instantly brushed it off. I wouldn't let sadness spoil this moment. No matter how much it stung.

"There is that, but I wasn't pregnant." He smirked and forked another bite.

His light mood took the sting out of my words. I took in a deep breath and glanced at the blazing fire. In the background, the rain pinged against the windows. Chill bumps rose on my skin. Everything was exactly as it was supposed to be, even if it did hurt sometimes. "I'm really thankful for all of this."

"I'm thankful too." His gaze landed on mine and his endearing expression melted my insides.

Heat climbed my neck, and I averted my gaze. How could a single look from this man turn me to mush?

Joe went back to his steak, and we sat in mostly blissful silence until we finished. I placed the last bite into my mouth just before the waitress approached our table and cleared our plates. "Would you like to see the dessert menu?"

"I think we're good. Thank you."

Once Joe paid the bill, we headed out for a walk. The air was damp when we stepped outside. The rain had momentarily stopped, but the huge gray clouds in the sky looked ready for another downpour. That didn't matter, though. I would enjoy every moment of this day even if we got totally drenched.

We strolled along the promenade, exploring the shops. We tried on different outfits and purchased a few knickknacks for Joe's house. Someday it would be my home, and I liked shopping for it and dreaming about adding a woman's touch to the place. It was nice to leave the sorrow of the last year behind and start thinking about the future again. But what about Joe? Most of his life lately had been about supporting me, making sure I was taken care of. He deserved to dream too.

We stepped out of an antique shop, and a large gust of wind rustled my hair. "What about your dreams, Joe?"

He stopped mid-step and turned toward me. "What about them?"

"You said earlier you haven't seen me write lately. Well, I haven't heard you talk about your dreams lately either."

He took hold of my hand and dragged me forward. "Let's go down to the beach."

Was he ignoring my question? "You didn't answer the—"

"Could you trust me for one time today?" He threw a playful smirk and continued to drag me toward the ocean. Small droplets fell from the sky.

When we made it to the sandy shore, Joe turned to me. He looked at me for a long moment, searching my face. "Earlier today, when we sat in front of the ocean holding each other ..." A flurry of wind blew around us, and the raindrops grew in size. "So many dreams filled me. One day I want to own my own restaurant, and I want it to be here, or a town just like it. I know how much the ocean means to you, and that's the thing, Tamara. Every dream that I have has you at the center of it. Starting with us at the altar, promising our lives to each other." Joe knelt on one knee.

What was he doing? We were already engaged. The rain fell heavily around us.

He reached into his pocket and withdrew a tiny black box. "Tamara Christine Jensen. I love you with all my heart. I want to spend the rest of forever giving you the life and happiness you deserve." He popped the box open and an elegant diamond solitaire ring shimmered at me.

Tears spilled down my cheeks, mingling with the rain.

"Marry me?" he yelled over the wind.

I knelt in the wet sand with him. "You crazy man. I said yes six months ago."

He slid the ring on my finger. "You deserved this kind of proposal." Then his arms were around me, his lips meeting mine with hunger and passion.

A few moments later he drew back, and I slowly opened my eyes. His dark hair was drenched, and rain dripped down his gorgeous features. The desire that shone in his countenance caused heat to pulse through me despite the frigid rain.

"You're soaked," he whispered in my ear, then stood before helping me to my feet. "Let's go get you warmed up."

On the walk back to the car, I thought about my future with Joe. I saw it exactly the way he described. Us living in a small town on the ocean. Running our own business. Raising a family...

My throat tightened around the word *family*. The returned letter and all of its daunting implications filled my mind. Over the last few months, I'd dealt with my pain with Kyle, the date rape and giving up Hope for adoption, but this one massive question mark still hung over my head. Would I be able to fully go forward with my life with Joe while having such an unresolved past?

I really wanted to, but if I was truly being honest with myself, I wasn't so sure.

CHAPTER 2

November 29, 7:00 p.m.

JOE

On our ride home, Tamara snuggled into my shoulder and fell asleep. I glanced down at the ring shimmering on her hand and smiled. What an incredible day. I'd had the ring for a while, but wanted to wait until we were past the grief to give it to her. My throat felt thick as I thought back over the last few months. Watching her grieve over the loss of her baby was brutal, but in some ways, I was thankful to have witnessed it. In my life, I had never seen a greater display of love. Tamara, knowing full well the pain it would cause her, went through with the pregnancy and then the delivery, literally laying down her body for Levi, Sarah, and Hope. It made me love her more than I already did. I was thankful I had the rest of my life to show her how much.

I turned on soft worship music and silently prayed over Tamara and our future. Our relationship had been tried in the fire, and yet we were more in love than ever. We were on a journey that was destined for a lifetime. I didn't need to be in a hurry, but a part of me was ready to start our future together. For her to be there when I got home from work, to be able to hold her through the night, and, when the timing was right, start our own family.

A little after 7:00, we drove into Tamara's apartment

complex, and I parked the car. She was still wrapped around my arm, snoring lightly. For a moment, I studied her soft features. She was so beautiful. Peaceful. It pained me a little having to wake her. Perhaps I should carry her inside. I smiled, and images of her in a wedding dress and me carrying her over the threshold filled my mind. My heart expanded as I lingered on the thought. If nothing else, it was time to set a date.

Tamara stirred and moved away, gazing at me with a sleepy smile. "Home already?"

I tucked a lock of hair behind her ear. "Somebody was tired. You slept the whole way home." I kissed the end of her nose. "Let's get you inside so you can sleep on a real bed."

She slid her hands around my neck. "I don't want to say goodnight."

"You sure? You seem pretty tired."

Big drops of rain pelted the windshield.

"I was just relaxed and happy." She gave me a small kiss. "Thank you for today. It was really special."

"This is the kind of life I want to give you." I took her left hand in mine and ran my finger over the diamond ring. I loved the way it looked on her small hand.

"The night is still young. Do you want to snuggle and watch our show?" she asked.

"That actually sounds wonderful." During the trials of the last few months, we had started watching *The Office* for the comic relief. We both fell in love with the show. Throughout the years, I'd watched it here and there, but I'd never seen it all the way through. Neither had Tamara. Now there were three more episodes left in our queue. "Maybe we could land that bird tonight."

"Yeah!" Tamara's green eyes lit up, then she reached for the door handle. "Let's do this."

Before I could respond, she opened the car door and bolted toward her apartment. I chuckled as she splashed through the parking lot. It looked like she'd have to dry out another time today. She could have at least grabbed the umbrella, but that was Tamara. Impulsive. Adorable.

I opened the car door, climbed out, and sprinted after her. By the time I reached the small front porch, she already had the door unlocked. She turned toward me with a huge smile and then kissed me as the wind and rain whipped around us.

After a minute, she drew away. "Thank you again for the most perfect day ever."

"You sure like being soaked, don't you?"

Rain dripped down her lovely face. "Only when I'm with you."

I dragged her inside. "You realize, you may have a dresser full of dry clothes here, but mine are across town."

She giggled. "You can always wear mine."

I tickled her. "Oh, you would just love that, wouldn't you?"

Her laughter became more intense. "You know it." She poked my sides. "You can wear whatever you want out of my underwear drawer."

"You're just full of it tonight, aren't you?" I grabbed both of her arms to keep her from tickling me.

She took a minute to catch her breath. Her gaze caught mine, her energy changing, desire painting her expression.

I swallowed and tried to suppress my own yearning. "You should go get into some dry clothes."

She nodded slowly, her focus on my mouth. It took all the self-control I had not to crush my lips against hers. I released her hands.

"I have a few of your hoodies in the top drawer if you want to change your shirt." She went to her dresser and threw me a sweatshirt before taking out fresh clothes for herself. She walked across the room and into the bathroom, closing the door behind her.

I changed into the hoodie, but my jeans were still damp. Oh well. Getting a little wet was worth seeing Tamara's playfulness finally return. Her spontaneity was one of my favorite things about her. I turned on the television, found the queue for *The Office*, and heated water for hot chocolate.

As I poured cocoa into the mugs, the bathroom door creaked open. There were footsteps across the floor.

Tamara slid her arms around my stomach and rested her head on my back. "I love you, Mr. Phillips."

I turned around and embraced her, breathing in her scent—a combination of strawberry, mint, and vanilla. "I can't wait for the day that I call you Mrs. Phillips."

She let out a quiet sigh. "I like the sound of that."

I leaned back a little to look at her. "Let's set a date."

"Um... yeah." A look I didn't understand fluttered across her features.

Hesitation? Was she *still* not ready? I didn't want to push her, but I was more than ready. Shaking off the doubt, I ran my hand through her damp hair. "I was thinking March seventh, our one-year anniversary."

She smiled, but a sadness overshadowed it.

"Or we could just head to Vegas." I peaked at my watch. "You could be my wife in less than twenty-four hours."

"You're crazy!"

"Crazy for you, baby."

She slid her arms around my neck. "March seventh sounds perfect."

"Really? You sure?"

"Absolutely. It's a date." Her lips softly met mine. I drew her closer and allowed myself to get lost in her—lost in us. A slow burn began in my stomach, and I withdrew. "We should probably get to that show."

She nodded. "Yes, let's do this."

Grabbing our hot chocolates, I followed Tamara to the loveseat. I set our mugs on the chest that doubled as a coffee table and settled in next to her. I pressed play and the familiar images of Scranton shown on the screen. The theme song started and Tamara adjusted her position, snuggling into the crook of my arm.

"No falling asleep."

"I won't. I already took a nap, remember?"

"Sure, you won't."

She smacked me playfully on the leg. "Oh shush, you going to tease me all night or are we going to watch the show?"

I chuckled and turned my attention to the television. The main storyline of this episode was about Andy finding the courage to quit his job to follow his dream to become a singer. In the end, he finally left and serenaded the entire office with a cover of "I Will Remember You." He wasn't half bad.

I glanced at Tamara to check if she was still awake. Were those tears streaming down her face? I snagged the remote and pressed pause. "You okay?"

She peered at me, eyes glossy. "Yeah, it's just a really good song."

I gave her a sad smile. It was adorable that she was quoting Angela from the show, but it seemed deeper than that. "Are you sure?"

"Yeah, I'm good. Let's just keep going." She waved me on.

"Okay." I pushed play and let the episode finish and roll over to the next one.

We watched in silence as I held her close. At the midpoint of the episode, I looked over at Tamara. Her tears were gone. I grabbed a sip of my chocolate drink that was now cold. We let the episode finish and the last one started. "Here we go, the final one. Are you ready for this?"

"Let's kill this bird."

I leaned over to kiss her. "I love your needlessly violent comments about ending shows."

She snickered and nuzzled into me. The end to the show was, in my opinion, the best ending to a sitcom I'd ever seen. Though *Parks and Recreation* might take a close second. As the credits rolled, I looked down at Tamara.

She was crying again.

Hopefully, they were happy tears. I wiped her cheeks with the wrist of my hoodie. "What's going on, T?"

"I don't know. The last few shows just brought up a lot somehow."

"Like what?"

"It's just from Andy's song to Michael Scott coming back to be there for the wedding, and everyone getting their happy ending."

I ran my hand along her arm, searching for the right words to say. "I think I understand. You've been through a lot, and we've been through a lot together, but I promise you we are going to get our happy ending too."

More tears ran down her face. What did I say? Was I making it worse? "Talk to me, T. Did I say something wrong?"

She wiped away a tear. "I just don't know if that will happen for me."

Her words crushed me. In my heart, she was my happy ending. Was I not enough for her? I put a finger under her chin and brought her face toward mine. "I don't understand."

She stood and walked into the kitchen and grabbed an envelope off the counter. "This was returned this morning." She held the letter out toward me. "I know this probably won't make sense with my family history, but in my perfect ending my relationship with my family is healed and they're at our wedding ... together and happy."

Return to sender. A lead balloon expanded in my stomach as I read the words next to the stamp. "This came this morning and you're just now telling me about it?"

She looked down at the floor. "I didn't want it to ruin our day."

I stood and pulled her into an embrace. "It wouldn't have, T. I thought you understood that you could trust me with stuff like this."

"I know." She leaned into me. "But sometimes it's easier to

be swept away in the moment. Sometimes I want to let you make me forget."

I pressed my lips against her forehead. After the last few months, I wished so badly that I *could* make her forget. Who knew how long it would take to track her family down? If she couldn't find them, would she push back the date? Would our wedding be on hold indefinitely? I leaned back and cupped her beautiful face with my hands. "Don't worry about the letter. We *will* find them, Tamara. I'll do whatever it takes. I promise you that." I swallowed hard at the words I'd just spoken. The weight of them created a knot in the center of my sternum. I wanted to be strong for her and reassure her, but what if this was a promise I couldn't keep?

CHAPTER 3

November 30, 9:07 a.m.

TAMARA

For a long time that night, I tossed and turned, thinking of the returned letter and my conversation with Joe. Finding my family after these many years felt like an insurmountable canyon to cross, but I couldn't let it go. They were the last piece of the puzzle of my becoming whole. Finally, I prayed, lingering on each one of their names as I drifted off into slumber.

As I slept, I dreamt about my sister, Dakota. The backdrop resembled a nightmare I'd had a thousand times but not in years. The sky was dark and hazy, and the smell of cigarette smoke lingered in the air. It was usually me walking up the sidewalk to the dingy apartment, but this time it was Dakota, her hair stringy and the skin around her cheekbones sunken in. The streetlight flickered as if it was about to go out. Before unlocking the door, she checked to see if there was anyone around. Dark circles surrounded her blue-green eyes. The door swung open and Ryan stood there glaring, thin lips curled into a scowl. He grabbed a hold of her and dragged her inside. I desperately wanted to break into the scene, but I was frozen outside, watching as Ryan struck her again and again. Dakota fell to the floor, and Ryan hovered over her, hands locked around her neck.

I woke with a start, and sucked in a large breath to calm my racing pulse.

Dull gray light poured through the window at the end of my daybed.

What was that about? I hadn't thought of Ryan in over a year. Ever since I lived in Ocean Shores. For years, that nightmare had been an omen pushing me forward before Ryan could find me and exact his revenge for stealing over two grand from him. Last I heard, he was in prison for selling drugs. And why had Dakota been the star of that dream? Sure, there wasn't a day that went by that I didn't think of her, but she rarely made an appearance in my dreams.

I rolled over in bed and noticed the clock. Already past nine. I hadn't slept this much since my first trimester of pregnancy. I stumbled out of bed, the effects of the nightmare still weighing heavily on my mind. Dakota's sullen face and darkened expression made my heart ache. Was there any truth to that dream?

I fumbled through making coffee as my mind continued to whirl around thoughts of Dakota and the rest of my family. I'd told Joe I wanted them at our wedding, but could there ever be that much healing for us? I'd forgiven my dad months ago, but did forgiveness mean letting him into my life again? A part of me thought it did. Maybe now, I'd be strong enough to be a light to them—a catalyst for healing.

I pressed the start button on the coffee maker. Dark fluid dripped into the carafe, and a rich aroma filled the air. While waiting for it to brew, I ran to the bathroom. After washing my hands, I brushed my teeth and threw my hair into a messy bun. Standing in front of the mirror, staring at my reflection, thoughts of my sister and the nightmare struck me again. What if Dakota *was* in some sort of trouble? What if she needed me? What if the dream was God trying to tell me something was wrong?

I thought I had worked through the guilt of abandoning

her, but suddenly a fresh fire stung my insides. I never should have left her. But what could I do about it now? Anxiety pinged against my insides. Sucking in a sharp breath, I ran my finger over the engagement ring Joe gave me yesterday. I couldn't keep torturing myself about my past. Not when God had given me a glimpse of such a beautiful future. I didn't know how I was going to find my family, but Joe had promised me we would. For now, I needed to let go and trust.

$\mathscr{November}$ 30, 9:32 a.m.

JOE

My mind ran through the list of what I needed to purchase at the grocery store as I turned onto 124th Avenue. The diner was running low on a few things, and the shipping truck wouldn't be there until tomorrow morning.

The dense clouds overhead were dumping so much rain, the windshield wipers were on high. Despite my efforts not to think about her, Tamara crossed my mind. Earlier this year, when I tried talking her into eloping, she had told me she needed to work through some things first. At the time, I thought she meant the date rape and pregnancy. For the most part, that was behind us now. Kyle was in jail and would be for at least five years. Tamara had been in counseling for months working through the damage of what he did to her. Giving up her baby seemed to be the hardest part. For weeks afterward, there were many times I'd find her crying, clutching onto the picture the hospital took of Hope.

Lately, though, she seemed to be doing better. Over the last few weeks, the grief had faded, and a new joy appeared. I thought maybe it was a sign that she was finally ready to move forward with the wedding. I hadn't realized that the wedding plans were contingent on finding her family.

I took a left on Mill Plain Boulevard, then drove into the supermarket parking lot. I turned off the ignition and watched the raindrops as they splashed against the windshield.

It had been over six years since Tamara had spoken to any of her family. Fear trickled into my stomach—ice cold drops starting in my core and rippling out through my body. Would we even be able to find them? I leaned my head against the steering wheel. How in the world was I going to make good on my promise? Especially when I wasn't sure I wanted to. Tamara had been through enough at their hands. Tracking them down could cause so much more damage inside of her. *God, help me.* I let out a long exhale and tried to shake off the heavy feeling. This would drive me insane if I let it.

I opened the car door and climbed out. I ran through the rain to the store, splashing through the puddles, getting drenched from every angle. The kid in me loved the rainy weather. It reminded me of my mom. When I was a kid, she would put on her boots and splash in puddles with me on rainy days. What did those kinds of days look like in Tamara's house? Sadness bit at me as I walked through the double doors and wandered to the bread aisle.

Four loaves of rye bread, a few bags of onions, and three pounds of pastrami should get us through the day. I placed the bread in the shopping cart and headed off to the veggie aisle.

"Joe?" A man's voice behind me.

I turned and there was Levi Taylor standing behind a shopping cart, a baby strapped to the front of him.

Tamara's baby.

My heart did something strange at that thought. "Levi, so good to see you." I hadn't seen Levi since the day Tamara had given birth to Hope. I really did miss him. We had gotten close in the months leading to the delivery.

"You too, my friend." Dark shadows circled his eyes, but he wore a grin as if losing sleep was worth it.

My focus fell to Hope. She'd almost doubled in size. Her

eyes were wide and full of wonder, her cheeks plump and pink. She was beautiful. Just like her mother. For a second, all I could do was stare, taking in the uncanny resemblance, emotions overwhelming me. The memories of holding Tamara as she wept over giving up her baby rushed through me in a split second. The crushing weight of it settled in my chest.

"She looks like her, doesn't she?" Levi beamed.

I nodded and tried to smile back. He was, without a doubt, a great father. My heart ached again for Tamara, but this time it was different. What would her childhood have been like if she had a dad like Levi? I'd never want to change her, but if I could, I would've put her in a place where she'd have known she was loved.

"How's Tamara doing?" Levi caressed the top of Hope's head.

"She's doing okay." I wasn't sure how honest Tamara would want me to be.

Levi tilted his head to the side, lines appearing in his forehead, a question in his countenance.

"At first it was a bit rough," I admitted. "But I think the worst is behind her now."

He nodded and took hold of Hope's tiny hand. "Sarah and I can't even begin to express how grateful we are. What she did changed our lives forever." His gaze landed on Hope. "Yeah, baby girl. You're our whole world."

She kicked her feet, and her face lit up. A twinge of jealousy flitted through me. At the beginning of Tamara's pregnancy, before Kyle returned and we found out his secret, I believed I was go to be a father to her baby. I was there with her through the whole pregnancy, feeling Hope kick and squirm inside Tamara's growing stomach. If things had played out differently, I would've been raising this child.

"Joe, you all right?"

"Yeah, it's just been a strange morning." More like a strange twenty-four hours.

"How so?"

I looked around the store. It was fairly empty, but a few people milled around the bins of fruit and veggies. This wasn't the best place for this conversation, but when would I have the opportunity again? Levi was one of the wisest people I knew. I leaned in a bit and spoke quietly as I shared the short version of last night's conversation with Tamara and the emotions that had been berating me since. "I just don't know what to do. When I'm being really honest, a part of me was relieved the letter was sent back. She's already been through so much this year. Finding them could unleash a whole lifetime of pain. I don't know if she's ready for that." Heck, I didn't know if *I* was ready for that.

Hope began to fuss. "It's okay, sweetie." Levi reached for a pacifier hanging on the front of her outfit and stuck it in her mouth.

"Am I upsetting her?" My voice had escalated there at the end.

"She's good. Probably just getting a little tired." Levi refocused his attention on me. "I understand your fear with Tamara. It's hard to see someone you love walk through so much." If anyone knew about watching a loved one suffer, it was Levi.

"I just wish I knew where to start. Tamara's efforts have led to a dead end. Maybe I should try to talk her out of finding them."

Hope fussed again, and Levi bounced her a little. "Tamara is a strong person, and I've witnessed a tremendous amount of growth in her life. I haven't seen her in a while, but last time I did, she seemed to be doing well. In my opinion, if she's taking the initiative to track down her family, you need to fully support her."

I crossed my arms in front of me. "What if we find them and it's a complete disaster? They've already done so much damage in her life."

"That's possible, but finding her family could bring another level of healing."

Or finding them could bring even more harm. "I understand what you're saying, but what am I supposed to do? I don't know where to start. They could be anywhere."

"That is hard. It could be an uphill battle, but you and I both know Tamara is worth it."

I nodded. She *was* worth it, but I still wasn't convinced this was the right thing for her.

Hope's binky fell out of her mouth, and she began to cry.

"I better go. She's probably getting hungry. Just know that Sarah and I are praying for you two. You both are special to us."

"Thanks, I appreciate that." As I walked away, I thought about how much prayer we were going to need for this to work out.

CHAPTER 5

November 30, 6:00 p.m.

TAMARA

Days like today made me hate my work schedule. Three days off in a row could give a girl way too much time to think. I spent the morning cleaning my apartment and trying to read the book David suggested during our last counseling session, *Stronger than the Struggle* by Havilah Cunnington. It was a good book, but it kept leading my mind down a road I was wanting to avoid. My family. Particularly my sister. Finally, I gave up and headed out to run some errands and get ready for my evening with Joe.

While shopping for dinner, I headed down the magazine aisle and picked out three different wedding magazines. I checked out and then headed over to Joe's house and let myself in with the key he'd given me months ago.

For hours, I sat in Joe's living room, pouring over the magazines. It was hard to focus with thoughts of my family swimming around in my head. Why would they have moved? We'd lived at that trailer park our whole lives. I turned the page and saw a woman wearing an elegant mermaid-style dress that hugged her curves like a fitted glove. The dress was overlaid with fine lace, and diamond-type gems embroidered the neckline. I loved it, but couldn't quite see myself in it. Honestly, I had no clue what I really wanted.

When I was a little girl, I didn't dream of weddings or finding Prince Charming. I was too busy ducking out of the way of my father's backhand. I still remember my last night at home as if it were yesterday. Lying there, body throbbing from the beating, tears streaming down my face, waiting for the house to go completely quiet. I was sure of one thing that night as I jumped out my bedroom window—I was never going back.

Light reflected off my solitaire engagement ring, and I flipped another page of the wedding magazine. I was less than six months from marrying the best thing that had ever happened to me. I should have been happy. No, scratch that. I should have been ecstatic, but for reasons I couldn't comprehend, all I could think about was them.

Over the last few months, as I looked back over my childhood, I was able to see it in a new light. Yes, there was anger and neglect, but now that I'd forgiven my dad, I could see he wasn't entirely bad. During the summer, we kids would take turns going on the road with him. On those trips, he was a different person. Not so stressed. The only people he'd yell at were the "idiots who didn't know how to drive." As we drove, we'd crank the radio and sing at the top of our lungs. That's where I got my love for eighties music. One time when driving through Arizona, he made a two-hour detour just so he could show me the Grand Canyon.

As we stood on the edge of the vast ravine, my tiny hand in his, he knelt down so we were at the same eye level. "You got more potential than any of them, kid. You can really make something of yourself. You can break the Jensen curse."

That was one of the reasons I left that night those years ago. With one single lie, I broke my dad's heart just as much as he had broken mine. I couldn't look him in the eye every day with him believing I'd actually brought drugs into his house.

Though my family had been full of dysfunction, they were still part of me.

I pushed aside the wedding magazine and grabbed Joe's laptop from the coffee table. I turned it on and waited, my mind racing as I stared at the Google search engine. The internet might give some sort of clue of why my family would have left their home after living there most of their lives, but where would I start? I'd already checked the different social media platforms and came up with nothing. Staring at the screen, I whispered a prayer for help.

The wind howled and a stray tree branch smacked against the window.

I slowly typed *Quilcene WA news*, hesitating before I clicked search. Our town was so small that any news could help me figure out what had happened.

The first article was about the high school football team and how they were excelling this year. Coach Hynix was still there after all these years. Good to know that some things stayed the same. I scrolled through several sites. On the fourth page, a headline caught my eye. "Local Trailer Park Burns to the Ground." Apprehension churned around in my core. There were only two small trailer parks in Quilcene, and my family had lived in one of them. This article could hold news I wasn't ready to hear.

My finger hovered over the track pad.

Moment of truth.

The front door crashed against the wall, and I jumped. Footsteps came down the hall and then Joe walked around the corner, hair dripping wet. "Sorry, the wind blew the door out of my hand."

I took in a slow breath. "It's okay. I'm just on edge."

"Oh yeah?" Joe kicked off his shoes and set them in the hallway.

"I found something. Something big."

"Sounds serious." He took off his wet hoodie and hung it on the coat rack before sliding next to me on the couch.

"This is an article about a trailer park burning to the ground in my hometown. It could be the one my family lived in."

He put his hand over mine, reluctance in his demeanor. Anxiety rolled off him, adding to my stress. I almost wished he wasn't here for this.

I clicked on the link and bit my bottom lip as I waited for the page to load. The cursor swirled and an article popped up. The date at the top of the screen said it was written in January almost five years ago. I scanned the article. My heart stopped when I read the address. Bowen Street. From what I remember, there were only seven mobile homes in the tiny park. Every one of them had burned to ash. Including my parents' trailer.

I slammed the computer shut, pulse thundering in my ears.

"What are you doing?" Joe asked, sounding confused.

"I can't do this. I thought I was ready, but I'm not. What if this whole time they've been dead, and I was too full of my own selfishness that I wasn't there?" Tears threatened to come.

"Hey, you don't know that. Everyone could have gotten out safely." Joe drew me into him. "Would you like me to read it? It could give us some sort of lead."

I withdrew from his embrace. "Not right now. I'm not ready to deal with this." I stood, my fingers aching to hold a cigarette. It had been over nine months since I'd had one, but my nerves were on edge. I needed help to calm me down. "I think I'm going to go."

Joe grabbed my hand and tugged me down onto his lap. "Don't go." His gaze searched mine. "You seem really shaken. Why don't you stay here tonight?"

What was he saying? My pulse quickened at the thought of spending the night in Joe's embrace.

"I don't want you being by yourself tonight after this. You can sleep in my bed. I'll sleep on the couch."

I tried not to let the disappointment show in my face.

"What's wrong?"

I slid my hand over the tight muscles on his shoulder. "I was thinking it would be nice for you to hold me tonight."

Joe's breathing changed slightly. The desire in his expression caused my stomach to tighten. "We both know that would be dangerous territory."

A smile crept over my lips. "You have no self-control."

He wound his fingers through the tips of my hair. "Not when it comes to you."

I leaned my head against him, feeling the familiar intoxication this kind of touch brought. Truth was, I probably couldn't handle cuddling through the night either. I pressed my lips against his and for the briefest moment, I forgot everything that hurt.

CHAPTER 6
November 30, 11:45 p.m.

JOE

That night, I stared at the ceiling, unable to sleep, my mind circling around the article Tamara had refused to read. I ached to hold her. Sneaking upstairs and climbing into bed with her would be so easy. Instead, I rolled over and adjusted my pillow. Her staying was pushing the boundaries we had set, but what choice did I have? I couldn't send her home to deal with this news by herself. Though having her this close, knowing she was in my bed, caused my mind to go places it shouldn't. I shifted my position again. Finding a comfortable spot on this couch was impossible. Or it could've been the desire for her making me uncomfortable anywhere else.

I couldn't wait to be married to her so I could hold her every night without having to be afraid of crossing lines we shouldn't.

She still had so much to work through before she was ready for marriage. Over the last six months, she'd come so far, I hadn't realized how much this stuff with her family was still affecting her. That article had brought a level of fear that I hadn't seen in quite some time.

At the beginning of this year, before I knew her full story, she would get this look in her eye that made me think the demons of her past were still engulfing her soul. Tonight, the same look had been there. After the last few months of grief, I believed the worst was behind us. But now, thinking about her family and what she'd found today, I wasn't so sure.

I glanced over at the laptop, still on the coffee table where Tamara had placed it. She may not have been ready to find out what was in the article, but I had to know. I sat, grabbed the laptop, and flipped it open. With a deep breath, I began to read. Halfway through, it said that there were no fatalities and the tightness in my chest eased a bit. At least there would be good news to report to her in the morning. I read on.

The article stated the circumstances of the fire seemed suspicious. I scanned further, and my gaze landed on Dakota Jensen's name. She had been one of the suspects in the arson. Arson? She must have only been fifteen at the time. My mind did a huge jump and then another idea struck me. I cleared the search engine and typed, *Dakota Jensen arrest record*. A bunch of sites with public records popped up. I clicked on a link and typed in Dakota's name again. Apprehension built as I followed the instructions on each page until it brought me to the final section where it charged me $29.99 to give me the information I requested.

I grabbed my jeans at the end of the couch and dug out my wallet. Only one tiny transaction between me and the truth. I took out my card, typed in the numbers, and hit enter. It took several excruciatingly long moments for the next page to load. Dakota had been arrested seven times over the last six years, but only convicted of a minor in possession and a petty theft charge. Under her list of offenses was her current address on Muncie Avenue.

Muncie? Why did that street sound familiar?

A scream tore through the night air, and instantly I was on my feet. I took the stairs two at a time.

Tamara sat up in bed, skin pale, body rigid.

I crossed the room in an instant and drew her into my arms. "Baby, what happened? What's wrong?"

She was on fire and her breathing was fast and hard—as if she'd been running for her life. For a moment, she seemed shell-shocked as if she were still caught in whatever nightmare she'd just escaped from. "The trailer. It was on fire. My family was there. I tried to save them, but everything burned." She sobbed into my shoulder. "I ran outside and then I was powerless to help. I stood there screaming as I watched them burn."

I rocked her back and forth. "You're okay, sweetie. It was only a dream." Her tears rolled down my bare skin. "I have you."

My heart broke for her. A part of me wanted to tell her that her family was safe, but then I would have to tell her about her sister. That would be too much information for one night. Exhausted, I leaned back in bed with her, pulling her as close as possible.

She slid her hands around my waist and rested her head firm against my chest. I wouldn't be leaving her side again tonight.

After a few minutes, her breathing changed, and her body relaxed.

I prayed for sleep to come for me too, but all I could do was lie there, feeling Tamara so close. It was wrong to be here like this. The only thing that separated us was the oversized T-shirt I'd given her to sleep in. But to me, nothing felt more right. Two halves of a whole coming together to make something perfect. I ran my fingers through her hair, kissed the top of her forehead and prayed. *Lord, surround Tamara with your peace as she deals with this situation with her family. Give me strength and wisdom to be there for her the way she needs me to be.*

CHAPTER 7

December 1, 9:20 a.m.

TAMARA

For a split second when I woke, my world didn't make sense. I was in Joe's very comfortable California King Bed, his blankets swaddled around me. Smells of bacon and coffee filled the air, and my tummy growled. Then I remembered Joe inviting me to stay the night after reading part of the article and then the nightmare about my family. I'd been so terrified of what I'd find that it made its way into my subconscious. Joe had been there, though. I pushed my head into his pillow and took in the scent of him, jasmine and the sweet spice of his cologne. If Joe was there to keep me strong, I could handle any news about my family.

Before heading downstairs, I rolled out of bed and dressed in the same clothes that I'd worn yesterday.

Joe was in front of the stove, flipping bacon, wearing only a pair of jeans that hung low on his waist.

I stood there for a moment admiring the defined muscles of his back. I tiptoed across the room and touched him.

He jumped a little.

I giggled.

He set the fork down and turned toward me, giving me a

crooked smile. Something was off in his eyes though. "Coffee's just finished brewing and breakfast will be done shortly."

"Coffee sounds really good." I grabbed two cups from the cupboard and brought them to the end of the counter. After pouring the coffee, I put ample cream and sugar in both and set his on the counter next to him.

Joe placed two over-easy eggs on a plate with some bacon and toast, then handed it to me. I carried my breakfast and mug to the table and sipped the hot drink while I watched Joe put the finishing touches on his plate. He joined me with his breakfast.

I took a bite of my bacon and let out a quiet moan. It was perfect, crispy edges, but not overdone. This was the first time we'd ever had an overnight, and I loved starting my day like this. Was this what our future would be like?

Joe took a sip from his steaming mug. "I need to tell you something."

My stomach lurched at his tone. It was too serious for morning banter. "Yeah?" I took another bite of the cooked-to-perfection bacon and tried to ignore the anxiety attacking my insides.

"Last night, I couldn't sleep. I kept thinking about that page. I'm sorry, T, but I had to read it."

My heart stuttered as thoughts bombarded my mind. What did he know? Was my family okay? I swallowed the fear that clawed at my throat. "Are they dead?"

Joe reached for my shaky hand. "No. There were no deaths. Everyone was safe."

I let go of the breath that I had been holding, relief washing through my body.

"But there's more you should know."

"Just tell me!" I blurted out, frustration coming out in my tone. This roller-coaster of emotions was killing me.

"The article said it was arson and that Dakota was a suspect."

"What? That can't be right." Tears of regret threatened to come. Why had I not searched harder for her the night I left town for good? I could have forced her to come with me. It wouldn't have been easy for us both to be on the run, but it would have been better than this. What was going on in her life now? Was she in jail? The pit in my guts opened into a ravine.

"After reading the article, I found Dakota's arrest record." Joe rose to his feet. "You need to see this." He left the room and returned seconds later with his laptop and placed it in front of me.

I scanned the page of Dakota's arrests and convictions. It wasn't as bad as I thought it would be, but it was bad enough. At the bottom of the last arrest a few months ago was her current address.

Muncie Avenue?

Bile caused my throat to burn. I knew that address all too well. The room spun, and my vision blurred a bit. This couldn't be happening. No wonder I had that dream about her. Dakota was in serious trouble.

"Tamara, are you okay?"

"It's worse than I thought." My chest felt tight, and my hands tingled

He placed a gentle hand on my back. "Just take a deep breath."

I tried to but it was hard to take air into my lungs. Two desires were at war inside me. One part of me wanted to do whatever it took to help my sister. She was obviously in some kind of trouble and had been for a while. The other side of me wanted to pretend I'd never seen any of this. To go back to my happy life with Joe and forget my family entirely. In the last twelve hours, I'd uncovered two tragedies in my family history, and a tingling in my gut told me there was more. Fear sank its fangs deep in my heart. I wasn't strong enough to fight whatever battle that lay ahead.

"Just breathe," Joe repeated, his hand making circles on my back.

I leaned into him and inhaled slowly. His strong arms encircled me, and, in that moment, he felt like my only safe place. His familiar scent calmed me a little. Maybe this was my answer, moving forward with Joe was the safest option for me. Going back was too painful. Too terrifying.

"Talk to me, Tamara."

I pointed to the address on the bottom of the screen. "Those were Ryan's old stomping grounds, a known drug house."

Joe tensed next to me.

I leaned forward and closed the laptop. "I think I've seen enough. It was stupid to look for my family. There's only sorrow back there." Dakota was in trouble, but what could I do for her after so much time had passed? She probably hated me for leaving her in the first place. If I showed up there now, after the hell she'd been through, she'd most likely slam the door and lock me out. No, moving forward in my future with Joe was the right thing to do. "I think you were right the other night."

Joe's brow creased. "About what exactly?"

"About Vegas. We should just jump in the car and drive. We could be married by tomorrow morning if we drive through the night."

"Baby girl," he said, tone soft, cupping his hands around my face. "You know how badly I want that, but you're not thinking straight. This is a lot to take in, but in some ways, it's good news. This is a huge lead. Surely, your sister knows where your parents are."

A thousand memories of my childhood carrying a lifetime of grief unleashed something that had been locked away for months. "You don't understand. I thought I could deal with this, but I can't. You don't know what it was like in my house growing up. There's a reason I stayed away so long. And now I find out their house burned down, and my sister is possibly living with a bunch of druggies."

My last night at home came back to me again, but this time the scene was different. Before Ryan picked me up that night, I had snuck into the living room where Dakota slept most nights. She was fast asleep, arms wrapped around the teddy bear I had bought her for Christmas the year before, her features childlike in the moonlight. I stared at her for a few minutes, memorizing the way she looked in that moment. "I love you, sis. Please don't forget that." I softly spoke over her, careful not to wake her.

Joe's voice whispering a prayer brought me out of the memory.

I fought back tears that threatened to come. Crying wouldn't help a thing. I withdrew from Joe and searched his face. It held a deep regretful emotion I couldn't figure out. Had he finally realized I was too broken to be his wife?

He touched my hand, caressing the tops of my fingers and tracing the outline of my ring.

"Tell me what you're thinking." I said.

"Honestly, I'm scared. I don't think it's a good idea for you to pursue this any further. But a part of me thinks it will eat you alive if you don't. There is no good answer here."

"What should I do? I need you to tell me what to do."

"You are the one who has to decide."

The emotion in Joe's eyes added to my fear. He had always been my rock, but this seemed too big for him. He didn't have the answers I needed, but I knew someone who did. I stood. "I'm going to go for a drive."

Joe flashed a concerned look. "Where to?"

"I don't know. I think I just need to sort this out with God."

"Okay." Joe stood and kissed the top of my forehead. "I'll be praying. I love you."

I gave him a half-smile and then walked down the hall,

grabbing my purse on the way out of his house—my heart heavy with the weight of this burden.

Dakota was in trouble, and I couldn't help but feel responsible.

CHAPTER 8

December 1, 10:40 a.m.

TAMARA

For a while I drove, listening to worship music, searching for the right answer. It wasn't long until I pulled into the place where my journey with God had begun. I walked up the steps, pushed through the double doors and quietly slipped into the sanctuary of Hope Chapel. The room was empty, and soft worship music played in the background. I took a few steps down the aisle toward the front row, allowing the music to wash over my soul. This was the right place to come. The one place I hoped to be able to find answers.

I ran my hand along the chairs as I walked. The last day I'd set foot in this sanctuary was three days before giving birth to Hope. In the few short months Joe and I attended here, it had become our home. I hadn't wanted to leave, but this was where Levi and Sarah attended. Seeing them every week with the baby I had carried would have been too much. I needed space to heal, but no other church we'd tried since leaving felt like home.

I sat down in the front row, staring at the spot I had knelt the day I surrendered my life to Jesus. I had let go of so much sadness that day, I didn't think there was any more left inside of me.

God, I need you.

My mind quieted as I focused on the music that played in the background. The song was *Everything and Nothing Else* by Chris McClarney. Tears welled as I meditated on the lyrics about trust and surrender. That article had busted me wide open. I may have escaped all those years ago, but what about Dakota? When we were kids, it was always me taking care of her. I was the one who had helped her get dressed in the morning. I was the one who had taught her how to manage her unruly hair. I was her protector on the playground. And I was the one who took the beating for her that night. But what about now? Was I strong enough to help Dakota out of the life I had abandoned her in? Fear wrapped around my chest like a boa constrictor, crushing the air from my lungs.

"God!" I stood from my chair and walked to the altar. "I need your help." Images of my childhood crashed through my mind, one painful scene after the next. The beatings. The poverty. The neglect. Thoughts of that ugly brown couch with my siblings squished together, watching *Nick at Night*, blaring the television to drown out our parents fighting. The scene in my mind shifted to my older brother, Gabriel, putting a comforting arm around me, telling me it was going to be okay. There were a lot of bad moments, but there were good moments too. And now those memories were gone, buried in a heap of ashes. It seemed parabolic of my childhood. Wouldn't it be pointless to go back and sift through the wreckage? Besides, what would I find?

Nothing but grief.

A song I'd never heard before began to play. The Holy Spirit settled over me as I listened to the lyrics about second chances and new beginnings. For a moment, I was brought back to that place where God had first found me. Love rushed over my being and my fears melted. The next line of the song overwhelmed my soul like a waterfall crashing over a cliff with raw power. *Beauty for ashes, beauty for ashes.* The line reverberated inside of my spirit. In my mind's eye, I could see the spot where my parents' trailer used to be. The ashes had settled into the earth, and flowers grew in their place. The plot that was once barren became a beautiful garden.

My eyes snapped open, unable to comprehend what I had just seen. The picture didn't make sense. Was God telling me that I should go face my past? Or was he saying that he would take the sorrow of my past and make it into something beautiful? My life with Joe was already beautiful. But was that enough?

I rose from my knees, walked up the center aisle, and pushed through the double doors, pondering these things.

"Tamara?" Off to the left, David stood near his office door.

"Hey, Pastor David." I crossed the room and gave him a hug.

"You doing okay?"

I looked around the foyer. No one was around at the moment, but I felt a bit uncomfortable having this conversation out in the open. "I found some leads on my family."

"That's a good thing, right?"

I shrugged, head down. From our counseling sessions, David knew a lot about my family history. "There was some pretty disturbing stuff actually."

"Sorry to hear that." David checked his watch. "Would you like to talk? I have about forty minutes before my next appointment."

I nodded and followed him into his office. The room was a light beige with high ceilings and trimmed with crown molding. The lighting was soft, and there were scents of hardwood mixed with hints of floral. David took a seat behind the large cherry-wood desk, and I sat in the oversized leather chair.

David wasn't the average counselor. His appearance reminded me more of a high school basketball coach. Tall and lanky, with a shiny bald head and kind gray-blue eyes. "You were saying you found some information?"

I played with the string that dangled from my hoodie. "I

found a news article that stated my childhood home burned to the ground."

Concern shown in his expression. "Was anyone hurt?"

"No, but the same article said my sister Dakota was a suspect in the arson."

"That is ..." He paused for a moment, seeming to look for the right word. "Very difficult."

"Yeah." I averted my gaze. "The thing is the night before I found out, I had a dream about Dakota. And she was in serious trouble. And then this morning Joe tracked her down. Her last known address is listed as an old drug house."

Worry lines appeared in David's forehead. He knew about how much guilt I carried over leaving my sister. He had helped walk me through it. "That is a lot to process. How are you doing with it?"

"I'm not sure what to do with the information. I want to go find her. To help her in any way that I possibly can. I want her to know how sorry I am for abandoning her."

David leaned back in his chair, eyebrows furrowed. "What if she's not ready for help?"

"What's the danger in going to talk to her?"

He was quiet for a moment too long. Was he expecting me to answer my own question? "What do you feel God is leading you to do?"

"I don't know." It was confusing to say the least. Everything had unfolded so fast I could barely catch my breath. There were the two nightmares, the article, and then the vision in the sanctuary. Somehow, they seemed to point in the same direction. "I think that if I don't at least try to do something, it would seriously mess with my head."

More silence from David.

I fiddled with my ring. If only someone that I trusted would tell me what to do.

David let out a long sigh and finally spoke. "I can't in good conscious tell you it's a good idea for you, but I will say, and I'm not saying this as your counselor, if it were my sister, I would move heaven and earth to try to help her. But, Tamara, I haven't walked the road you have. You're still in the process of healing. This could open some pretty big wounds."

In so many ways it already had. "I don't think I can ignore what I've found. I need to figure out a way to help her. She deserves that much." I stood with a new resolve. I wasn't the person I used to be. I wouldn't run from this.

David rose from his chair. "Tamara," he said, his countenance full of concern. "Please be careful."

"Thanks, David, I will be." I threw him a wave and headed out of his office before his misgivings could talk me out of it. I would never forgive myself if Dakota was in some sort of danger and I didn't try to stop it.

I'd already failed her too many times.

Rain pelted my skin as I ran to my car, but it barely phased me. Thoughts of Dakota, the drug house, and my nightmare tore through my mind with every step. Ryan may be in prison but only God knew the kind of evil she was surrounded by now. Guilt twisted my insides as I climbed in my car—a painful gnarl that started in my stomach and shot through my skull, giving me a splitting headache.

I slammed the door shut. Raindrops smashed against the windshield. I flipped the wipers on and sped out of the church parking lot. As I merged onto I-205, everything in me wanted to head north on I-5 and then hit Highway 101 until I reached my hometown. I'd leave no stone unturned until I found my sister, something I should have done six years ago.

I gripped the steering wheel tighter and pressed the accelerator. *God, please keep Dakota safe wherever she is. Help me find her and help Joe understand why I need to go.*

Anxiety consumed me as I turned into the Highway 99 Diner. How was I going to make Joe understand that I couldn't wait another day? I had to start looking for Dakota immediately.

I parked the car and entered the restaurant through the back. The place smelled like bacon, pancakes, and deep-fried onions. The combination hit me in an odd way, and my stomach recoiled. Howie, the cook who had replaced Anthony, had at least four orders on the grill and the order wheel was completely full. Through the cook's window, I could see Claire bustling from table to table. I thought about going to see if she needed help, but I was too anxious to talk to Joe.

She could handle it.

There had been plenty of times it had been busy and it had been just me. It wasn't easy, but I'd managed. Claire would be fine. I walked down the hall to the office and pushed open the door.

Joe sat behind the desk, looking at his laptop. "Hey, you." He grinned, and waved a hand, beckoning me. "Come take a look at this."

I forced a smile and walked across the room. On the screen was a list of restaurants for sale near Cannon Beach. My chest constricted. He was dreaming about our future, and all I could think about was my past.

"You okay?" He stood and put his hand on my back. "I thought this might make you happy."

It did, but also a little sad. "I'm all right." What a lie. "I went to Hope Chapel to pray."

"That's certainly a good place to start."

"I think I have to go to Quilcene. I have to find her."

The color drained from his face. "Now?"

"Yeah, of course now."

"I don't know, Tamara. This doesn't feel right. Maybe we should slow down."

"Slow down? You just don't get it. I, more than anyone, know the risks. That's why I have to try to help her. What would you do if this was your sibling? Would you just go on with your happy life even though you knew she was in some sort of trouble? Even David said that if it were his sister, he'd move heaven and earth to help her."

Confusion lined his brow. "You talked to David about this?"

I nodded. "I ran into him at Hope Chapel."

"And he said you should track her down?"

"Yes. Is that so hard to believe?" They weren't his exact words, but close enough.

"Maybe. It just doesn't make sense." Joe sat in the chair next to the table and was quiet for a long moment. Too long. Too quiet.

Guilt nagged at my insides. I shouldn't have lied, but if I told Joe about David's caution, it would just add more ammunition for Joe to resist this. "Tell me what you're thinking," I said finally.

"Okay, so both you and David think it's a good idea, but why now? Life is just now stabilizing for us, T. I was hoping to enjoy it for a little bit longer."

"Joe, you promised you'd help me find my family."

"And I meant it." He took in a deep breath. "But what are we supposed to do? Just drop everything and head there immediately?"

"It will only be for a few days. If I don't try to help her and something worse happens, I will regret it for the rest of my life."

"You haven't been there for six years. How is rushing to find her going to change anything?"

"Why are you resisting this so hard? We have no obligations other than the diner, and Claire is more than capable to run the day to day."

A strange expression flitted across Joe's features. "I don't know..."

"If you're worried, we could always have Trudy check in on her."

"I hear what you're saying. It's just—"

"Just what?"

He stood and paced the length of the room before turning to me. "I can't say."

"Come on, Joe, since when do we keep things from each other?" Another pang of guilt caused me to pause. It wasn't like I was being forthcoming, but what choice did I have? "And if it's keeping you from finding my family, you have to tell me."

"There are certain secrets that are not mine to tell."

"So now you are hiding Claire's secrets?"

"Of course not, it's just ... One of our rules at AA is that anonymity is sacred, so I can't say, but I just don't think she could handle the diner alone."

What was he saying? Claire was an addict? That was why he didn't want to leave the diner with her? He couldn't be serious. "Don't you think that's a tad hypocritical?"

Joe rubbed his forehead. "Okay, fine, the truth is she's struggling with her sobriety. I don't feel great about putting undue pressure on her."

"Undue pressure?" Anger pulsed through my veins. Wasn't he the least bit concerned about Dakota? "Claire is stronger than you give her credit for, and it will only be for a few days."

Joe crossed his arms. "I just don't think she's the right person for the job."

I threw my hands up in exasperation. "Find someone else then, because tomorrow morning I'm going to Quilcene with or without you." I turned toward the door.

"Where are you going?" His voice pitch changed, sounding alarmed.

"To help Claire with the lunch rush. I wouldn't want her to collapse under the pressure." I slammed the door on the way out of the office.

CHAPTER 9

December 1, 12:45 p.m.

JOE

For a long time, I stared at the closed door, paralyzed, anger and fear taking alternate punches at my insides. Should I go after Tamara? Did I even want to? This wasn't like her. Not the Tamara I'd known since finding her kneeling at the altar at Hope Chapel. What did she mean she was going to Quilcene without me? That would *never* happen. I opened the door and walked down the hall, hoping no one had heard the door slam.

Yeah, right.

Everyone heard it.

By the end of the night, the rumors would be out of hand, and I'd have to do damage control with Trudy.

I continued down the hall. Howie had six burgers on the grill and was melting cheddar cheese over each one. I walked past him into the dining room.

Claire bustled around the room, taking care of the patrons. But no Tamara. Where had she gone? My heart dropped into my abdomen. What if she'd already left?

No. She wouldn't do that.

I headed to the back for my phone and called her. It went to voicemail after three rings, and my pulse spiked. Maybe she *had* taken off. "Hey, uh, where are you? Call me as soon as you get this." Images of her speeding up the interstate filled my mind. I batted the thought away and pressed my phone against my head. That wasn't who she was anymore. *God, please help.* I grabbed the keys off the desk and headed out to my car.

Unease bit at my core. What now? I started the car and prayed again. My phone vibrated. *I'm sorry. I shouldn't have stormed out. I'm just upset and need some space.*

I breathed a sigh of relief. I wasn't sure how to respond so I set the phone down and backed out of the parking spot, heading toward Caleb's. I needed someone to talk to.

Twenty minutes later, my emotions had settled a bit, but a weight still sat in the center of my stomach. It wasn't fair of Tamara to put that kind of demand on me and storm out like that. But I guess it wasn't right for me to expect her not to want to go up there. I turned onto 87th Street and hoped Caleb would be home. Odds were, he would be. The guy had no job, lived with his parents, and this was his day off school.

Despite it being cold and a bit damp, Caleb was in his driveway, wearing his signature baggy shorts and a T-shirt, dribbling a basketball. I parked the car on the street and climbed out. Caleb pivoted a few times, acting as if he was defending against imaginary players, then did a jump-shot. The ball bounced off the rim and into the basket.

"Nice one. You're well on your way to that basketball scholarship." I snagged the ball as I walked toward the house.

"Hey, man." Caleb turned and came in for a sweaty side hug. "It's been a while. What's new?"

"Oh, you know." I set down my wallet and keys and moved to the same place Caleb had shot from.

"More women issues?"

"Ha, I guess you could say that." I modeled the same moves he did, then jumped and shot the ball. It hit the rim and bounced in.

"Not bad, Phillips." Caleb grabbed the ball on the return bounce. "I'm taking a psychology class this term. Maybe I can help." He spun around and attempted a shot but missed the basket completely.

Just then his mom popped her head out the door, smiling brightly. "Hi there, Joe, can I get you a drink? Water, orange juice, or soda?" She wiped her hands on her cherry print apron and stepped outside.

"Hey, Judy." I walked across the driveway and gave her a firm squeeze. I wasn't thirsty, but if I resisted, she would press. "Water sounds great."

"I'll take a soda, Ma."

She threw him a wry glance. "You know where the refrigerator is."

I chuckled.

She winked at me and headed back inside.

"Why psychology? Did you change majors again?" I grabbed the ball and dribbled it a few times before making a clean jump shot. Caleb had been a perpetual student ever since the big layoff at Entec. He'd changed his major a few times in the last three years, accumulating all sorts of debt. His dad was constantly on his case about it, but I think his mom liked having him at home.

"No, no, I'm still doing marketing, but a psychology class is required. Supposedly, it will help me be a better boss when I climb the corporate ranks." Caleb grabbed the ball, mirrored my last move and missed.

"If only it helped you with your game. That gives you an *H*," I said.

Judy came out with the drinks. She handed me the glass of water, then taunted Caleb with the soda before relinquishing it.

"Thanks, Judy."

"You're welcome." She blew me a playful kiss and headed back inside.

"She definitely loves me more." I threw the ball, but it bounced off the backboard.

"Whatever. All women love you more." He took a swig of his drink and successfully made a shot with his other hand.

Impressive.

"That's cause I'm nicer than you." I gave a cheesy smoldering look. "And way better looking."

He snatched the ball and threw it hard at my torso. "You keep telling yourself that, bro."

"Ouch." I coughed out a laugh. "I'm just messing. Aren't things going good with Jessica?"

"Dude, turns out she's crazy."

I raised my eyebrows. Heard that line more than once. This could be amusing. "Do you care to expound upon that?" I walked to the same place he'd shot from and tried to mimic his one-handed play but completely missed the basket, and the ball bounced into the bushes.

"Now you have an *H* too, Phillips," he said and went to fish the ball from the shrubs. "But yeah, apparently it was a bad idea to leave my phone in the car when I went in to pay for gas." He set down his drink and shot from the side. It was a perfect shot, all net.

"I'm not following." I grabbed the ball and walked right next to him.

"There were 'allegedly' several threads with other women on my phone."

"Allegedly?" I set down my drink next to his and then took my shot. Another miss.

He raised his hands in the air. "I will neither confirm nor deny these allegations. And that miss makes you a *H-O*."

"Oh, I'm the ho? I think chatting with multiple women while in a relationship actually makes you one." I laughed. "You're lucky you're still alive."

He grinned and dribbled a few times. "Dude, I know you didn't come here just to shoot hoops and mock my love life." He attempted a simple throw, but the ball bounced off the backboard and back to him. He tossed it to me.

I exhaled and threw it from where I was standing. Another miss. "It's Tamara."

"Shocking."

"Oh, come on."

"Sorry. What's up?" He moved back close to the basket, this time making his simple close-range hook.

I scooped the ball with one hand and moved closer to where he'd shot from. "She found some information online about her sister. She's living in some drug house."

"Wow."

"Right? She wants us to just drop everything and drive there to save her or something." I took the shot and missed again. I was so off my game.

"That's *H-O-R*. Sounds like an adventure to me, but if you don't want to go, then just tell her *no,* man."

"I can't do that."

"Why not?" Caleb tried a creative backward over-the-shoulder throw and missed.

"Because it's important to her." I caught his air-ball mid-bounce, shot from where I was and made it.

He shrugged. "Then go with her." He walked over and duplicated my shot with ease.

"I don't know, there's just a lot that could go wrong."

"Like what? In reality, what's the worst that could happen? You go to the bizarro-land drug house and, if her sister doesn't want out, then you just come home." Caleb snagged the ball on the return bounce and threw it to me.

I grabbed the ball and walked toward the sidewalk. "It's not that easy. We've had a rough few months. I just want to enjoy my fiancé for a minute without the intensity." Was that too much to ask for? I attempted a shot from the edge of the driveway and missed.

Caleb retrieved the ball. "All I'm saying is you have to make a decision, and then you tell her what's going to happen. Period.

End of discussion." He tossed the ball, and it swooshed into the basket.

I snorted. "Why did I even tell you about this? You don't know a thing about women." I snagged the ball and threw it but missed again.

"Maybe, but it doesn't take a rocket surgeon to know you need to grow a pair."

"The phrase is rocket scientist."

"It's a marketing thing I'm trying out. Merging two phrases into one to make something new, like Picasso did. Taking a bike seat and handlebars to create his bull sculpture." Caleb grabbed the ball. "But seriously, Joe, you're too much of a puppy when it comes to women. Susan and now Tamara. You have a tendency to get lost in them." He shot again, another swish.

Was he right? No, of course not. There was a reason he was still single at twenty-six and living with his parents. I moved into position and took the shot. Complete miss. That was it for my letters.

Caleb raised his hands in victory. "Another game?"

"Nah, I have to get back to the diner and figure this mess out." I took my stuff from the ground.

"So, you're going to go?"

"Probably. I really don't want to, but I have to." Another round with Tamara's demons... Wasn't it time to start *our* happily-ever-after?

Caleb shook his head. "I'm beginning to think you're the crazy one, Phillips."

"You literally have no idea. One day I hope love smacks you so hard you can't see straight. Then you'll know what it's like."

"Oh jeez." Caleb's eyes rolled into the back of his head. "I'm just saying ya gotta be all in or all out. Our perceived reality can be tricky, and perception is often nine-tenths of the flaw."

"Ok, Mr. Miyagi. Is that another marketing phrase?"

"Yes, Daniel-san." Caleb placed his hands together and gave a slight bow.

"It's terrible." I turned and walked to my car.

"But so true!" Caleb yelled. "You need to figure out what you want or that woman will eat you alive."

I put my keys in the car door. "Whatever, dude. Thanks for the game. Have a good one."

"Anytime." He saluted me before taking another shot.

I slipped into my car, trying to shake the feeling that part of what he said may be true.

CHAPTER 10

December 1, 4:35 p.m.

TAMARA

Standing in the middle of my living room, I held the pack of Camel 99s in my hand and imagined ripping off the cellophane. One cigarette wouldn't hurt, would it? I mean, seriously, after finding out about my sister and fighting with Joe, a couple of drags was understandable. I played with the tiny tag and then tore it off. I opened the lid on the cardboard box and removed the foil covering the smokes. The familiar aroma of pressed tobacco filled my nose, and my stomach turned.

This was so dumb. I'd quit this smelly habit almost a year ago, but nothing was touching the shock of uncovering this info about my sister. I slowly pulled the cigarette out of the pack and brought it to my lips. Maybe Joe was right. Maybe I needed to slow down. What was going there now going to do anyway? Dakota probably hated me for abandoning her.

I grabbed the lighter I'd bought and flicked it a few times before it ignited.

A tap on the door. I threw the lighter down and shoved the cigarettes under the couch cushion. The lighter landed by my daybed, so I kicked it underneath on the way to answering the door. I opened it a crack, and there was Joe, a bouquet of long-stemmed red roses in his hand.

Seriously? I'd been such a jerk to him at the diner and he was bringing me flowers? I opened the door the rest of the way, head down, heavy from shame. "I'm so sorry for how I acted earlier."

Joe kissed me tenderly on the cheek. "I'm sorry too. I know this is hard for you."

The sweet scent of fresh cut roses hit my nose as I rested against him.

The cigarettes under the couch cushion invaded my thoughts. "That doesn't give me the right to treat you like that." I took the flowers from his hands, went into the kitchen, and grabbed a vase. "I don't know what's wrong with me."

Joe followed me. "This is difficult, T. I can't imagine what's going on inside of you right now."

I placed the flowers in the vase and turned toward him. His kind eyes were full of understanding. Guilt berated my insides. I shouldn't have lied to him earlier. And what about the cigarettes hidden in the couch? Should I tell him? I leaned into him, pressing my head against his shoulder. His arms came around me, and I melted further.

"I talked to Claire this afternoon. She can cover while we're gone, but it will take a couple of days to get her ready."

So that was it? I had bullied him into this decision and now he was fully on board? Another bucket load of guilt filled my belly. "I need to tell you something."

"Okay...?" Apprehension tinged his voice.

I ducked out of his embrace. "David didn't exactly tell me I should find her. In fact, he cautioned me against it."

He was quiet for a long moment. "Why would you lie to me?" He didn't sound angry. Just hurt. Which was so much worse.

"I don't know. This whole thing is exploding inside of me. I don't feel like myself right now. I'm really sorry."

"I forgive you, but Tamara." He played with a lock of my

hair, his expression sad. "I just thought we were in a place that you could tell me anything. We're in this together."

"I know we are. And you've been so great through everything. It's just seeing that stuff on the internet messed with my head. I didn't tell you this either, but I had a nightmare the other night about Dakota. It was the night before I found that article." My voice broke, and I swallowed back the shards of glass raking against my throat. "I'm afraid if I don't do something, I may not have a sister."

Joe pulled me to him once more. "It's going to be okay. We'll head there in a few days. I promise you, Tamara. We'll get through this together."

His words settled over me. Truth was, I knew *we* would be okay, but what about Dakota? What could I possibly do to help her?

Honestly, I didn't know.

CHAPTER 11

December 3, 2:45 p.m.

JOE

"Have I shown you the call list just in case?" I sat in my office with Claire, going over the last-minute details. A huge ball of anxiety sat on my sternum, a feeling I hadn't been able to shake for the last few days. Something was off about this trip, but I couldn't place my finger on what.

"Like five times." Claire said, shifting in her seat.

"Sorry." I tapped the tip of my pen against the table. "Just want to be thorough."

She shot me an irritated glare. "Your lack of confidence is insulting."

There was a knock at the door. Betty popped her head in. "Hey, Claire, there's someone out here asking for you."

"Be right there." She gave her cell a quick glance before standing. "Are we done here?"

"Yes. Thanks again for doing this."

"Absolutely, I'm glad to help."

I followed Claire out of the office, down the hall, and through the kitchen. Howie hovered over the grill, pushing food around with his spatula. The order wheel was filled with tickets. Lunch rush was in full swing.

The dining room was almost to capacity. There were only

two empty booths and one free table. A man with a bad comb over stood by the door, holding a briefcase. He wore slacks and a trench coat.

Claire gave Betty a questioning glance.

Betty tilted her head toward the man.

He was obviously not here to be seated.

Claire walked toward him. "May I help you?"

"Claire Hoffmann?"

"Yes?" Her voice sounded shaky.

He opened his briefcase, pulled out a Manila envelope, and handed it to her. "You've been served." He then turned and walked out the door.

Claire stared after him, mouth gaping, envelope clutched in her hand. She grabbed the closest empty chair and sat down, the color slowly draining from her face.

"What is it?" I asked.

She looked at me. "I'm not sure."

I glanced around the busy diner. "Let's go back to the office."

Claire followed me to the small room and sat down. She hesitated for a moment, then opened the envelope and slid out the paper slowly. She froze. A look of horror briefly crossed her features before she shoved the papers back in. A cement block dropped into my stomach. What was in there? And more importantly, was Claire going to be able to run the diner for the next few days? "Are you okay?"

Claire straightened herself and cleared her throat. "Oh yeah, I'm good. My ex can be a real drama queen sometimes." She waved the envelope nonchalantly. "All this to tell me he wants to change the visitation schedule. Trade Wednesday's for Saturday's. That's it." She stood abruptly, her chair making a screeching sound. "Aren't you supposed to be meeting Tamara soon?"

"Ummm, yeah." I checked my watch. "Are you sure you're still good to run the place?"

"Yes, of course." She smiled, but it seemed forced.

She was without a doubt lying to me, but what could I do? Tamara would have left days ago if we could have. We couldn't postpone the trip because Claire had personal drama going on. "All right, well, if you need help, Trudy is only an hour away."

Claire waved me off. "Get out of here."

I threw her a wry smile and headed out the back door.

Worry churned in me as I started my Jeep and drove out of the parking lot. What if that envelope contained information that was earth shattering? Would Claire be able to handle the stress of the diner? Would she be able to keep her sobriety?

I grabbed my phone. Maybe I should call Trudy. No, Trudy didn't need to be hassled with this. Claire would be fine. The diner would be fine. I'd already done the ordering for the week. The only thing she would need to do was make the drops and make sure the customers were happy. Surely, she would be able to handle that. I pressed on the accelerator and prayed that I was doing the right thing by everyone.

CHAPTER 12

December 3, 3:45 p.m.

TAMARA

The sun shone bright on this cool, crisp day. It was the first day in weeks that it hadn't rained, and I hoped it was a sign.

Joe seemed nervous as he loaded my duffel bag in the back of his Jeep. He usually had this childlike faith that made my reservations disappear. Seeing Joe's nerves, though, filled me with doubt.

Over the last few days, I'd circled the options in my mind a thousand times and always drawn the same conclusion. Driving the three-and-a-half-hour trip was our only viable choice.

I tugged on his hand, and he turned his gaze on me.

"You okay? You seem off."

"An incident happened at the diner before I left." He closed the hatch before walking around to my side of the car and opening the door for me.

His mood wasn't about the trip? That was a relief. I followed after him. "What was it?" I climbed into the Jeep and buckled myself in.

"Hold that thought." He walked around to his side and climbed in. "Claire was served some sort of legal papers from her ex-husband."

No wonder Joe had been tense. "Sounds serious."

"She said not to worry, but I don't know." Joe started the vehicle and backed out of the parking space. "You should have seen her face when she opened the envelope."

I felt bad for Claire. She had become a good friend over the last few months. She'd been there for me through the pregnancy and adoption. Now she was going through something big, and I was leaving town. Should we postpone the trip? I pondered the thought for a few brief moments. No. This thing with my sister was too important. Dakota needed me more than Claire did right now. "I'm sure she will be all right."

"I hope so," Joe said.

I cranked the radio to drown out the guilt that was bludgeoning my stomach and rested my head on Joe's arm, weaving my fingers through his. Claire would be fine. I should have taken this trip years ago.

We made our way through traffic, heading North on I-5. As the road flew by, I imagined what seeing my sister after six years would be like. A vision of Dakota standing before me, eyes burning with resentment before slamming the door in my face, played through my head. My heart became heavy—the force of a ton of bricks landing in it. This right here, the unknown future taunting me with my past mistakes, was the exact reason I'd never attempted going back. Most of the time, my mind conjured the worst of images.

I couldn't think that way now. God had let me see this for a reason. It was time to at least try to make things right—even if Dakota rejected me. This way I could at least say I did the right thing on my end. If she didn't want me back after everything that was her choice. Being afraid of rejection wasn't going to hold me back because a different outcome was always a possibility. She could be happy to see me. To know I was alive after all this time. And maybe, just maybe, I could help her. I thought about the vision I'd had at the church, and a hopeful feeling flitted through me.

Joe squeezed my hand. "What are you thinking about?"

I glanced at him. He seemed a bit more relaxed. "The other day when I was praying, I had some sort of vision, like a short movie playing inside my head."

He turned down the stereo. "What did you see?"

"I saw the spot where my parents' trailer used to be. The ashes had settled into the earth, and flowers bloomed in their place, becoming a beautiful garden. It kind of felt like a promise."

"Beauty for ashes," Joe said, his tone contemplative. "Interesting. I just read that verse the other day."

That's in the Bible? "What verse?"

"It's in Isaiah, Chapter 60."

I opened the Bible app on my phone, found the verse, and read it out loud. A hopeful feeling rose from deep within as I stared at the words. So many signs were leading me in this direction. It had to be the right decision.

CHAPTER 13

December 3, 6:20 p.m.

JOE

We made good time on the drive. The GPS said it was a three-hour trip, but with the traffic being clear I was able to set my cruise control for five miles over the speed limit. Once we hit Highway 101, we had to slow down a bit because of the winding road. The scenery was breathtaking. The road snaked its way along the Olympic Peninsula, water on one side and tall evergreen trees on the other. Tamara found a feel-good country station and leaned back in her seat. We passed through a tiny town called Brinnon and then headed up a mountain.

The phone rang through my Bluetooth speaker with Betty's number on the screen. A dart of anxiety hit me as I tapped the green icon. "Hello."

"Hey, Joe," Betty's nasally voice came through the line. "I've tried calling you several times, but it went straight to voicemail."

"I'm sorry, the service on the peninsula is a bit spotty."

"Claire's not doing well."

Tamara and I exchanged a worried glance.

"What's going on?"

"After you left, she locked herself in your office for over an hour. When she came out, her eyes were puffy like she'd been crying. I don't know what was in those papers she was served, but whatever it is, it's affecting her. I don't think she's in any place to run the restaurant."

Not good. I knew it was worse than she'd let on. "All right, Betty, thanks for letting me know. I'll take care of it."

"I don't know, Joe. I just wish you were here—" The line went blank.

I looked at my phone to see what had happened. No signal.

Tamara shifted in her seat. Her lips turned down, a line forming between her brows. "Sounds like we should just turn around."

"No, T. We're literally minutes away. I'll just call Trudy."

"We can't." Tamara's voice was flat. "We have no signal. When I was here before, Quilcene was a total dead zone."

"It's been years since you have been here. The whole town can't still be without signal."

"Well, it's obviously still spotty."

"I'm sure we'll be able to find service somewhere. But if not, I'll call Trudy from the first landline we see. For right now, where do you want to start?"

She sighed. "I don't know."

"It's getting late. Why don't we go check out that house first?" Ahead of us, the small town came into view. On this end, there wasn't much to it. A few houses between the evergreen trees and a garbage dump.

"Okay." She nodded. "I'm sorry. I'm just nervous all of a sudden."

"Understandable." I squeezed her hand. "Where do we need to go?"

"Keep going for another mile on this road."

On the left, we passed a restaurant that looked more like a large log cabin. "That's the Timber House. My mom used to work there." The tone in her voice was sad. Tamara didn't speak much about her mom, but from what I knew, she worked a lot, always leaving the kids home alone to fend for themselves.

"Maybe she still does."

"No, she quit a long time ago. She couldn't stand her boss. When I left, she was working two jobs in Port Hadlock.

We drove past the Mountain Walker Inn, where Tamara and I would be staying, and then another restaurant named Loggers Landing.

"Right there, where the road curves, just stay straight on to Linger Longer Road," Tamara said.

I wasn't sure if I liked the energy of this town. It had a certain amount of quaintness and charm, but there seemed to be an ominous black cloud that blanketed its beauty. I followed Tamara's directions down a road that wound around a swamp with a fence around it. Next to the fence was a sign that said, *Your tax dollars at work.*

Tamara pointed ahead. "Over that bridge, we're going to take a right."

I flipped on my signal and turned onto Muncie Avenue. Most of the houses, though small, were taken care of, with the yards clean and manicured.

"That's it on the right." She pointed to a grungy grey house right ahead of us. My stomach tightened. The house was out of place in the neighborhood. Paint peeled around the windowsills, revealing an odd dirty-red underneath. The yard was overgrown, and a few rusted old cars cluttered the driveway.

Pulling forward, I did a U-turn, and parked on the opposite side of the road before facing Tamara. Her features held years of sadness. Nothing in me wanted to let her go near that house. I placed my hand gently on her arm. "We can do this tomorrow if you're not ready."

"No." She took in a deep breath. "Just give me a minute."

I caressed her arm. "Take all the time you need."

After a few moments, she reached for the door handle. I climbed out, hurried around the car, and took hold of her hand as soon as I reached her. We walked across the street and down the gravel driveway. The dark cloud I sensed earlier felt heavier as we grew closer to the house.

Tamara stepped up to the door and knocked three times.

Someone peeked out of the blinds. Footsteps. The door opened a crack, and a blast of marijuana hit my nose, mingling with the stale smell of alcohol and cigarettes.

A twiggy blonde woman with dark shadows under her eyes and a few sores under her mouth stood in the doorway. "Can I help you?" Her focus shifted as if she was seeing more than just us standing there.

Tamara gave me a nervous glance. "Um, I'm looking for Dakota Jensen."

"Dakota?" She said her name like a curse word, opening the door a bit wider.

A guy sat on the ratty couch behind her, puffing on a cigarette. Or a joint.

"Who's looking for her?"

"I'm Tamara, her sister."

The guy in the background seemed to perk up.

Blondie let out a snort. "Dakota doesn't have a sister."

Tamara looked down at her feet, a pink color climbing her neck. "It's been a long time. I'll be in town for a few days at the Mountain Walker Inn."

My grip tightened around Tamara's hand. What was she thinking, giving this girl that kind of information?

"I don't know where she's at. She took off with Ryan a few days ago."

Alarm bells rattled my brain. Was that the same Ryan Tamara had been running from years ago? He was supposed to be in jail.

Tamara's face went a dismal ashy color before she turned and took a few steps toward the car.

"Thank you for your time," I said, then followed after Tamara. I caught up with her and put my arm around her waist.

She was shaking, and inwardly I was too because I knew exactly what was going through her mind. Dakota had disappeared a few days ago with the man from Tamara's nightmares.

CHAPTER 14

December 3, 6:50 p.m.

TAMARA

My mind felt like it was under water as I climbed into Joe's Jeep. Dakota was with Ryan? How could he be out of jail? I had read that article when I was in Ocean Shores. He'd been arrested for dealing drugs. The article had said if he was convicted, he would spend up to ten years in jail.

"Oh no!" I put my head between my knees, mind spinning.

Ryan was never convicted. He'd been roaming free this whole time.

"You're okay, Tamara." Joe placed his hand on my back.

I wanted to scream. I was definitely *not* okay. Just like in my dream, Dakota was in danger, off somewhere with that psychopath, and I was powerless to help her.

The car started to move forward.

What if Ryan was punishing her for what I had done years ago? I would never forgive myself if she was in trouble and somehow it was my fault. "We have to find her, Joe. If he's done something to her—" I couldn't choke out the rest of the words.

"We *will* find her," he said emphatically. "I promise."

"How do you know that?" I lifted my head to see him.

His expression was gentle, sincere, and full of faith. I had thought earlier that his faith had faded, but here it was when I needed it the most. Would he have enough for us both?

Images of Ryan choking the life out of Dakota sent a fresh wave of dread through me, and both of my limbs went numb. I sucked in a large breath to calm my racing pulse.

I was vaguely aware of my surroundings as Joe steered the Jeep into the Mountain Walker Inn and parked it near the office. Leaning over, he put both of his arms around me, drawing me in close.

I took in a few long inhales, letting my body melt into his.

"Do you want to come in with me to check in?"

"No. I'll just wait out here."

He kissed my forehead before exiting the Jeep. I looked around at the place to distract myself from thinking about Dakota. They had done a lot of improvements to the inn since I'd been here last. They'd painted the outside and upgraded the landscape. A lot nicer than I remembered.

Thoughts of the nightmare returned. Ryan's angry scowl as he dragged Dakota into the house, striking her multiple times. So much time had passed, and I was right back in the same place I'd started—a scared, helpless little girl. Only this time it wasn't me I was afraid for.

A door slammed across the parking lot, and I jumped. Going down the old dark pathways in my mind wasn't going to help. Minutes passed, and I wished I would've gone in with Joe. What was taking him so long? He'd already paid for the room online. All he needed to do was sign the paperwork and get the key.

A minute later Joe emerged from the office, his expression disturbed. He climbed in the car. "So, I have good news and bad news."

"I can't handle more bad news."

"I'll start with the good then. My phone had service in the lobby, and I got ahold of Trudy."

I checked my phone. Two bars. Not too bad.

"She's going to be checking on the diner this evening," He continued, "and will be staying in town until we get back. I should have just called her in the first place."

I thought of Claire and what she was going through. Joe was right. "What's the bad news?"

Joe lifted the room key into the air. "They made a mistake on the room reservation. We got a king bed instead of two queens."

My eyebrows shot up. Sounded like great news to me. "They couldn't change it?"

Joe bit his bottom lip. "Nope. Completely booked. To top it off, it happens to be the honeymoon suite."

I bit back a laugh. "I could think of worse things."

"I'm sure you could." He muttered to himself.

I did appreciate how he guarded over our purity, but sometimes I wished he'd lighten up about it. "We could go somewhere else."

"No, not tonight anyway. You need to get some rest."

Joe backed the car to our room and parked. We unloaded our two bags and brought them inside. It was a simple room for being the honeymoon suite: blue carpets, a king size bed with a red comforter and mirror on the ceiling. Other than that, it was your basic motel room with a mini-fridge and microwave.

After going to the bathroom, I slumped down in the bed, the discoveries of the day weighing on me.

Joe came over and knelt in front of me, taking hold of both of my hands. "How are you?"

God, I loved this man. I didn't know what I did right in my screwed-up life to deserve him, but I would hold onto him for all he was worth. "I'm not sure." My tummy grumbled.

"You hungry?"

"A bit. I'm more tired than hungry."

"You need to eat, T."

"I don't want to go anywhere."

89

"You don't have to. I'll walk over to that restaurant and get us dinner."

"That sounds amazing." My stomach growled again. Loggers was right next door, so it wouldn't take long, and it had been years since I had Loggers food. "If I remember correctly, they have an excellent BLT."

"One BLT coming right up." Joe kissed my forehead on the way to his feet.

I gave him a tired smile. "You take such good care of me."

"That's my job." He kissed me again. "Do me a favor and lock the door when I leave."

Being raised in such a small town, we hardly ever locked up, but because he insisted, I followed him and strung the chain across the door before heading to the bathroom. I turned on the shower and undressed quickly.

I tried not to think as I stood in the stream of hot water but couldn't hold back the onslaught of images I'd suppressed for years. The day I found out Ryan was a drug dealer played through my mind like a movie. It had been close to two in the morning, and I'd been sleeping for hours. I woke to the sound of Ryan screaming at someone about owing him money. Following the commotion out to the garage, I found him standing over a young man, kicking him repeatedly, yelling about fronting him drugs and now he was going to pay. In my mind's eye, the young man Ryan was beating transformed into Dakota, and I practically doubled over in the shower.

God, please make these pictures stop and keep Dakota safe, wherever she is.

I turned off the shower and grabbed a towel. It was thin and half the size of my towels at home, but it did the job.

After drying off, I threw my hair into a loose ponytail and applied the slightest amount of makeup. I was dabbing on lip gloss when I heard a tapping at the door. *That was quick*, I thought, walking across the room. *Maybe Joe forgot his wallet.* I took off the chain lock and swung open the door. "That was—"

A man stood in front of me wearing an old gray cap, head tilted forward so the bill covered his face.

My pulse sped, pounding in my ears.

His head slowly rose, a sardonic grin twisting his grizzled features.

My heart jumped into my throat. Every nightmare I'd had for the last six years appeared before me, but this time it wasn't a dream.

Backing away, I screamed.

CHAPTER 15

December 3, 8:15 p.m.

JOE

A panicked shriek filled the air as I left the restaurant. I dropped our food and bolted out of the parking lot.

As I rounded the corner, I noticed the door to our room was wide open. Adrenaline pushed me faster.

It didn't make sense. She'd locked herself in as I'd left.

I darted through the door.

A man had Tamara pinned against the wall, his hand covering her mouth. Her eyes were wide, like a wild animal caught by its predator.

I crossed the room, yanked him off her, and slammed my fist against his jaw.

He took a few steps back and swung at me.

I ducked out of the way and then jabbed him in the abdomen. Before he could swing again, I pounded him with an uppercut, knocking him to the floor. I jumped on him and shoved my knee deep into his ribs. He cursed and flailed his arms, but I dug my knee deeper and slammed my fist into his face again. Thoughts of killing him almost overtook me. Who was this guy? What was he trying to do with Tamara? After a few more hard slams to the jaw, he slowed his resistance.

"Joe, stop!" Tamara's voice cut through my murderous thoughts. "He's not worth it."

"Call 911!" I flipped him over and twisted his hands around his back, close together so he couldn't budge. Behind me, Tamara rattled off details to the dispatcher.

He squirmed and fought underneath my grasp, a string of expletives exploding from his mouth.

"Who is this?" I asked as she hung up the phone.

"It's Ryan." Her voice trembled with fear. "I thought he was going to kill me."

Anger, in blasts of heat, pulsed through my veins. This was the animal that caused the one I loved so much torment. What would he have done to her if I wasn't here? My stomach recoiled. I tried to shake away the disgusting images playing through my head. I would kill him if he ever touched her again. Forget that. I should kill him now and end this.

CHAPTER 16

December 3, 8:25 p.m.

TAMARA

Mind racing, I stared down at Ryan squirming under Joe's restraint. His skin was pallid, and his eyes were bloodshot with shaded dark circles around them as if he hadn't slept for a week. He was stronger than he used to be, but in the six years since I'd seen him, he seemed to have aged fifteen.

"You have a lot of nerve coming here." Ryan's voice was guttural, inhuman, demonic.

"Shut up," Joe said through clenched teeth. "Don't say a word to her."

In the distance, sirens sounded.

"Joe, maybe he knows where to find my sister."

Ryan laughed, a sick menacing sound that made my stomach clench. "You wanna know what happened to your sister, baby?"

The lines of anger on Joe's face deepened, and he shoved Ryan's head harder against the floor. "I said shut up!" Joe turned his gaze to me, his expression softening. "Maybe you should wait outside."

"No, Joe, I want to hear what he has to say."

Ryan squirmed under Joe again, whipping his head around

so he could see me. "I killed her." He laughed again. "I watched as the bonfire swallowed her whole."

What? No! It couldn't be true. Three days ago, she went missing with Ryan, just after my nightmare. Was I too late?

"He's lying, Tamara." Joe smashed Ryan's head further into the carpet. "Don't listen to a word he says."

The sirens grew closer as they pulled into the motel parking lot.

"I wouldn't lie to you, baby," he said through gritted teeth. "And just so you know, I'm gonna kill you too."

"You will never touch her!" Joe slammed his face against the floor.

"Joe, stop!" I cried out just before the police officers stormed into the room.

"I'll kill you. Do you hear me? I will kill you!" Joe shouted.

Two tall men in uniform, wrestled Joe off of Ryan.

An officer turned toward me. "Miss, could you tell me what happened here?"

For a second, I couldn't speak. I couldn't make sense of what just happened. Or the words Ryan had said. A sharp ringing shot through my ears.

"Miss? Are you okay?"

I sat down on the bed, unable to stand for another moment. "She can't be dead," I whispered.

"Excuse me?"

I looked around the room, suddenly aware that Joe and Ryan were gone. "He said he killed her."

CHAPTER 17
December 3, 8:40 p.m.
JOE

The officer pushed me against the car, twisted my hands behind my back, and slapped handcuffs on me. My right hand throbbed, and blood trickled down my knuckles. I wasn't sure if it was Ryan's blood or mine.

"You have the right to remain silent."

I crooked my head around, searching for Tamara as the officer read me my rights. From the corner of my eye, I could see Ryan's battered features through the back window of the other police car.

He stared at me, his expression full of loathing. The hair stood on the back of my neck. No wonder Tamara had been scared of this guy. He was pure evil.

"Officer, I didn't do anything wrong."

"When we came in, you were assaulting a man and threatening to kill him."

"That psychopath attacked my fiancée."

"Sir, I would advise you to stay quiet until you have a lawyer present."

A lawyer? He couldn't seriously be arresting me. "My fiancée will tell you what happened."

"My partner is questioning her right now."

I twisted my head again. Where was she? My hands twisted in the cuffs. "Officer, please let me explain. I'm not a violent person." I thought of Tamara in that motel without me. Terrified out of her mind that her sister might be dead. I had to get to her. "I was just protecting the woman I love."

"Okay, son, that's enough."

Son? Did he call me *son*? "Sir, can I please just go talk to her to make sure she's okay? He said he killed her sister."

The officer turned me around.

Through the door, I saw Tamara sitting on the bed in the hotel room, hunched over, head buried in her hands, body convulsing.

"You're telling me Ryan Cooke confessed to killing someone." The officer waved to the car Ryan was in, beckoning the other cop to come to us.

A younger man in uniform approached us while his partner stayed behind with Ryan.

"Tell Officer Moore what you just told me."

"He said he killed Tamara's sister, Dakota Jensen. Said he watched her burn in a fire."

Fear flickered across the young man's face.

"He threatened to kill Tamara too."

The older cop opened the car door. "Thank you for the information. We need to do some investigating, but for now, I need you to have a seat."

I climbed in the back seat without resisting.

The officer closed the door and stood guard outside while Officer Moore left to go check in with Tamara.

Her arms were enfolded around herself, and she rocked slightly back and forth.

My heart split in two. I needed to be in there with her. I hated that I could see her in this much pain but could do nothing to comfort her. *God, please help me get out of this.*

I let out an exhausted sigh. I couldn't believe I was in the back of a cop car with handcuffs on. Could this day get any worse?

The cop spoke on his CB radio several times, talking in codes I couldn't understand.

A few minutes later, Officer Moore walked out of the room, his expression grim. He took the older officer aside, far enough away that I couldn't hear. After a few minutes, Officer Moore returned to his car and drove away.

Ryan's beady-eyed gaze stayed on me as they drove out of the motel parking lot. They were taking him in. Would I be next?

The officer's partner came out of the hotel room and closed the door, leaving Tamara alone.

The car door swung open. "We have your girlfriend's statement on record, and it confirms your story. We'll be using them both in our official report."

"Whatever you need, sir."

He helped me out of the back of his car and unlocked my handcuffs. "Ryan Cooke has been a thorn in our side for years, but we've never been able to nail him. Slippery as a snake, that one. With enough evidence, we might actually be able to put him away for a while on this one."

"What about Dakota?"

He tensed. "Can't say. She's got a history too, so anything is possible. We'll file a missing person's report on her and start an official investigation. We'll be in contact as soon as we have any more information." The officer handed me his card. "If you hear from her, give me a ring."

I nodded and took the card, uneasiness filling my stomach. Dakota couldn't be dead.

Tamara wouldn't recover from it.

The officers climbed into their vehicle.

I walked toward the room, body heavy, hand aching.

Tamara stood when she saw me, looking as if she might

break in half. I hurried toward her, drew her into an embrace, and she collapsed against me.

For what seemed like hours, we quietly lay in the hotel bed. There was nothing to say, so all I did was hold her.

Tamara finally broke the silence, her tone lifeless. "Do you think God is punishing me?"

"What? No?" I swept my hand over her beautiful tear-stained face.

"I feel like it's my fault." The depth of sadness in her eyes was hard to bear. "I just don't understand."

I searched for the right response but came up short. How was I supposed to tell her it was going to be okay when I wasn't even sure myself? "I'm so sorry, Tamara."

"You've been the one good thing in my life." She averted her gaze and spoke through quivering lips. "Sometimes I'm afraid I'm going to lose you too."

I gently caressed the outline of her jaw. "I'm not going anywhere, T. I love you so much."

She rested her head back on me. "Have you ever seen that movie *The Butterfly Effect*?"

"I don't think so."

She sighed heavily. "It's about a guy who time travels to different places in his life, but in doing so it changes the circumstances in the present. Every time he goes back to make things better, he does something that makes other people's lives worse." She paused as if momentarily caught in her thoughts.

I didn't like where this was headed. Not even a little bit.

"In the end, he realizes that it would have been better if he had died at birth. That way none of the terrible things his life had caused ever happened."

"Tamara." The emotion stuck in my throat, making it impossible to speak.

"Look at the damage I caused. If I had never run away or stolen money from Ryan, Dakota would be safe."

How could she think this world would be better without

her in it? She was the one who brightened my world. The one who gave me the energy and reason to push forward on difficult days. I moved her face toward mine. "There's no way you could know that for sure. Ryan is feeding you lies to mess with your head."

Her bottom lip trembled. "Joe, you don't know Ryan like I do. Sure, he's a liar, but I wouldn't put this past him."

"Listen, I need you to hear me. I love you so much. This is killing me right now. On the off chance he *is* telling the truth, we will get through this. I promise you whatever the next moment holds, I will be with you every step."

"I *do* hear you," she said, her voice hoarse. "Thank you for being here, for loving me the way you do."

I ran my fingers through her hair and brought my mouth gently to hers. She slipped her hands around my neck, pulling me in closer, inviting the kiss to become deeper.

My phone rang on the nightstand.

We both ignored it.

Tamara wove her fingers through my hair, and her lips became urgent against mine.

What was she doing? I hadn't seen it going in this direction with the sadness of the day lurking over us. I drew back slightly, fighting the hunger within me.

Tamara crushed herself into me, and the small amount of resistance I did have crumbled. The passion that I'd been suppressing for months suddenly took over.

I was slightly aware of the faint ringing of Tamara's phone.

She withdrew her mouth from mine, slowly kissing the line of my jaw to my ear.

Tap, tap, tap. A light knocking at the door.

Tamara stiffened and leaned back, taking in a few ragged breaths.

I glanced at the clock. *10:47 p.m.* Perhaps it was an officer returning to check in with us.

Another round of knocking. "Tamara." A woman's voice came through the door. "You in there?"

Tamara's eyes grew wide, she jumped out of the bed and bolted to the door.

"Tamara, wait." I caught hold of her. "Let me get it." I pushed myself past her before she could protest and opened the door a crack.

A woman stood there, her back turned away from us, her long, dark hair moving in the breeze. She was smoking a cigarette. A puff of smoke came off her as she turned around.

Whoa! The resemblance was uncanny. I shut the door quickly and slid the chain lock off, reopening it as quick as possible.

Beside me, Tamara gasped. "Dakota?"

Though Dakota was the younger sister, she looked older. She didn't carry the same resilience as Tamara. Tamara had experienced her fair share of suffering since she'd left home, but the hollowness in Dakota's gaze told me she'd gone through more.

"Well, well, well. The prodigal daughter finally returns home." Dakota took a long pull from her cigarette and blew it toward Tamara.

Tamara coughed, but then rushed toward her, throwing her arms around her. "You're alive!"

My phone rang again.

I didn't want to leave Tamara's side for a second, but I needed to check it. This was the third time someone was trying to reach out to us at almost eleven at night. I walked across the room and answered my phone.

CHAPTER 18

December 3, 10:55 p.m.

TAMARA

Relief replaced the fear that I'd fought back all night. Dakota was alive. I was touching her. "Ryan said that he killed you."

She stiffened under my embrace as the smoke of her cigarette swirled around us. "Yeah, well, we both know Ryan is a liar." She stepped away and took a drag of her cigarette. "Who's Romeo in there?"

I glanced over my shoulder.

Joe was on the phone with someone, his features agonized. Was it more trouble with the diner? I couldn't think about that now. I had my sister back. "That's Joe, my fiancé."

Her mouth twisted into a sneer. "Fiancé? Sounds like you got your Prince Charming fairytale life while I've been stuck here fighting off the dragons."

"I'm sorry I left you."

She took a final drag off her cigarette, threw it to the ground, and stomped it out. "You gonna stick around for a while so we can swap horror stories, or are you just passing through?"

"Dakota, listen, I know you must hate me for leaving you like I did, but I'm here to make this right. I want to be here for you now."

Dakota rolled her eyes as she pulled out her pack of cigarettes. They were Camel 99s, the brand I used to smoke. Flashes of how God used that number to reveal himself to me returned. Maybe he would do the same thing for Dakota. "I'm gonna need another smoke for this conversation." She held one out to me like a peace offering.

Honestly, a cigarette sounded great. I shoved my hands in my pockets. "No. I quit."

She lit her smoke, took in a long drag, and blew the smoke toward me. "Good for you, big sis. Maybe I'll follow in your footsteps one day." Her tone had a sarcastic ring to it.

"Hey, Tamara." Joe's voice came from behind me. "I need to talk to you for a minute."

"Can it wait?" I asked.

"I'm sorry, sweetie, but it can't."

I turned around, unable to ignore the grim tone in Joe's voice. His expression was strained. I glanced back at Dakota, and she waved me off with the hand that held the cigarette.

I followed Joe into our room.

He turned around and clutched onto both of my hands. After taking a few deep breaths, he swallowed hard and spoke. "The diner was robbed tonight, and Trudy was shot."

His words struck me with the weight of a semi-truck. "Is she okay?"

"I don't know. Claire was hysterical on the phone. Trudy's undergoing surgery. I hate to say this, Tamara, but we have to go."

I thought about Trudy lying in a hospital bed, possibly dying, and then Dakota outside, smoking. She was dying too. A slow, painful death in this life she had created for herself. "I can't, Joe. Dakota needs me. She's needed me here for a long time. I just found her. If I leave her now, who knows when I'll see her again? You go back for Trudy. I have to stay here."

"No." Joe shook his head, countenance hardening. "There

is no way I am leaving you here. Not after what happened today. I won't allow it."

He wouldn't allow it? What was he, my father? I tried to suppress the anger that was beginning to boil under the surface. "Then stay with me."

"You know I can't do that. Trudy's like a mom to me. If she dies—" He looked down at the floor, unable to finish the sentence.

My heart ached. I wanted to go with him, to take away his hurt, to be there for Trudy, but I couldn't—not after thinking Dakota was dead for the last few hours. "I love Trudy too, but I can't leave Dakota, not now."

His eyes met mine again, and the look in them was hard to bear. "Tamara, I feel like our world is imploding. In the last four hours, you were attacked and now Trudy's in the hospital with a gunshot wound. Trudy is like a mother to you, too! What if she dies?"

His words jolted me. "Joe, please, try to understand. If things were different, I'd leave with you without question, but less than five minutes ago, I thought my sister might be dead. There is no way I'm leaving her now."

Hurt flitted over his features. "Okay. Fine." He crossed the small room and threw his duffel bag over his shoulder.

I followed him out the door.

Dakota leaned on the side of the building, playing some sort of game on her phone.

"Dakota, have a good night." Joe stormed by her.

She threw me a strange look. "Leaving so soon, are you, sis? I guess I should be used to it by now."

"Not me. Just him. I'll be right back."

"Wow. This night is just full of surprises." Sarcasm laced her words.

Tension weighed down every step as I followed Joe out to the Jeep. I hated his leaving like this, but there was no other choice.

He put his duffel bag in the back seat and turned toward me. "Last chance. Are you absolutely sure?"

"Yes." I wanted so badly to hold him and kiss him before he left, but he didn't look like he'd receive that comfort.

He climbed in his vehicle without another word.

A lonely feeling crashed through me as I watched him back out of the motel parking lot. Taking in a deep breath, I walked back to Dakota, who still stood by the door.

"That was dramatic," she said with a dismissive attitude.

I nodded. "Yeah, one of our close friends was badly injured tonight." I didn't want to freak her out about the details of Trudy being shot. It would just make it more real, and I wasn't ready for that yet. I could only deal with what was right in front of me now. "She's in the hospital going through surgery as we speak."

"Why didn't you go with him?"

Sad that she even had to ask the question. "I just found you. I wasn't ready to leave you yet."

"Aw, sis." She pressed her hand to her chest. "I'm touched." More sarcasm. "What do you say we head over to Logger's Landing, grab a drink, and catch up?"

"Um, okay. I'm not much of a drinker anymore, but—"

"Oh, come on. We need to celebrate. It's like a full-on family reunion. The estranged Jensen sisters reunite."

I thought about Joe driving back home by himself, Trudy lying on the surgery table, and Claire scared out of her mind. Celebrating was the last thing I wanted to do, but taking the edge off an incredibly jagged day sounded like a good idea. "Let me go grab my purse." I said a quick prayer as I walked across the room. *God, please be with Trudy and Joe. And please be with me.*

I joined Dakota outside, and we walked toward the bar. Tons of questions ran through my mind, but did I have the right to ask them? There was something I had to know though, for my own sanity and sense of safety. "You're not dating Ryan, are you?"

"Oh, hell no." Dakota threw me a disgusted look. "What would make you think that? I mean, no offense. He was better looking when you were with him. Now he's just a demented meathead with rotting teeth."

No doubt. Drugs had done a serious number on his mind and teeth.

"But hey, now you have Romeo, and you're getting married. Let's see that ring."

We stepped to the entrance, and I held up my left hand for Dakota to see.

She took hold of my hand, brought it close and let out a low whistle. "This thing must be worth a fortune. Romeo must love you bunches."

"His name is Joe." And *yes, he loves me like I've never experienced before.*

"He looks like Romeo to me."

Rolling my eyes, I swung the door open. "Since you're not dating Ryan, are you with anyone?"

"I like to keep my options open."

We took a right toward the bar side of the restaurant and walked through another set of double doors.

"Dakota," the guy behind the counter said as we walked in the room. "Looking good, baby."

Dakota leaned against the bar, smiling seductively. "Hey, sugar, how 'bout you pour me and my sis here a few Long Islands and make 'em strong." She winked at him.

"Um, ah, I was just thinking a beer would be good," I said cautiously. "And maybe some food."

Dakota turned toward me, lip curling in disgust. "A beer? No, no, Jerry makes the best Long Islands. But first, we need a round of shots. We got six years to catch up on."

Shots? I tried to smile, but it felt more like a grimace. Dakota lived at a way higher speed than I did. I hadn't even drank for over a year. Before I could protest, Jerry grabbed a bottle of Tennessee whiskey and sour apple schnapps, and free poured both into a mixing cup with ice. He added cranberry juice and shook it before grabbing two shot glasses. "Two Washington Apples for the lovely ladies."

"You're such a doll." Dakota lifted both shots and handed me one. "Here's to you, sis, for finally coming back to this hellhole."

I hesitated for a moment, unease working its way through my core.

Dakota raised her eyebrow in what seemed like a challenging expression.

I clinked her glass and shot back the contents in mine. The whiskey burned my throat on the way down, and I coughed as I slammed down the shot glass.

Jerry and Dakota exchanged a glance as he set down both Long Islands. Dakota pushed the drink closer to me. I took a long swallow to stop the burning, but this drink was even stronger. I coughed again.

Dakota let out a hoot. "Jeez, girl, you can't handle your liquor."

"I told you I don't drink much anymore." Like, ever.

Dakota's face grew serious. "Now are you going to tell me why you're here?"

"What do you mean? I told you I came for you."

"But why now? It's been six years. You disappeared, Tamara. Where in the hell have you been?" Her voice held the judgment I expected mixed with sadness.

How could I even begin to answer? I set down my Long Island and reached over to take her hand. "It's definitely been a long and winding road. At first, I just bounced from town to town, trying to keep one step ahead of Ryan."

Dakota gave me a knowing look as she removed her hand from mine and took a gulp of her drink.

"I settled in Ocean Shores for almost a year. Got my heart

broke. After that I landed in Vancouver, Washington. Then earlier this year, I got pregnant."

"With Romeo's baby?"

"No." I wished it were his. "Just a guy passing through the Highway 99 Diner, where I work." One day I hoped to tell her the whole story, but now wasn't the time, and this certainly was not the place.

"Sounds scandalous. Where's the baby?" Dakota stirred her drink with the straw.

Throat tightening, I looked at the floor. "I chose adoption." I reached for my drink and took another gulp.

"You abandoned it?" Her voice was cold. Accusing.

Of course, she would see it like that. I had abandoned my baby the same way I abandoned her. "No. It's an open adoption. I know the parents. They are everything I wished we had had growing up. And through all of it, I found God."

"Oh, jeez." She gave an exasperated sigh and a dramatic eye roll, then slapped her hand down on the bar. "Jerry, we're going to need another round of shots."

"You got it," he said.

"I'm good." I raised my hand to protest. I was already feeling a bit swirly.

"Don't listen to her, Jerry. She definitely needs another one." Dakota looked at me again. "Don't tell me you think God told you to come back to this cesspool."

What could I tell her? That I found out where she lived on the internet? It would be way too much way too soon. "No, it's not like that. But, between God, placing the baby for adoption and planning for my wedding," I took another sip of my drink and continued, "I started thinking about our family. It felt like it was time to make peace with my past."

Jerry placed two shot glasses in front of us again, and Dakota reached for hers. "Good luck with that." A dark cloud hovered over her features. "I've been here the whole time, and I still haven't made peace." She gulped back the contents of the glass.

"Maybe we could do it together."

Dakota looked down at the floor and was quiet for a long beat. "It's a bit too late for that, sis."

"I don't believe that."

Her head jerked toward me. "That's 'cause you weren't here! You have no idea how bad it got after you left."

"I can imagine."

"I'm pretty sure you can't. After you left, Mom turned into a shell. She cried every night for a month, hoping you'd come back." Dakota was quiet for a moment, seeming to retreat into some ominous thought.

Guilt settled in deep. Over the years I'd never let myself think of how my leaving must have affected Mom. It hurt too much. I grabbed the shot that was in front of me and downed it. "Where are they now?"

Dakota glared at me. "I have no idea. Haven't seen any of them for years. Is that the only reason you stuck around tonight?"

"Of course not, Dakota. It's not like that."

"I need a smoke." She headed for the door.

I followed her outside, the room tilting a bit as I walked.

Dakota pulled out a cigarette and lit it.

"Could I have one?" Even with the drinks, my nerves were on edge. Maybe a cigarette would help.

A crooked smile crept up her lips as she handed me the smoke she had already lit.

"What?" I took a tentative drag. Surprisingly, I didn't cough. Just like riding a bike, I guess.

"Remember that time we stole those smokes from Gramma." She took another cigarette out of the box.

I returned her grin. "Oh yeah, I remember taking the fall for it and Dad beating my butt until the board broke."

She chuckled, struck her lighter, and held it to her cigarette.

"Yeah, you were always a good sister like that, until you weren't." She averted her gaze and just like that the walk down memory lane was over.

Until I wasn't ... that was a hard sentence to overcome. In so many ways, she was just like me a little over a year ago. I could almost see the invisible barrier she had built around herself to keep people out. To shield herself from the pain life had brought her.

I took another drag and prayed for a way to break through.

CHAPTER 19
December 4, 12:10 am.

JOE

The day's events circled around my mind as I sped down I-5. Even now, as I hit the Oregon border, I had to fight the urge to turn around for Tamara and make her come home with me. Leaving her in that place alone with her sister left me cold inside. But what choice did I have? Trudy was in the hospital fighting for her life. I couldn't let someone else so important to me die without me at least being there doing what I could.

I slammed my fist against the steering wheel. How could everything go wrong this quickly? All I wanted was to be strong for Tamara as she went back for her family. Instead, I almost got arrested and abandoned my fiancée in a town where drug dealers roamed free. What was Tamara even thinking? The sad fact was that Dakota needed a lot more than the support Tamara could offer.

A dark feeling overshadowed my mind as thoughts of Tamara being attacked by Ryan overtook me. My hands tensed around the steering wheel, and I shivered. "God, I don't understand what's happening right now." Taking Tamara to find her sister seemed to have triggered a field of landmines. And now whatever move we made was bound to set more off.

Shaking the thoughts away, I flipped on the turn signal and

merged onto I-84. *Tamara will be okay. She had to be okay. It's Trudy I need to worry about.*

The last eight hours needed to go straight back to hell, where they belonged.

I turned down the street to the hospital and moments later into the parking lot of Providence Portland Medical Center.

I shut off my car and rested my head on the steering wheel. "Lord, give me the strength to deal with whatever is in front of me." Sitting back, I exhaled, thinking about the last time someone I loved had been in this hospital.

She hadn't come out alive.

Here I was again, and just like when I was here with my mom, I was alone. I ached for Tamara. The one time I needed her to strengthen me, why wasn't she here? I tried to pray again. Trusting God in this was the only answer, but suddenly there was a blockage inside of me. Wiping away the tears, I reached for the door handle.

I walked into the hospital. Claire said she'd be in the waiting room of the Trauma Unit. I walked down a long hallway and took the elevator to the fourth floor, my mood growing heavier with each step. Around the corner was the waiting room. I pushed the door open.

Claire was in a seat, arms wrapped around her waist, with an empty look on her face. Frank sat beside her, fidgeting with his hat.

Where was Roger? I would have thought Trudy's man would have been here.

Claire bolted out of her chair, ran toward me and hugged me tight. "I'm so glad you're here."

Frank came and stood beside us. "Where's Tamara?"

Claire pulled away, eyes glossy.

My gaze fell to the floor. "She stayed in Washington."

Frank and Claire exchanged a glance.

"She'd just found her sister and needed to stay." Tamara

could tell them the horrific details of that story later if she wanted. "Any news on Trudy?"

Claire opened her mouth, lips trembling. "She's still in surgery. They came in with an update about twenty minutes ago." She swallowed hard and spoke, her voice empty. "She has lost a lot of blood."

I wasn't ready to hear this. "Where's Roger?"

"We've been trying to get ahold of him," Frank said. "He's off on some fishing expedition with his brother." Frank walked over, head down, his voice low. "It's bad though, Joe. The doc said they lost her a couple of times on the table. We need to prepare ourselves for the worst."

The air was knocked out of my lungs. Prepare for the worst? I'd heard those words before, and I wasn't ready to hear them again. I looked at Claire. "How did this happen?"

Claire shook her head. "I don't even know why she was there."

"Betty called me and said you had locked yourself in the office after I left."

A scowl overtook Claire's features. "Betty needs to mind her own business! I had it handled." She paced the length of the room before turning back to me. "So, you had such little confidence in me that you sent Trudy to check on me?"

"It wasn't like that. I was concerned about you."

"You were concerned about the restaurant, not me. But like I said, I had it handled."

"Can you please just tell me what happened?"

Darkness clouded Claire's countenance. "I had just locked the door and was counting out the till when Trudy showed up. I let her in but must have forgotten to lock up again. Then this guy came in the front door, demanding money. He said he had a gun. Trudy thought it was a bluff, but it wasn't. When she refused to give him the money, he shot her." She finished with a sob, pressing her mouth against her fist.

"Jesus," I said, half-prayer, half-expletive. "How could this happen?" I asked myself more than them.

"Damn it, Joe. None of this would have happened if you had just trusted me."

"Betty said you weren't doing well. What was I supposed to do? You could have at least been honest with me."

"Hey, now, nobody needs to blame anyone," Frank interjected.

The room felt three times smaller than it had two minutes ago. I sat down on a chair and rubbed my temples, throat aching. Guilt and sorrow swam around in my stomach, making me nauseous. I should have never left the diner. I knew in my gut it was a bad idea, and now our lives were falling apart. This was my fault.

So. Many. Mistakes.

The fault lines in my soul cracked. *Hold it together, man.* I shoved down the emotions that threatened to overtake me. *You're stronger than this.* I popped my knuckles and said a silent prayer. Trudy would make it through this. She had to. Pressure grew in my chest. I imagined myself taking a shot of whiskey, but batted away the thought immediately.

"Joe." Frank said.

I looked up at him.

He had a business card in his hand, extended toward me. "I know this is a lot to take in, but here is the card of the officer in charge."

I nodded and took hold of it. The name in the corner said *Officer Gibbs.*

"He said the diner would be closed for the next twenty-four to forty-eight hours to process the crime scene."

Crime scene ... what a nightmare. Seemed like over the last few hours my whole life had become a crime scene.

CHAPTER 20

December 4, 7:45 a.m.

TAMARA

Light poured through the crack in the curtain, waking me. I clenched my temples, head throbbing. My mouth was dry and tasted like I'd licked an ashtray. "Ugh." I groaned as I rolled over. Shame and nausea weighed down my stomach like a thousand-pound anchor.

How had I let Dakota talk me into drinking so much? And then smoking too?

My eyes squinted open, and I looked around the room. "Dakota?" I called out.

Silence.

I flipped off the blanket, stumbled out of bed and then into the bathroom. No sign of her. Where was she? I walked back to the bed.

A little note was folded next to my purse.

I unwrapped it, and my heart plummeted as I read the five words she had written. *How does it feel, sis?*

I looked around for my phone, but it was nowhere to be seen. I dug through my purse and then emptied it out on my bed. Where was it? I scanned the room and then the bathroom.

Nowhere.

Had Dakota jacked my phone? I looked through the pile on

my bed and then opened my wallet. The two hundred fifty dollars I'd put in there before the trip was gone.

Dakota stole from me? I ran over to the door and flung it open. She was probably long gone, just like I'd done to her. Leaving in the middle of the night without even a goodbye.

An empty feeling overtook me. Did this mean that she wasn't coming back? I wished so much that Joe was here now. I let him leave to be there for Trudy without me for this? To be abandoned by my sister in the middle of the night? So she could play her sick little revenge game on me. If Trudy died, I would never forgive myself.

How does it feel, sis?

Her words felt like a dirty scalpel twisting in my chest. I grasped the note with shaky hands and did a double take of my left ring finger.

My engagement ring was *gone*.

I crumpled over, my lungs on fire, hands tingling. Did she steal my ring too? The one material possession that meant the most to me. The symbol of Joe's and my love. How could I let myself get so trashed that she could get it off my finger without me noticing? My pulse thudded in my ears. Joe would never forgive me for this.

Hopelessness crashed over my soul. Joe was gone, my sister was gone, and my ring was gone. What could I do now? I sat down on the bed and cried. *Jesus, please help me.*

The hotel phone rang, and I jumped. I stared at it while it rang two more times. If it was Joe, I *did* want to talk to him, but I wasn't ready to tell him the truth. I answered after the fourth ring.

"Hello." I tried to keep my voice steady.

"Hey." Joe's voice came through the phone, sounding sad and tired. "I've been trying to call your cell. Are you all right?"

I looked at the pile of stuff on my bed from my empty purse. "Sorry, my phone was on silent." The lie left a bitter acrid taste on my tongue, but I just couldn't tell him what she'd done. Not yet. "What's going on with Trudy?"

He was quiet for a long moment. "She's made it through surgery, but she's in the ICU in critical condition."

"Critical condition?" How could this be happening? I should have just left with him last night. "What does that even mean?"

"It means she could die." His tone was hollow. I could just imagine him sitting there in the hospital, in utter torment as he waited for news.

"I'm so sorry, Joe." I ached to be there for him. For once, to be the one who held him together like he always did for me. I looked down at my hand where my ring should have been, tears threatening to come.

"The thing that hurts the most is that it's my fault." His voice was rough and broken. "If she dies—"

How could he possibly think that? "Trudy's strong, Joe. She'll make it through this." I didn't know if I believed the words, but I willed myself to. For him.

"I hope so."

"You sound tired. You should get some rest."

"I'd rather just come and get you. I don't like how we ended things last night."

I looked at my left hand again. A part of me was selfish enough to ask him to do that. "Me neither, but there are still some things I need to do here."

There was a long pause. "How did it go last night with your sister? Did she have any more information about your family?"

I pinched the bridge of my nose. Dakota had been angry at the mention of the rest of our family, and now she was gone with my engagement ring. That was as big a message as any. She wanted nothing to do with me and was willing to do whatever it took to keep me out of her life for good. "Not as much as I would have liked." I hated keeping things from Joe, but I couldn't add to his suffering now. "I better get going. I'll check in with you soon."

"Okay. I love you."

"I love you too."

"Oh, and T, you just say the words and I'll be there to get you."

I smiled sadly as I placed the phone on the receiver. This man loved me too much for his own good, and at this moment I couldn't see why. My own sister didn't want anything to do with me. She would never forgive me for leaving her, and I wasn't sure if I'd be able to forgive her for what she'd stolen from me. Maybe taking my ring settled the score with us in her mind. But I hadn't intentionally hurt her. The other day God had told me He'd give me beauty for ashes, but there was no beauty in this.

I grabbed my bottle of antidepressants and wondered if Dakota had noticed them. Seemed like she would have. I shook out a pill and swallowed it dry then shoved a few things into my purse. What happened with Dakota was the reason I'd stayed away from my family as long as I had. Loving them only brought sorrow into my life.

God, I don't understand. This hurts too much.

David and the words he spoke to me at Hope Chapel before I left flitted across my thoughts. Both he and Joe had cautioned me about coming here, and they'd been right. Between Dakota and Ryan, my soul had been ripped wide open, and I didn't have a clue where to start picking up the pieces. I reached into my wallet and looked through the pockets before grabbing his business card. At least she left me my debit card and my purse. I lifted the phone and dialed David's number.

He answered quickly. "Hello, David speaking."

"Hi, it's Tamara."

"Hey there." His voice was soft. "I thought I might be hearing from you today."

"Really?"

"Joe put Trudy and you on the Hope Chapel prayer chain. It wasn't specific, but I've been praying for you both this morning."

His words soothed my soul. Did that mean Levi and Sarah were praying for me too? "Thank you. I could use some extra prayers right now."

"Do you mind me asking what's going on?"

"Can you promise whatever I say will stay between just us?"

"Absolutely. That's part of my job description."

"I know, but we're not in your office."

"I am, and I'll pretend you're right here with me."

I smiled for the first time this morning, but it quickly faded as I launched into the story about the drama with Ryan, Trudy getting shot, and then my sister leaving in the middle of the night with my ring, money, and phone.

"The shame of it is eating me alive. I told Joe to trust me, and what do I do? I get drunk with my sister to the point of passing out. I guess I deserve getting my stuff stolen. It was like I opened the door wide and invited the devil himself to come take my stuff." I wrapped the telephone cord around my finger. "I haven't told Joe any of this. I don't know if he'll be able to forgive me."

"Tamara, there's one thing I know about Joe and that is he loves you. He'll forgive you, and God already has."

I looked down at my left finger where my ring should be, throat tightening. I hoped he was right. "I just don't understand. There was that vision, and Joe had read the scripture verse about beauty for ashes. I thought God was talking to me, like maybe I was actually hearing his voice."

David was quiet for a few moments. "I wouldn't rule that out. Sometimes when God gives us a promise, it's because we're about to encounter some hardships and we need His words to give us faith to get through the battle. Think about it. God knew what you were about to go through, and he gave you a promise. It means that you're going to come out the other side.

If I were you, I would repeat this promise over and over like a declaration. Doing so will strengthen you and help you find the beauty."

"I don't know, I'm not sure how much more of this battle I can take." I was already exhausted. The last twenty-four hours had served to prove how weak I was.

"You're stronger than you think. You'll be all right. You and Joe will get through this."

"What about Trudy? Will she make it through?"

Another long pause. "I can't answer for sure, but I've seen miracles happen, and I'm believing in one for her."

"Me too." She had to pull through.

"What can I do to help?"

"Just keep praying."

"I will. Keep me posted."

When I hung up, I could breathe again, but sadness still weighed down my steps as I got ready to leave the hotel room. After what Dakota had told me last night, I couldn't give up on finding my family, especially my mom. There had to be some sort of clue in this town as to where they could have gone. I didn't have much time though. Not when Trudy was fighting for her life.

CHAPTER 21

December 4, 1:37 p.m.

DAKOTA

I tossed the keys to Lisa's '87 Monte Carlo into my purse and entered Max's pawn shop. The hour drive to Port Angeles was a bit out of my way, but worth it if I could secure the money I needed. Over the years, the owner had helped me out of a bind or two. Here was hoping he'd come through for me today.

Max, a big hairy guy with broad shoulders, beer gut and a missing front tooth, stood behind the glass counter, sharpening a Bowie knife, as I pushed through the wooden door. The store had a cold feel to it and smelled like old carpet and chewing tobacco.

I stepped to the counter and placed the ring on the glass.

He set the knife down, snatched the ring, and looked at it with caution. "Sorry, Dakota." He kept his focus on the ring as he spoke. "You know I don't peddle hot merchandise."

"What? Max, no, it's not like that. This was my mother's ring. She died last month."

"Your mother's?" Max's dark gaze leveled on mine. "And you seem so devastated."

I shot him an injured look. "It's not like we were close."

"Uh-huh." He gave me a wry glance as he took out his magnifier. The ring sparkled under the pawn shop light as Max inspected it, his dark bushy eyebrows pinching together. "I'll give you four hundred for it." He gave a half-grin, revealing gappy, tobacco-stained teeth.

"Yeah, right. This thing has to be worth at least three grand." Four hundred was not near enough to get Ryan off my back. I was just lucky he was in jail for a little while, though probably not long. That was the thing with Ryan, he always had a way of slipping through the cracks. And when he got out, I had to get him the money I owed him. Otherwise, he'd make good on the lie he'd told Tamara.

I snatched the ring out of Max's grizzly hand. I swear the dude was half-gorilla. I shoved the ring into my pocket and turned toward the door.

Admittedly, stealing Tamara's ring was a new low, even for me, but the way I saw it, I was doing her a favor. She came home looking for the truth. *Sorry, sis, but Jack Nicholson said it best— you can't handle the truth.* Her engagement ring was a small price to pay to keep her as far away from my gnarly demons as possible. If she only knew how big of a favor it was.

I ran to Lisa's car and jumped in. I twisted the key, and the engine roared to life. Already two in the afternoon, and still about six more pawn shops in Port Angeles to visit. Lisa had wanted her car back by three, but she owed me. She was part of the reason I was in this mess to begin with. If I didn't get that twelve hundred dollars to Ryan by the time he got out of jail, Lisa would be going down with me. I slammed the gear into reverse and peeled out of the parking lot.

CHAPTER 22

December 4, 4:13 p.m.

TAMARA

After a few hours of walking around town, I was still nowhere closer to finding my family. I'd ran into a few old acquaintances, but no one had seen any of them for years. It was time to give up for now. The bus was scheduled to come in a little less than an hour. At least Dakota left me with my wallet and debit card to be able to secure a ticket. Joe would have come and got me, but I needed the extra time to sort out everything in my head before I saw him.

I checked out of the hotel room and walked to the community center where the bus would stop. I wished I had my phone to distract my mind from the thoughts bombarding it. I paced the parking lot to pass the time.

An old guy with his dog walked by and waved. A few cars passed and then a semi.

I was *so* ready to leave this one-horse town. I gazed down the highway, looking for the bus. Surely, it was getting close to time.

A maroon minivan pulled into the parking lot, driving toward me.

What now? Couldn't this town just let me leave in peace?

The van came closer and the tinted window rolled down. "Tamara Jensen? Is that you?" A dazzling smile greeted me.

"Maddie Mog?"

Her smile grew wider. "It's Buck these days." She lifted her hand in the air, flashing her wedding ring.

My stomach tightened at the site of the beautiful diamond encased in rose gold. "That's wonderful. Congratulations."

She shut off the van and climbed out the door.

My gaze fell to her enlarged abdomen. She had to have been at least seven months pregnant.

"Vanessa Hutchins said she saw you earlier, but I didn't believe her." She gave me a firm squeeze.

"I don't remember seeing her."

Pulling away, she flashed a playful grin. "That's 'cause she's gained about a hundred pounds since high school."

"No way."

Maddie lifted her hand in the air. "I swear."

I chuckled. "Oh my." Seeing Maddie was like taking a breath of fresh air.

"Yep, too many Ho Hos and soap operas for that girl. But look at you. You look great. What are you doing here?"

"I came back to find my family."

A strange look flashed across her face, but then it was gone so fast I wondered if I had imagined it.

"I found Dakota, but that didn't go so well."

Her expression turned sympathetic. "I can imagine."

Down the road, the bus came around the corner. "There's my ride."

Maddie turned. "The bus? Where are you heading?"

"Vancouver, Washington."

Her blue eyes grew wide. "You can't be serious. That would take you forever."

"I don't really have any other options."

"I'm on my way to Shelton right now. I could take you as far as the Olympia Bus station."

"You would do that?"

"Of course! I'll even treat you to dinner when we get there. It will give us time to visit."

"That would be amazing. Thank you." I always loved this girl. She hadn't seemed to have changed much since high school. Back then, she was the kind of person no one ever messed with, and she always had a sweet spot for underdogs like me.

I followed her around to the back of the van and put my bag in.

"What possessed you to find your family after all this time?" She asked as we got in.

I stretched the seatbelt across my lap. "It's a long story."

"We have time." She hooked her iPhone into her system and soft guitar strums played in the background.

"I never thought I'd come back, but about six months ago I found God. Well, it's more like He found me."

"That's great." She smiled.

"You think so?"

"Hell, yeah, girl, I love God."

I laughed. Not your typical response, but it seemed appropriate for Maddie. I noticed then that the music coming out of the speakers was Christian.

"What artist is this?"

She turned up the volume. "Will Reagan and United Pursuit. It's Live at the Banks House."

"I like it."

I listened for a moment as the band sang about finding our own flame. "Tell me more about your life."

"Not long after you left town, I got pregnant." She rubbed her swollen belly. "My son just turned five. His sperm donor was a real piece of work. You know how it is. I was just young and dumb."

I could so relate to that.

"The dad's not a part of our lives. Jake adopted him."

"And this baby is your husband's?"

"Yes." She pulled out her phone and swiped across the screen. "Here's a picture of us."

In the picture, their heads were leaning against each other, both smiling. Jake's head was shaved, but it seemed to work with his handsome features.

"You guys are so cute." I wished I had my phone to show her Joe.

"Thanks. He's a bit older than me, which freaked me out at first, but we got through that."

"Yeah, my fiancé is older than me too." But Joe still had his hair.

"Fiancé?" Maddie's voice brightened.

"We have a date set for March. That's another reason I'm trying to track down my family."

Maddie nodded, but I glimpsed the same expression from when I had mentioned them earlier.

"What do you know about them? Dakota said she hasn't seen them in years, and everyone else in town said the same thing."

She looked at me from the corner of her eye and then back at the road. "There's not much to tell."

"Come on, Maddie, if you have information regarding my family, please tell me."

She was quiet for a long moment. "Did Dakota mention anything to you about Gabriel?"

"What about him?"

Maddie turned down the radio. "About a year after you left, he disappeared."

Her words echoed in my head for a moment, not making sense. "Disappeared?"

"People assumed he ran away like you did. No one has heard from him for about five years. Your parents came under the town's suspicion after that. Everyone wondered what was going on in your house to make two kids run off. A few months later, their trailer burnt down, and they left town."

An uneasy feeling crawled along my spine. The car was suddenly too quiet, and I wasn't sure what to say.

Maddie turned up the volume and I zoned out on the music.

It seemed the more I uncovered, the worse I felt. Had Gabriel run away like I had? Or had a worse fate befallen him?

The music bellowed out of the speakers and struck my heart. Resting my head against the window, I said a prayer as the song washed over me. *God, I choose to not lean on my own understanding. My life is in your hands. I give it all to you and trust you will make something beautiful out of this.*

I straightened in the seat and refocused my attention on catching up with Maddie. My life, as shattered as it felt at the moment, was in God's hands.

CHAPTER 23

December 4, 9:40 p.m.

JOE

My eyes shut involuntarily, and my head jerked me back awake. I returned my attention to Trudy, her ribcage rising and falling in synchronization with the noises. When she'd come out of surgery, the doctor had put her into an induced coma to allow her body to heal with the least amount of pressure, but other than that there was no change.

Being at the hospital for this long, with the beeping of the heart monitor and the whirring of the breathing machine, was enough to drive me insane. Over the last twenty hours, I'd dozed off several times but fought to stay awake, as if somehow watching her could keep her alive. A part of me wanted to go home and sleep for days, but the majority of me could not bring myself to leave her side. I didn't want to miss her waking or ... taking a turn for the worse.

"You should go get some rest." Anita, the kind graveyard nurse, walked into the room and checked monitors before turning to me. "She's in good hands."

I looked at her, giving a tired smile. "I know." But I didn't want to leave her alone. Frank and Claire had left hours ago, and Roger still wasn't here. We'd finally gotten ahold of him, and he was en route.

"I will call you myself if there is any change in her condition."

I checked the clock on the wall. 9:45 p.m. Getting some shuteye was probably a good idea. "Thanks, Anita. I'm going to stay with her for a few more minutes."

"Okay. But you need to take care of yourself. You promise me you'll get a good eight hours of sleep before coming back here?"

"Yes, ma'am."

Anita walked around the bed to check the monitors one more time before leaving me with Trudy.

I stood and walked to her bed, placing my hand on her arm. "I'll be back soon. Please stay with me, Trudy. Tamara and I need you." Bowing my head, I prayed a silent prayer, hoping this time God would answer.

The whole day I'd been in the bargaining stage. I'd do anything if He'd heal her. Nothing had changed, though. Her levels were the same, and she was still classified as critical condition. I leaned over and kissed her on the forehead. "See you in the morning."

At least I hoped. I left the room, feeling unsteady.

Once outside the hospital, I checked my phone. I hadn't heard from Tamara since this morning, and I was starting to worry. Seemed like she would have called to at least check on Trudy. I jumped into my Jeep and started the engine. Everything in me wanted to drive to Quilcene and bring her back with me. I shot her a quick text.

I miss you

On the way home, I blasted worship music and tried to release the knots in my stomach to God. I wanted to trust him. I thought I'd come a long way in the last six months, but trials like this made me see how much I'd been fooling myself.

Trusting God was a bigger mountain than I realized, and I had a lot more climbing to do.

I turned into the driveway of my townhouse and stared at the empty building. *Lord, help me trust you. Right now, in this moment, I'm not sure how.*

Feet dragging, I exited my Jeep and walked up the sidewalk. When I got in the house, the first thing I noticed was Tamara's sweater draped over the couch. Memories flooded back of her staying over a few nights before we'd left. I would give my right eye to have her here with me now.

I kicked off my shoes and hauled myself upstairs. A shower was probably a good idea, but I didn't have the energy. I peeled off my shirt, unzipped my pants, and stepped out of them before climbing into bed. As I settled into my pillow, I caught a whiff of Tamara and longing caused my chest to ache. It didn't matter what she said, tomorrow after checking in with Trudy, I was going to bring her home.

CHAPTER 24
December 4, 10:15 p.m.

DAKOTA

I parked Lisa's car in the darkest corner behind the casino and dug out the last of the dope. I took out a pocket mirror, carefully poured powder onto it, and cut it into two thin lines. I snorted the first line through a rolled-up dollar bill and sat back in my seat, waiting for the familiar rush to zing through my veins.

The whole day was a total crap shoot when it came to selling Tamara's ring, but now I had a new plan. It wasn't foolproof, but unfortunately, it was what I had.

I looked down at the last line, and a scornful laugh rose from the sick places inside of me. This was what Ryan got for trusting an addict with selling his drugs. I mean honestly, he should have known better. He was, without a doubt, losing his mind. Or maybe us Jensen sisters were his Achilles heel.

I railed the second line and put the mirror away.

We might be Ryan's weakness, but as soon as he was released from jail, I'd be his whipping boy. He'd not only make me pay for the drugs I used instead of selling, but he'd take the anger he held toward Tamara out on me too. And his rage would have grown exponentially.

I strung my purse over my shoulder and climbed out of the

Monte Carlo. The two hundred and some change that I'd stolen from Tamara was still tucked safely in the side pocket of my handbag. If I played my cards right, or, more literally, the roulette wheel right, I could possibly make twelve hundred tonight.

My phone vibrated, and I dug through my purse. I pulled out the wrong phone and noticed a message. My phone continued to rattle as I opened the message in Tamara's phone. It was from Romeo. A simple *I miss you.*

Aww. Doesn't that just warm the cockles of my jaded heart? Romeo sure does love her. I thought about her engagement ring in the bottom of my bag. The teensiest amount of guilt twanged at my insides, but I quickly shrugged it off. Tamara would be fine. Romeo would buy her another ring even better than the first, and they'd slip off into the sunset together.

I put Tamara's phone back into my purse and grabbed mine. Another missed call from Lisa. She was probably furious about the car being eight hours late, but what was I supposed to do? I had to figure this mess out.

I walked through the lobby of the casino. Dennis, the security guard, threw me a friendly wave. I headed straight to the roulette table.

Rhoda, my favorite dealer, stood behind the wheel. "Dakota, good to see you. Where have you been?"

"Oh, you know. Around." I took a fifty out and tossed it down on the table. "I'll take blue." There were two other people I didn't recognize sitting at the table. An older woman dressed to the nines sat at the end, a stack of pink chips in front of her. To my left sat a nerdy guy with a big nose and thick glasses, drinking a scotch on the rocks.

I ordered a Long Island and watched for a few spins before I decided I was ready to play. It hit red three times in a row, so I put half my chips on black and waited for the others to bet.

Nerdy-glasses guy scattered his chips over the board, and

pink-chips woman put ten bucks worth on the zeros. Rhoda dropped the marble, and I held my breath as I waited.

It landed on red.

I watched my chips as they were taken away. Not a good start.

The waitress came back with my Long Island, and I took a large drink. I watched a few more rounds. The next spin, Pink Chips won big on the zeros, and then it hit red again. Nerdy-glasses guy lost both times. He cursed and shot back the remainder of his scotch.

Okay, my turn to win. I put twenty-five dollars' worth of chips on black and bit the inside of my cheek as I watched the marble spin around the wheel, bouncing in and out of the numbers.

Beside me, a man's hand dropped a twenty on the table.

The marble landed in black and excitement filled me as Rhoda doubled my chips.

"Good to see you, Dakota."

I turned toward the husky voice.

Timothy Moore stood beside me. Or should I say Officer Moore? Except now he wasn't in uniform, and a five o'clock shadow lined his perfectly etched jawline.

"Officer Moore," I said curtly, arching an eyebrow. He hated it when I called him that, especially because of our history.

He leveled me with a smoldering gaze. "I'm glad to see Ryan was lying."

"Duh. Ryan's a liar." I turned my attention back to the game. Rhoda was waiting on me. I waved her on to let her know I was letting it ride.

Tim put five on the middle row.

I watched as the little ball spun round the wheel. It settled on number seventeen, black. We both won.

Tim grabbed his chips off the table, but I let mine ride

again. It hit black again. My luck was changing. I smiled, tossed Rhoda a five-dollar tip, and continued to let it ride.

A massive wave of adrenaline spiked inside of me as it once again hit black. Bam. Four times in a row, baby. I loved this game. Up two hundred in just a few minutes.

Tim slid a hand to the middle of my back. "You should give it a rest for a minute."

My skin tingled where his hand touched. I looked at him defiantly. "Thanks for the tip, but I don't need you watching out for me." A few more double downs and I'd have my twelve hundred.

He tilted his head to the side, his features holding a depth of emotion I couldn't quite understand. "You sure about that? Everyone needs a guardian angel every once in a while."

I moved my chips to red. "Whatever." This was not the time to slow my roll. I was on a streak.

I always hated when Tim got all serious and caring. He'd been this way since we were kids, long before he lost his baby weight and filled out in the right places. Back then, Tim was my best friend. His house had been my safe haven away from the fighting at mine until seventh grade when we started drifting apart. Well, it was more like a clean break. I started using drugs, he begged me not too. I told him to get lost.

He never did, though. Timothy Moore had always been on the periphery of my life.

The silver marble landed on red. Yeah, baby. Up four hundred dollars. I retrieved the other two hundred and exchanged it for chips. Six hundred total. Just one more win was all I needed.

Tim leaned in and spoke quietly, but the concern in his tone was palpable. "Be careful, Dakota. You keep playing games, and you're gonna get hurt."

Why couldn't he just leave me alone to live my own life? I slid my pile of chips to black and hesitated. Maybe I should stay on red. No, black.

Tim and his caution were seriously messing with my juju. I decided on black and Rhoda spun the wheel. I held my breath. The silver marble fell into the black, popped, and then settled into red. My heart stopped for at least three seconds and then started again.

Rhoda gave me a sympathetic look as she hauled away my stack of chips.

I glared at Tim. "Thanks for jinxing me!" I stormed off. So. Freaking. Close. I could taste the win, and now it was gone. Just like that, back to square one.

"Dakota!" Timothy shouted after me.

"Stay away from me!" I yelled over my shoulder. I lit a smoke as soon as I was outside, the air damp as usual. Exactly what I'd expect on a December night on the Olympic Peninsula.

The light rhythm of footsteps on the pavement sounded behind me. I took in another drag, wanting to punch something. "I said, get lost!" I checked to see if he obeyed, and my pulse accelerated.

Tim hadn't followed me out. Justin and Avery had. Or, as I liked to call them, Tweedledum and Tweedledee. A couple of Ryan's low life cronies. They were both as dumb as a box of rocks, but they could do some damage. I'd seen it firsthand. I quickened my pace. Great. Why did I have to park so far back? The car was close but still about twenty feet away.

"Come on, sugar. We're not here to hurt you. We just want to talk." Avery spun me around and grabbed hold of my wrist.

I wrestled my arm free.

He slammed me against the side of Lisa's car. "Are you stupid? I said we just want to talk."

Talk? Yeah right... I'd seen what they did to people when they said they *just want to talk*.

Justin brought out a switchblade and brought it near my face. "Why you running from us?" He pressed the blade against my skin. "You have a real pretty face, Dakota. I'd hate to have to ruin it."

My limbs went numb as panic coursed through them. "What do you want?" Where was Tim when I needed him?

"Ryan wants the money you owe him."

"You and I both know Ryan's in jail." I spat out the words, teeth clenched.

The blade pressed harder against my cheek. "And he needs bail."

Trepidation clawed at my stomach. I thought I had at least a few days to figure this out. What was I going to tell these guys—that I used the drugs with Lisa and her boyfriend instead of selling them like I was supposed to? They wouldn't even wait for Ryan to get out. They'd hack me with their switchblade and feed the fish in Dabob Bay. "I don't have it on me," I choked out. "I left it with some friends for safekeeping while I came to the casino."

Justin slowly withdrew the knife from me. "Take us to it then."

"Hey!" Tim's voice came from across the parking lot. "You okay, Dakota?"

Avery let me go, and I stood straight. For once I was glad to have my puppy dog following me.

Tim stalked across the parking lot. "What's going on?"

"We're, ah, good here, uh—" Justin tripped over his words.

Tim glanced back and forth between the two lowlifes, then flashed them his badge. "Dakota looks like she might be having a bit of trouble with you."

Fear shot across their faces. "Nope, officer. We're good here," Avery said.

I shook my head almost imperceptibly, but I was sure he saw it.

Anger flared in his eyes. "Both of you need to listen and listen good. If I see or even hear you've been within a hundred yards of her, you'll find yourselves in the back of my police car.

Understand?" His tone sounded more like a military sergeant than a cop. It was kind of sexy.

Avery and Justin nodded. "Understood," Justin said, and then they both walked away.

Tim turned toward me. "What kind of trouble are you in this time, Dakota?"

"Like I said before, I don't need a goody two-shoes guardian looking out for me."

He crossed his arms in front of him. "You sure about that?"

I could still feel where the knife had been against my cheek. I let out a deep sigh. "I owe Ryan money." Why was I telling this to him? "They were calling in the debt."

Fear tinted his features. "Damn it, Dakota. Are you trying to get yourself killed?"

His words stole the air from my lungs. Maybe I was. I was *so* sick of living this life. So sick of the lies and secrets.

His jaw tightened, and he averted his gaze. "Listen, Ryan's bail is set for one hundred thousand dollars. I can follow you home and run patrols of your house." He looked at me. There was a desperation in his expression as if he was seeing every bad scenario in his mind at one time. "But isn't there some place you can go? What about your family?"

I glared at him, every wall I had ever built erecting at once. "My family? They've never been there for me."

"I know." He hung his head.

I turned and opened the car door. "I'll figure it out." There were still options, but my family would never be one of them.

There was still Tamara's ring I could pawn. I just needed to find someone who'd be willing to pay a good price for it.

CHAPTER 25

December 4, 10:55 p.m.

TAMARA

The lights of Vancouver came into view. Another ten minutes or so and I'd be pulling into the bus station. I stared at my reflection in the window as the weight of defeat hung heavy on me. What was I even doing? Maybe I should just stop looking for my family now. Maybe this trip was enough. Maybe it was better to leave well enough alone. As I gazed past my reflection out at the changing scenery, I thought about Dakota and the rest of my family. I'd gone to Quilcene wanting to find her, and I left missing a ring and now a brother. If he had left five years ago, who knew where he might be now? Or worse yet, if he was even alive.

David's voice whispered through the grief. *When God gives us a promise, it's because we're about to encounter some hardships and we need his words to give us faith to get through the battle.*

I pulled out my journal and wrote the words at the top of the page, followed by the phrase, *beauty for ashes.* I stared at the words. Seeing them written out seemed to give them more power, as if they were somehow more real now. Though, after everything I'd already gone through, I would need more to hold on to than a few simple phrases. *Lord, speak to me.*

I leaned back into the seat.

In my mind, I saw a picture of Joe standing at the altar, tall and debonair in his tuxedo. My whole body came alive with joy as I took in the tenderness and awe on his face as I walked down the aisle toward him. The vision shifted a bit, and I noticed that I wasn't walking alone as I had always assumed I would be, but my arm was wrapped around a strong, sturdy arm. I looked up, and there next to me, walking me proudly down the aisle, was my dad. There was more grey in his hair then the last time I'd seen him. His countenance was soft, full of kindness and pride. My heart jolted. Where in the world did that image come from? There was absolutely no possible way that could ever happen. Especially after the last few days. But when I was being honest with myself, that was one of the motivations of this trip—family reconciliation. And that picture of my dad walking me down the aisle would be the deepest kind of reconciliation. It would mean complete forgiveness on both sides. A new beginning for all of us—that was my hope.

Was this another promise, God?

I wrote it down in the journal, but then scratched it out.

Don't do that to yourself, Tamara. I couldn't let hope flicker again, not after what had happened with Dakota.

The bus slowed down and then came to a complete stop. I touched my left hand where my ring should be. It was well after eleven, but I didn't care. I had to see Joe. I could feel that he needed me as much as I needed him.

After exiting the bus, it took a few minutes to find a cab, and then another fifteen to get to Joe's house. I dug his key from my purse, quietly unlocked the door, and crept inside, relocking the door immediately. The scent of everything Joe hit my nose, and a warm and wonderful sensation happened inside my core. Coming here was home for me. I felt along the hallway and then up the stairs into his room. The streetlight shone through his window, and there he was, bare chested and sound asleep.

A few seconds went by as I watched him breathe. He was so

beautiful. And he was mine. I kicked off my shoes, tiptoed across the room, and slid into bed next to him. Yet again I was crossing every boundary we had set, but I needed to be with him after the weekend I'd had.

I put my hand around his waist and pushed myself close into him.

Joe stirred. "Tamara?" His voice was groggy. Suddenly he was embracing me. "Am I dreaming?"

"Shhh. No. It's me."

"I missed you so much."

"I missed you too. Sorry for waking you."

His sleepy gaze ran over me. "How did you get here?"

"The bus."

"I would've come to get you."

"I know."

Joe ran his hand down my arm. My body subtly tensed. His touch felt amazing and terrifying as his fingers caressed the top of my hand, the way he usually did before weaving them through mine. He froze. "Baby, where's your ring?"

He wasn't supposed to notice that tonight. I just needed one peaceful night with Joe holding me close to rejuvenate my soul, to gain strength to tell him. "It's gone," I choked out before a knot in my throat made it impossible to speak.

Joe sat up in bed and flicked on the light, a look of horror on his face. "What do you mean?"

"My sister stole it along with the money in my purse." I was unable to hold back the tears. "I'm sorry, Joe. If I had left with you, I'd still have it."

His expression softened, and then his arms were around me, strong yet tender. "There's no way you could have possibly known that."

"It just seems like an omen, like somehow I'm going to lose you too."

Both of Joe's hands cradled my face. "You are never going to lose me, Tamara. Do you hear me?" His voice was strong.

Passionate. He took my left hand in his and placed it on his chest. "My heart is completely yours. I don't need a ring or a piece of paper to prove it."

I searched his expression, so full of warmth and tenderness. "I thought you might hate me."

"How could you ever think that?" He wiped the tears away from my face, then kissed my cheek where the moisture had been.

Every part of me melted at the softness of his lips. How in the world did I get so lucky to have a man like him? "I will never deserve you," I whispered.

"Don't talk like that about the woman I love." His mouth came over mine, sweet and tender.

I ran my hand along his bare skin. The kiss became deeper, less controlled.

"Tamara." He whispered my name through the kiss, his breath jagged. "I love you so much." His fingers wound through my hair and he drew me closer. His touch felt different, more aggressive—like the desire he'd been suppressing for months had been unleashed.

I could feel myself losing control, my body coming alive with need. A part of me knew that we should stop. That we were getting way too close to the point of no return, but I couldn't make myself. His touch melted away the disappointment and hurt of Quilcene and renewed a flame that life had tried to put out. Our gazes met.

The battle behind his eyes was the same one that was swallowing me whole. Then his lips were on mine again, and there was no more fighting, only surrender. I pushed myself closer to him and let him cross every line we swore to never cross before marriage. I gave him all I was holding back, and we fully lost ourselves in each other.

CHAPTER 26

December 4, 11:30 p.m.

DAKOTA

I parked in front of the dark house and prepared myself for the worst. The headlights in the rearview mirror gave me some comfort. For reasons I would never be able to comprehend, Tim cared about me.

I lit a smoke and headed inside, bracing myself for Lisa's fury. The door was locked, so I rifled through my purse to find the key.

The door swung open, and a cloud of marijuana smoke flooded out. "Where in the actual hell have you been?" Lisa spat out. "I had to walk to work in the rain, you b—"

"Lisa, calm down—"

My sentence was interrupted by a string of expletives.

"I'm sorry I just—"

She stuck her pointer finger in my face. "Don't you dare tell me you're sorry. You're not sorry. You only ever look out for one person, and that is yourself, Dakota, you nasty two-bit crack wh—."

"That's enough, Lisa." Anger flared through my veins like a blowtorch. I wasn't the one who'd sold my body on more than one occasion for drugs. I dropped my cigarette and shoved her into the house. "I was out there trying to scrounge up the money for Ryan. You were there with me as we partied away the dope I was supposed to sell, and now he is trying to collect."

"Don't you dare lie to me! Ryan is in jail!" She stepped closer, just inches from me.

"He sent Justin and Avery after me to collect." I pushed her away.

She turned a purplish red. "How is that my problem? You owe him the money, not me."

"If he comes after me, I'm taking you down with me."

"That is *it*! Get out of my house!" she screamed.

"Your house? I pay half the rent."

"Yeah, well my name is on the lease. No one in their right mind would rent to you."

"Don't act like you're better than me. I know what you did to get into this place."

Lisa's hand slammed hard and fast across my cheek. Stinging pain radiated through my jaw.

"Get out! Get out! Get out!" She shoved me, each time she shouted the words.

Rage erupted in me. "You get out!"

She grabbed hold of my hair and tried to drag me outside.

I resisted, and we both landed against the television with a loud crash. More cursing from both of us.

"I'm going to kill you!" She wrestled to her feet and ran toward the kitchen.

I lunged for her legs and knocked her over.

She hit the corner of the coffee table on the way down, sending marijuana ash across the room. "I hate you!" She kicked at me.

Her foot connected with my forehead with a sickening crunch.

"Enough!" In the doorway stood Tim's tall silhouette.

He was still here? For a split second I was relieved, then Lisa's foot slammed against my neck.

"I said enough!" Tim stomped across the room, picked Lisa up under her armpits, and tried to drag her from the house.

"You can't come in here! This is private property!" She struggled against his hold, calling him every foul name in the book. "You don't have a warrant, pig!"

"I'm not here as a cop. I'm here as Dakota's friend. And you're lucky, because there's probably *plenty* in this house I could arrest you for."

His words seemed to knock the fight out of her. "I just wanted her to leave." Her voice cracked. Was she going to cry? "She can't stay here anymore."

I struggled to my feet, head throbbing.

"Dakota, get your things." Tim said, voice level, still holding Lisa.

"What? I'm not leaving. She can get out!"

"It wasn't a suggestion. Get your things." The authority in his voice made me move toward my room. He was right. Staying here wasn't a good idea for either of us. But everywhere else I could think to go felt more dangerous. People were afraid of Ryan and would turn me over to him without question. Tim might be the only person I could trust.

"If I let you go, will you remain calm?" Tim asked Lisa.

"Yes." Lisa's voice was terse, but I doubted she'd come after me again. For the second time tonight, Tim had saved me.

I shut my bedroom door, threw my clothes into a duffel bag, and placed the jar of ashes in the middle for safe keeping. That was the one thing that mattered now. I zipped the bag and threw the strap over my shoulder.

Tim stood by the door, gaze on the floor.

Lisa sat on the couch, legs curled into her torso, smoking a cigarette, tears streaming down her face.

A small part of me felt bad for her. We'd been through a lot together, and I sure as hell didn't want our friendship to end like this. But that was how my life went—relationships ending abruptly, punctuated by violence.

I followed Tim out to his truck and placed my duffel bag into his trunk. "So, what's the plan, Officer Moore?"

"You're going to come stay with me for a little while."

"You can't be serious." A wayward junkie staying with the po po? That seemed like a recipe for disaster. Or a bad sitcom.

"It's the safest place for you right now."

No arguing that. Ryan would never think to look for me there.

"But, Dakota, absolutely no drugs."

Drugs weren't an option at this point. "What about vodka? That's legal, right?"

He let out a deep breath and walked around the car. "Just get in."

CHAPTER 27

December 5, 7:35 a.m.

JOE

Last night as I held Tamara, I dreamt about us in the future, walking along the beach as we did on our first date. The weather was perfect in the dream—blue skies, with soft puffs of clouds floating in the horizon. With us were two young children. A boy around four years old, and a little girl around two who looked just like Tamara. Chin-length brown hair framed her cherub features. The boy looked more like me, except with chubby cheeks and a smile that brightened his whole face. Tamara splashed in the water with the children, laughing as they ran away from the waves. The little girl ran to me, arms extended. "Daddy, up." I lifted her and twirled her around, joy filling me.

The sound of my phone ringing interrupted the beautiful scene. I groggily reached for it and looked at the screen.

The hospital.

I reached out for Tamara, but she wasn't there. Where was she? Memories of last night rushed over my mind, along with a garbage heap of guilt.

What did we do?

Shame pressed hard against my guts, making me nauseous.

In that single act, I'd broken the one promise I had made to God, Tamara, and myself.

With everything in me, I wished I could go back to the peaceful feeling of the beach I'd just been on. With all that had happened over the last few days, that comforting dream felt like a gift from God—even after our mistake.

The phone rang again, and I answered it.

"Hey, Joe, Anita here."

I held my breath, bracing for the worst.

"I'm about to leave and wanted to give you an update on Trudy."

"Is she ..." I couldn't bring myself to ask the question.

"She's all right. She had a good night. She's stable, and they changed her status from critical to serious."

I let out the breath I was holding. "Thank God." Finally, some good news. I rolled out of bed and walked into my bathroom. The house felt eerily empty. Where in the world was Tamara?

"She's not completely out of the woods," Anita continued, "but the fact that she's leveling out is a good sign. If things continue to go well, they will start removing the drugs to bring her out of her coma."

"Thanks for the update. I appreciate you letting me know." I walked downstairs, still searching. Perhaps she'd gone to see Trudy.

"You're welcome."

"Hey, Anita, before you go, has anyone been to visit her this morning?" I peeked into the kitchen.

"Only Roger. He's been with her since six this morning."

After ending the call with Anita, I walked back upstairs, heart aching.

I scrolled through my phone and tapped on Tamara's name. The phone rang four times before it went to voicemail. "Hey, sweetie, where are you? Call me." I hung up and then shot her a text saying the same thing.

I sat on the edge of my bed and ran both hands through my hair. Perhaps she went to get us breakfast. But she didn't have her car. Images from last night filled my head again.

How could I be so weak?

"God, please forgive me." As soon as I said the words out loud, thoughts of the dream I had last night flooded through me, the one peaceful moment I'd had in days. Could that be us one day? Walking hand in hand on the beach with our kids? I didn't know, but the vision did give me the strength to want to keep fighting, to get back on the right path even after failing.

"God, forgive me." Feelings of hope overwhelmed my soul, chasing away the sadness. The vision had to mean something. It had to be a sign from God that he was still on our side. I opened my hands to him and surrendered to his forgiveness.

But what about Tamara? Where was she? Was she struggling through what we'd done? The last few days had been so much harder on her. How was she handling what had happened between us? Probably not that good if she couldn't stick around to look me in the eye this morning.

"God, be with Tamara wherever she is. Speak to her. Show her your love. Let things be okay with us."

I grabbed my phone again and shot Tamara another quick message.

Please get ahold of me. I love you.

I stared at the phone. Was she avoiding talking to me? Had she run again? "God, I can't lose her."

I looked at the picture of my mother that sat on my dresser. A tear slid down my cheek. It would be okay. It had to be. We had fallen down, but all was not lost. Trudy was doing better, and there was that wonderful dream.

Next to my mom's picture was the ring I'd given her for her birthday when I was twelve years old. For months, I'd saved my allowance, which at the time was only five dollars a week. It was a simple band with a large bronze heart attached to it.

I glanced at my phone again. Why hadn't Tamara responded to me yet? I couldn't just sit here waiting anymore. I had to find her. I slipped on a pair of jeans and a T-shirt before picking up the ring and heading out the door.

CHAPTER 28

December 5, 8:15 a.m.

TAMARA

I walked for a long time, trying to make sense of the mess my soul had become. When I woke this morning in Joe's arms, they felt wrong. For the last year, Joe had been my safe place. He was the one person I could always lean on when my world felt as if it were spinning out of control. This morning was the first time being with Joe that it hadn't felt right. I felt dirty. Guilty. Ashamed. I didn't know how to make it better, so I walked and walked until I ended up here. The one place I hoped I could find peace from the dark thoughts.

I pushed open the doors of Hope Chapel, and heat hit my frozen cheeks. I turned to the left, and my heart dropped into my stomach. Levi stood beside David, deep in conversation. I had come here for respite from the inner storm, not for more emotional turbulence. The last time I'd seen Levi was the day I gave him Hope. I wasn't ready for this. I spun around to leave, but before I could, David spotted me.

"Tamara." His voice was full of fondness, as if I was one of his favorite people in the world.

I turned back around and waved timidly, trying to force a smile.

Levi waved back, his signature genuine smile on his lips.

My insides settled a bit. I realized then how much I had missed him. Levi had played such a big part in changing my life for the better, and I'd been avoiding him. I walked over and gave him a hug.

He embraced me like a long-lost child. "So good to see you."

A knot formed around my voice box as I let myself cry. There were a thousand questions I wanted to ask him about Hope, but they stayed buried under my current pile of emotions. I pulled away and wiped at the tears.

David and Levi exchanged a concerned glance.

"Are you okay, Tamara?" David tilted his head.

I shook my head, and more tears came. I wasn't okay. I didn't know how to be at the moment. "I came to talk to you," I finally choked out.

"Why don't we step into my office?" He placed his hand on my shoulder. "Levi, let's talk later."

"Sounds good. I'll be praying for you, Tamara," Levi said.

"Thank you." Those words wrapped around me like a security blanket. One thing about Levi, he was a man of faith. I was sure God answered his prayers. I followed David into his office.

"I'm glad to see you made it home safe." David walked around his desk.

"I guess you could say that." I felt more like I was in a thousand different pieces and wasn't sure how to put them back together.

"What's going on?"

I looked down at the oversized leather chair that I usually sat in. I couldn't sit. I was too on edge. Instead, I paced, searching for the words to convey this tangled mess. "I feel like my whole world just exploded. I tried to help Dakota, and she hates me so much that she stole my freaking engagement ring. Talk about a clear message. She gave me no information on how to find the rest of my family, so I'm back to square one on that.

Oh, and by the way, Trudy is in the hospital with a gunshot wound fighting for her life." He already knew this information, but it spilled out of me like raw sewage from a broken septic pipe. Scared to look at David, I twisted my left empty ring finger and continued to pace. Then there was what happened between me and Joe... Should I tell David? Gosh, what was he, my priest? He wasn't a stranger inside of a box, though. What would he think of me? "I slept with Joe last night." I choked on the words. "I just missed him so much when I was in Quilcene, and after what happened there, I needed the comfort, so I went straight to his house." Face burning, I avoided eye contact.

Over the last six months this man had been my pastor, but more than that, he'd become like a father to me. It felt terrible to make so much progress only to let him down. "Joe's the strong one when it comes to us." I swallowed back the emotions building in my throat. "I think my showing up in the middle of the night caught him off guard. It's my fault, David. He's told me before how much of a struggle it is for him. And I basically threw myself at him. I climbed into bed with him in the middle of the night, for goodness sake."

"Tamara, please look at me."

My head turned to the sound of his voice, finally meeting his gaze.

His expression was soft. Tender. Sadness lined his countenance, but he didn't seem judgmental. More like a father who was concerned for a hurt child. "I'm really proud of you."

Proud of me? That certainly wasn't the sentiment I'd expected.

"Would you please have a seat?" He motioned for the chair.

I eyed the big recliner again and nodded. Without a word, I slumped into it. Taking in a deep breath, I looked out the window. A bird came and perched on a small tree that had lost its leaves. I felt like that tree—naked, exposed, barren.

"I am so, so sorry you are going through this right now. You knew trying to reconnect with your sister was going to be a risk, but your love for her outweighed that, and you went there anyway. That took courage."

"Courage, really? I made a complete mess out of the whole situation, and I don't know how to fix it."

"Honestly, Tamara, I am so very proud of you."

"How?" Confusion caused my eyebrows to furrow. His words didn't compute. "I may be new at this whole Christian thing, but I do know that sex outside of marriage is one of the big sins. It's pretty clear."

"Yes, but I was more referring to how you came in here ready to deal with your pain instead of running. The woman I met six months ago would have tried to find a way to shove that pain deep inside and run from it. But you came in here to deal with it. That takes courage."

I didn't feel courageous. And even if David was proud of me, what about God? Why couldn't I shake this feeling of shame?

"The Bible says that everything, and I mean everything, was paid for at the cross. Now He's welcoming you into His arms and is more than happy to make you feel clean again."

"But what about the other stuff?"

"That I don't know. But I do know God is good."

I barked out a laugh, though tears streamed down my face. At one time, I had sensed his goodness, but lately it had been muted by the familiar darkness I thought I'd beaten. If I were being honest, it hadn't been only the last forty-eight hours. Things had changed inside of me since the adoption.

David's phone beeped, and he glanced at it. "I'm sorry to cut this short, but it's time for my next client. Please know that I will be praying for you, and at our next visit I'd like to dig into this topic a bit deeper." David looked at his phone again. "Our next appointment is on the seventeenth. Does that still work for you?"

I nodded and stood. "Thank you for meeting with me."

David came around his desk and gave me a firm squeeze. "Thank you for trusting me with your pain."

Pulling away, I threw him a half-smile, and left his office. A couple sat on the leather sofa in the foyer. They stood when they saw me and went into David's office. I eyed the sanctuary door, soul filling with longing. I missed the closeness I'd felt to God at the beginning of my walk with him. Maybe somehow through this mess I could find him once more.

Without another thought, I pushed through the sanctuary doors and walked up the center aisle. The place was too quiet as I made my way down to the front. The last few days' events circled around my mind. Ryan, Trudy, Dakota, and Joe. Every name had a different emotion attached. Fear, concern, anger, and disappointment. All these weighed on me heavy as a millstone as I knelt down before the only one who could put me back together.

CHAPTER 29

December 5, 9:15 a.m.

JOE

I drove around town looking for Tamara, starting at her apartment. When I'd got there, her car was parked in her usual spot. For a brief moment, that gave me hope. Maybe she'd caught a taxi home and then shut off her phone to sleep. The feeling quickly faded though as I tapped on her door and then entered with the key she'd given me. The place looked exactly the same as it had when we'd left two days ago. I went to the diner, her favorite coffee house, and down to the pier.

No Tamara.

I messaged her again. *Please call me.*

Apprehension consumed me as I typed out another message, giving me that on-edge feeling. *I'm really worried about you. I'm so sorry. I love you.*

I stared at the phone for a few minutes, praying for a response. Where was she? I was completely out of ideas. I scrolled through my contacts and found Levi's number.

He answered quickly. "Hey, Joe. How's Trudy?"

"She's okay. Not out of the woods yet, but better." I'd been so focused on finding Tamara that I hadn't made it to the hospital yet. Perhaps I should go check there. "At this moment, I'm more concerned about Tamara."

"Oh yeah?"

A part of me wanted to tell Levi what I had done, but I couldn't bring myself to confess to this man who loved Tamara like a daughter. "She's disappeared, Levi. She's not answering her phone, and I've been all over town looking for her." My voice sounded desperate.

He was quiet for a long moment. "I don't know if I should tell you this—"

"Tell me what? Have you seen her?"

"Yeah. About an hour ago down at Hope Chapel."

Hope Chapel? Why hadn't I thought about that? Of course, she would be there. I pulled off the side of the road and spun around. "Thank you! I gotta go!" I hit end and sped toward the church, relief and fear filling my senses at the same time. Relief to know where she was—afraid to find out how she'd react to me.

The whole way there I prayed for grace to wash over Tamara and that God would prepare her to forgive me. A sense of déjà vu overtook me as I drove toward the church. It reminded me of six months ago when I'd found her there before I asked her to marry me. Ten minutes later, I turned into the parking lot and parked. I kept my head down as I walked up the church steps, praying I wouldn't run into David.

Before pushing through the sanctuary doors, I paused to say another quick prayer. I quietly nudged the door open and stepped inside.

There she was, kneeling at the altar, body convulsing as she wept.

She was hurting more deeply than I'd realized. My insides shattered as I tiptoed down the aisle, careful not to make a sound. When I reached her, I knelt down beside her and took hold of her hand.

She looked at me with a tear-stained face. Sorrow split me down the middle.

Without speaking she bowed her head once more.

I did the same. "God, please forgive me for breaking my promise to you and dishonoring your daughter. Forgive me for being weak—"

"It wasn't your fault, Joe. It was mine." She looked up at me.

"It's my job to protect you and guard over us. I hurt you, Tamara." My voice was hoarse and broken. "It won't happen again. I promise you that." I wiped her tears away. "I understand if you're angry with me."

Her brows pinched together. "Why would you think I'm angry with you?"

"You weren't there when I woke. I've been trying to call you all morning with no answer. I thought maybe you didn't want to talk to me."

Her lower lip trembled. "Dakota stole my phone along with the ring."

Didn't she say that her phone was on *silent* that morning? Had she lied to me? I shoved down the hurt and put my arm around her. That didn't matter now. "I'm so sorry that happened to you. We have been through a lot lately, but we're going to make it through this together."

She nuzzled closer. "You think so?"

I squeezed her a little. "I do. Last night I had the most beautiful dream. We were married, and this mess was behind us. We had two beautiful children. A boy and a girl, and we were playing at the beach."

"Sounds wonderful." Her lips tilted at the edges, but her eyes were weighed down.

I took hold of her left hand and brought out my mom's ring. "This ring isn't as beautiful as your other one, but it was my mom's."

I slipped it onto her finger. It fit perfectly.

Tamara ran her fingers over the bronze heart. "I love it."

Drawing her close, I held her tightly. "We're going to get through this."

CHAPTER 30

December 5, 9:40 a.m.

DAKOTA

A loud thud jolted me awake.

"Sorry." A male voice called out.

Where was I? The smell of freshly cooked pancakes and coffee made me recoil. For every high there was a low, but this low felt as if it might be the bottom. A dull ache worked its way through my head. The events of last night slowly made their way through the fog. Justin and Avery following me out to the car at the casino, holding a knife to my cheek. Tim saving me. Lisa and my huge blow up. Then Tim saving me again.

This couldn't be real. I was in Tim's guest bedroom?

I scanned the room. Plain soft-cream walls. A few totes stacked at the end of the bed and a dark wood dresser next to it, but that was it. The windows were small with blue curtains. Wasn't that nice? Barf.

I rolled over in the bed, put a pillow over my head, and prayed to the sleep gods to pull me back under. Maybe I could sleep for the next ten years and forget my whole life.

From the other room, Tim whistled while he cooked or whatever he was doing out there.

Annoying. The noise felt like a nail shooting through my skull. Or that could have been Lisa's footprint.

Another layer of smell wafted through the door. Some sort of sausage. Or was that bacon?

My stomach coiled into a giant knot. What I would give for another line. I couldn't believe I was in a cop's house. How in the hell had I gotten here? Ryan's face, full of murder, flashed across my mind. I cringed.

I was so screwed.

My purse rattled. What the? My phone was right next to me.

Oh yeah. Tamara's phone. I pulled it out.

One voicemail and six text messages. All from ... that's right ... good ole Romeo.

I listened to his voice message. "Hey, sweetie, where are you? Call me."

Had Tamara not made it home yet? Was she still here in Quilcene?

I clicked on the texts Joe had sent. They were somewhat simple, but the last one felt almost desperate. *I'm really worried about you. I'm so sorry. I love you.*

What could he have possibly done? Maybe Tamara's life wasn't as perfect as I thought. From the bottom of my purse, her ring seemed to scream at me. I shook away the guilt like the worthless insect it was. There were no other options. If I didn't figure this out soon, I would end up just like—

No, I couldn't think about that now.

It was Tamara's bad for coming back after all this time. A stupid move on her part. For years, Ryan had carried on about how if he ever had the chance, he'd break Tamara's neck with his bare hands. Good thing Romeo had been there when he found her.

I leaned over, dug through my duffel bag, and brought out the jar of ashes. A gaping chasm expanded in my soul. "I have to sell the ring," I said to the jar. "I don't want to, but I have no choice." Tears slipped down my face. "You're not here to protect me, and neither was Tamara." Suddenly I felt like that fourteen-year-old little girl, watching helplessly as Tamara took the beating for me. I looked at the messages on her phone once more.

Years later, and she was paying for my addiction again. I threw Tamara's phone across the room and wiped my tears away.

Crying was so stupid. Since Tamara left, no one was here to hear my cries anymore. I hated her for that. She was an idiot for trying to find me. If her life was destroyed because of it, she had nobody to blame but herself.

CHAPTER 31

December 5, 10:20 a.m.

TAMARA

Joe's hand felt like a vice grip around mine as we walked down the hall toward the ICU. The fluorescent lights overhead were too bright, making my head hurt right behind my temples. The pungent smell of disinfectant hit my nose, and my empty stomach tightened. What was I thinking, making him come here alone the first time when I stayed in Quilcene with my sister? This was the place he'd lost his mom. I could be so selfish sometimes. Only seeing what *I* needed in the moment.

A nurse in blue scrubs rushed by us, and I looked at Joe. His handsome features were painted with a hard yet solemn expression. Another round of self-loathing battered my insides. We reached the double doors, and Joe buzzed us in.

The doors opened, and we entered the ICU. More antiseptic, but this time something extra mixed with it—fear mingled with death. Joe led me to Trudy's room. The door was closed so he tapped lightly on it before slowly pushing it open. The curtain was drawn halfway, keeping Trudy shielded from view.

Trudy's boyfriend, Roger, sat at the end of her bed. He looked at us, and my heart fell. The look he wore was one of a tortured man about to lose the thing he treasured the most. He stood, crossed the room, and hugged Joe like a drowning man clinging to a buoy.

Joe held a stunned, sorrowful expression as he embraced Roger. "She's going to be okay."

Roger pulled away, gaze on the floor. "How could this have happened?"

"I don't know... She was at the diner and—"

"Why was she at the diner? She's never at the diner. I didn't even know she was planning on keeping the place."

Trudy was there that night because of me. I walked forward, around the pastel curtain. My throat felt suddenly dry. Trudy lay there lifeless, a tracheal tube in her mouth, feeding her oxygen. I was faintly aware of Joe and Roger talking in the background. I stepped closer to her and placed my hand on hers.

It was so cold. I checked the monitor to see her temperature. It said 99.9. Though that meant she had a slight fever, a glimmer of hope rose at seeing my number. Was God giving me a sign that Trudy would be okay? Saying a silent prayer, I covered her hand with the thin hospital blanket and bent closer to her. "I'm so sorry, Trudy. I should have come home with Joe." Earlier this year when she had been in the hospital, her eyes had sprung open, startling me. I wished so badly that they would open now. That she would wake up and tell me everything was going to be all right. For a moment, I just stared at her, listening to the constant whir of the breathing machine and beeping of the monitor—these beautiful miracles of modern medicine that were keeping her alive until she could sustain life on her own.

She had to pull through. Joe and I needed her in our lives. She truly was the only mom either of us had at the moment. Joe's hand on my back startled me out of my thoughts. I looked back at him. Roger was no longer in the room. "Where's Roger?"

"He went to get coffee."

I nodded and refocused on Trudy. "I'm so sorry, Joe."

"For what, baby?" he whispered.

"For making you come face this alone."

He wrapped his arms around my waist and rested his chin on my shoulder. "All is forgiven."

I turned around and snuggled into him. That sweet, safe feeling was back between us. I breathed him in and let it wash over me. His stomach growled, and I glanced at him. "You hungry?"

"Starved. I haven't eaten yet today."

"Me neither." I turned back to Trudy. "I'm not sure if I could eat though. I don't want to leave her."

"She's in great hands here, love. The nurse told me this morning that she had a good night. You need to take care of yourself. I think it's time we both get some food and much-needed rest."

I nodded, tears stinging the back of my eyes. Joe was probably right. And, if nothing else, it seemed like the most merciful thing to do for him. I leaned over and kissed Trudy's head. "We're praying for you, Trudy. You're going to pull through this."

CHAPTER 32

December 5, 11:25 a.m.

TAMARA

I pushed the last bite of French toast through a trail of syrup and sighed. Joe took another small bite of his half-eaten omelet. He didn't seem impressed with the quality of the hospital cafeteria food. I placed the bite in my mouth and then set down my fork. Mine wasn't bad, but it was kind of hard to ruin French toast. Though the room was bright and clean, depression hung in the air. The hospital staff were friendly and helpful, but many of the people who were there had a sadness in their countenance. Despite that, a part of me wanted to sit with Trudy for the rest of the day, but by the weariness in Joe's features, he was in need of some reprieve from the stress and the memories. "So, what do we do now?"

Joe set down his fork and leaned back in his seat, eyebrows pinching together. "I don't know. I was kind of hoping we could just relax."

"The weather is nice out. We could go down to the wharf and then window shop." Being by the water always rejuvenated my soul.

Joe scooted his plate away from him and threw his napkin down on the half-eaten food. "I'm pretty drained. I'd like to have a chill day with you and regroup."

"What did you have in mind?"

Joe shrugged. "We could head back to your place and find a new show on Netflix."

The entire day in my apartment with Joe? "I don't know if that's a good idea."

"What?" Hurt flashed across his face. "We can't spend time alone anymore because of one mistake? I would love to rest with you today. We've been okay every other time for all these months."

Swallowing, I look down at my empty plate. "Yeah, but then we didn't know what we were missing." Heat climbed my neck at the admission.

"So, it was good for you?"

I made eye contact again. His expression was doubtful.

Leaning forward, I whispered, "Do you really have to ask that?"

"I don't know." This time he averted his gaze.

Why where things suddenly so awkward between us?

"I feel like we probably shouldn't talk about it." Joe came forward, voice low. "But a part of me wants to know."

"I've never felt anything like it," I said quietly, face on fire. Our gazes met again. A thousand words passed between us before I looked away. "But you're right. We definitely shouldn't talk about it."

"Fair enough." A smile tinted his voice now. "But I can't not be alone with you. We'll pile pillows between us if we have to and only hold hands."

I burst out laughing. "Pillows? That's your plan?"

"Hey, I've barely slept in days." A grin spread across his gorgeous features. "That's all I got."

"I guess it's worth a shot." It was ridiculous, but charming.

"Like I said before." His expression went serious. "What happened last night won't happen again. I care about you too much. I don't want to hurt us."

I loved Joe for that. He was so much stronger than me in

that regard. "Okay. A relaxing day with you sounds wonderful. What series were you thinking?"

"Tommy keeps raving to me about *Game of Thrones*. We could give it a shot."

"I don't know... I've heard it's pretty graphic. How about a mellow show like *Gilmore Girls*?"

"You can't be serious, babe." He chuckled. "You're killing me."

I laughed. "You know what show I was thinking of the other day? *Party of Five*. It's super old, but when Dakota and I were kids, it was our favorite show." It would probably unearth more hurt to watch it now, but something in me almost needed it.

"I don't remember that one." Joe took his last drink of coffee.

"It's about a family with five kids ranging from one to twenty-years old who just lost both their parents in a car accident, and they're trying to figure out life without them."

"Sounds sad."

"It's better than you'd think. Dakota and I watched it because there were five of us kids. Plus, she had a thing for Scott Wolf."

Joe's eyebrows lifted.

"I was more into Matthew Fox myself."

"Oh, come on, Matthew Fox, *really*?" He rose, a playful smirk on his lips.

"Heck, yes! You know what? Instead of *Party of Five*, we could watch *Lost*. He's way better looking in that show." I stood.

"No way. I've already seen *Lost*. It was good until the fourth season. After that I was totally *lost*." He put air quotes around the last word and winked before pushing the door open for me.

"You're such a dork." I smacked his arm.

"That's why you love me."

"True." It felt so good to be light-hearted with him again. I followed him out to his Jeep, and we headed back to my apartment.

Twenty minutes after leaving the hospital, we entered my studio. Joe took my coat and hung it on the hook while I went into the kitchenette and put on hot water for tea. "Do you want herbal or black?"

"Better go with black. I need the caffeine." Joe took the three pillows off my daybed and placed them in the middle of the loveseat and grabbed the remote before sitting down.

"Really?" I leaned on the wall, shooting him a playful smirk.

Grinning, he raised his hands in the air. "Can never be too careful."

I shook off the urge to grab one of the pillows and clobber him with it. I smiled at the thought before turning back to the kitchenette and pulling two mugs out of the cupboard. After opening my tea drawer, I scanned the selection and grabbed a package of Earl Grey for Joe and Moroccan Mint for me. A wave of exhaustion hit me, and thoughts of the last few days invaded the tea-making routine. Trudy, Dakota, my missing ring... What happened after I left that had turned Dakota into the kind of person who stole her sister's engagement ring? Fear tingled down my spine as I thought of the possibilities. Maybe she was in league with Ryan after all. Or maybe Ryan had been punishing her this whole time for me stealing from him. An overwhelming weight crushed my chest. If that was true, I needed to find her and beg her to forgive me.

I looked down at the ring Joe had given me earlier and ran my finger over the bronze heart. Such a sweet gesture and in so many ways, it was more me than the fancy diamond ring Dakota had taken.

A lump formed in my throat. Whatever she had been through over the last six years didn't give her the right to steal from me. She could have told me if she needed money. Stealing my ring felt more like a message, as if she didn't want me back in her life.

Joe's hand on my back startled me out of my thoughts, and I jumped.

"I didn't mean to scare you." His hand caressed my shoulder, sending shivers down my spine. "The show is loaded and ready to go."

The show... I looked down at the ring again. I couldn't watch *Party of Five* right now. It would be too painful.

"About that. I changed my mind." I turned around. "The other day Claire was telling me about *Nashville*. It sounded like a good blend of music and drama. Why don't we give that a try?"

"If that's what my lady wants." Joe tilted his chin and pursed his lips. "I'll see if I can find it."

I gave him a gentle kiss. "You're the best."

His hands slid down my arms, and he threaded his fingers through mine. "Why don't you come sit with me while you wait for the water to boil? I miss you."

I searched his tender gaze. "How could you miss me? I'm right here."

"I don't know. Somehow you feel far away. It's like you've pulled away from me, and I don't know how to bring you back."

"I haven't gone anywhere, Joe. I love you more now than ever."

"You promise?"

"With all my heart."

The kettle finally whistled, and I drew away. Joe went back into the living room. I poured the steaming water into the mugs, my mind on Joe and what he had just said. I hated that he doubted us in any way. Life had hit us hard over the last few days, and it had certainly taken its toll on our relationship, but we were strong. We were getting married in less than six months, and nothing could change that.

CHAPTER 33

December 5, 2:00 p.m.

JOE

I tightened my hand around Tamara's and tried to focus on the show. Putting the pillows between us had been a stupid joke. Right now, I wanted to toss them aside and pull her close. There was nothing impure in the desire, only this aching need in my chest to hold onto the goodness that was us. Life was too fragile and too out of control at the moment, and she was the one thing that I was sure of. The one person I loved more than anything.

The third episode ended, and Tamara turned toward me. "What do you think?"

"I think I like it. The music's good. It's a bit high drama though."

"Yeah, I'm definitely intrigued. The characters are interesting. Deacon kind of reminds me of you."

I shifted my position toward her. "Why? He's a bit of a man whore."

She barked out a laugh. "He's only slept with Juliette."

"Exactly."

"Well, aside from his promiscuity, he definitely is Joe-ish."

"It's because he's a recovering alcoholic, isn't it?"

She smacked my leg. "Nooooo. You can tell he's a good guy.

179

He cares about people and he's still madly in love with his first love after years of being apart."

"Does that make you Rayna then?" I shot her a silly smile.

"Maybe. She's tough as nails and she *did* run away from home when she was sixteen."

"You're way hotter than Rayna James."

She smiled and leaned in for a kiss. "And you're way better looking than Deacon, so I think we're good."

I ran my hand slowly down her beautiful face. "But unlike Deacon, I'm never going to let you go."

Her gaze lingered on my lips. Thoughts of last night and what had happened between us crashed over me at once. I looked away, pushing back the onslaught of images, bringing my desire under control. "You ready for the next episode?"

She nodded, and I clicked play.

For the next few hours, we let the episodes play one after another. The show's intensity continued to build as every ending came with a more dramatic cliff-hanger. The only time we stopped it was for quick bathroom breaks and a call to order food.

When the pizza arrived, we paused the show and grabbed a few plates from the kitchen. I lifted the lid to the box and the smell of basil, garlic, and mozzarella cheese filled my nose. I grabbed a piece of the supreme pizza topped with extra cheese. A few pieces of sausage fell off, and I scooped them back on before taking a massive bite. I glanced over at Tamara. Her gaze was on her plate as she somberly picked at the toppings.

"What's wrong?" I asked around a bite.

"I don't know... this show." She was quiet for a long moment. "It's bringing up some things I wasn't expecting about my past."

"You mean your family?"

"No."

"What then?"

"The longer we watch it, the more some of these characters

remind me of people from my time living in Ocean Shores."

"Yeah? Is that good or bad?" I set down my pizza and wiped off my hand on a napkin.

"A little bit of both. I want to like Avery, but he reminds me a bit of Danny—a brooding musician with a dark side. Then Juliette is one hundred percent Shelby, a blonde bombshell who always gets the guy, but never knows how to keep him. As you know, they both hurt me pretty deeply when they cheated on me with each other."

I nodded. "I'm sorry those things happened to you."

"It's okay. It doesn't hurt like it used to. Now that I have you, I realized that stuff with Danny was shallow waters."

A ghost of a smile played on my lips. "I'm glad to hear that. But we don't have to continue the show if it's hurting you."

"No, no, it's not like that. It feels like a theme right now that I can't run from my past. This show is helping me see that some parts of my life don't hurt like they used to, which feels great. On a more positive note, what most surprises me is how Gunner reminds me of Charlie."

"Who's Charlie?" I wasn't sure I liked the way she said his name.

"I never told you about Charlie?" A fond expression flitted over her features, and a twinge of jealousy hit my insides.

"I am pretty sure you haven't."

She smiled again. "He was Danny's cousin and a good friend. A few weeks before I found out what was going on with Danny and Shelby, he came to my birthday party and gave me a bracelet." She stood, went to her dresser, and opened the top drawer. She took out the bracelet and brought it to me. "He also gave me a card but said I couldn't open it unless I decided to leave Ocean Shores."

I ran my finger over the charm that dangled from the bracelet. There were two tiny feathers etched into silver with a clear gem in the center.

"It means Godspeed. It was as if he knew I needed to leave.

181

The day I did, I opened the card and a thousand dollars was inside of it. His kindness made the next month of my life a lot easier to endure." She was quiet for a long moment, seeming to linger on the memory.

Another stab of jealousy. Had there been something going on between them? He obviously had feelings for her.

"I never got a chance to thank him for his generosity."

I shook off the nagging envy. What was wrong with me? The guy had done a great thing for Tamara that had led her to me. I should be thankful. "Maybe someday you will."

"Maybe." She picked a piece of sausage from her slice and popped it in her mouth. "It almost feels too late now."

"You never know." I took another bite of my pizza, searching for a way to change the subject, but I couldn't find safe territory in my mind.

A dark shadow flitted across Tamara's features. "It feels like I'm too late for a lot of things."

An ominous feeling snaked its way through my abdomen. "What do you mean?"

"Did I tell you what I found out about my brother?"

"No." She hadn't told me a lot about what had happened in Quilcene, but we hadn't had much time yet.

She shifted in her seat. "Dakota was being pretty elusive, but I ran into an old friend before I left town. She said Gabriel went missing about a year after I did. Everybody thinks he ran away." She paused for a moment, biting the inside of her cheek. "But I don't know. I can't imagine him leaving. He was nineteen when I left home, and he'd already stuck around after he could have left. Why would he have just suddenly gone?"

I pushed the pillows onto the floor and pulled her close, where she should have been the whole time.

"I keep thinking about him." Her eyes welled, and she blinked a few times before continuing. "A feeling in my guts tells me there's much more to that story, but it's probably better left alone."

At this point I couldn't agree more. Our lives had fallen apart the moment we went to track down her sister. Right now, we just needed to gather strength from each other and God and move forward. I rested my forehead on hers and said a silent prayer that God would put everything back where it was supposed to be. "Do you want to watch the next episode, or do you want to try a different show?"

Her smile was sad as she looked at me. "Are you going to put the pillows back between us?"

I slowly shook my head. "But I will if you want me to."

She put her head upon my chest. "Go ahead and press play."

I hit the button and put my feet on the wooden case in front of us. Now that Tamara was close like this, I could finally relax. In this moment, life felt like it was supposed to be—as if the other stuff didn't matter as much. The television became background noise as I traced circles on her arm and thought about the dream I'd had last night. Perhaps Tamara wasn't meant to find her family. Her redemption could be with me. Here, I would always treasure her and keep her safe.

Toward the end of the show, I could feel Tamara drifting off to sleep. That was probably my cue to leave, but I was weighed down by my own exhaustion. I let the show flip over to the next episode while I leaned my head on the back of the loveseat, feeling myself fade into sleep.

"Joe, wake up," Tamara whispered, shaking my shoulder. "You can't stay here."

I yawned deeply. "I know, I'm just tired." I stumbled to my feet.

"Are you okay to drive?" Tamara followed me to the door.

"I'll be fine." I kissed her on the cheek. "I'll be here around ten in the morning so we can check on Trudy together."

"I love you."

"I love you too." I hated the fact that I needed to leave but staying wasn't an option.

CHAPTER 34

December 6, 9:15 a.m.

TAMARA

After Joe left, I staggered to bed, but I tossed and turned as the events of the last few days swirled in my mind. Meeting with David and the prayer after had helped at the moment, but once I was alone, my recent mistakes and discoveries crashed down on me with an avalanche of emotion.

When I drifted off, I dreamt of Gabriel. At first, I didn't recognize him. His dark hair was different, shorter than he normally wore it. His clothes were worn, with frayed ends and scattered holes. He stood on a gravel road leading to nowhere I recognized. Large evergreens lined the road, their green limbs blowing in the wind.

"Tamara?" He smiled when he saw me. "Where have you been, girl?" He ran toward me and hugged me, lifting me and spinning around.

"Where are we?" I asked as he set me back down, gravel crunching under my feet.

His smile faded. "That doesn't matter." He grabbed hold of my wrist. "There's something you have to know."

"Where are you? Where are Mom and Dad?"

His grip tightened around my forearm. "You have to find them." His features held a solemn conviction.

"But what about you?"

"Don't worry about me—" His words were interrupted by a muffled ringing.

"What do you mean?" How could I not worry about him? He was out there, just like I had been, lost in the world without his family.

Gabriel hesitated for a moment, a war raging in his eyes. "Trust me. You have—"

The ringing noise drowned out his words. I reached over to my nightstand for my phone but then remembered Dakota had it. Joe's phone? I threw the blanket off, rolled out of bed, and stumbled toward the ringing. I tucked my hand between the cushions of the loveseat and ran it along the seams until I found the phone and pulled it out. It was Joe's, but the person had already ended the call. I slumped down on the seat, a sad feeling gnawing at my insides. I had sent Joe away so abruptly last night that he'd forgotten his phone? He'd been really tired. I hoped he was okay. A notification popped up saying whoever it was had left a message. Should I listen to see if it was important? No. Joe would be here soon enough.

I set the phone down and went into the kitchenette to start the coffeepot. After filling the reservoir with water and the filter with coffee, I grabbed the box of Cinnamon Toast Crunch out of the cupboard and poured myself a bowl. Joe always teased me about my breakfast choices. If it wasn't Cinnamon Toast Crunch, it was Peanut Butter Cap'n Crunch. I poured milk over the cereal and grabbed Joe's phone again before sitting at the kitchen table. I took a few bites and then scrolled to find the messages he had sent me yesterday. Sadness welled in me as I read them. It sounded like maybe he thought I had left him. All that I'd put him through earlier this year, rolled over me in a second. My brokenness and knee-jerk reaction had hurt him deeply. I was so thankful we'd found our way back to each other.

I studied the messages. Had Dakota read them? Did she

even still have my phone? If she did, maybe this could be a way to reach out to her. I took another bite of my cereal. Did I want to communicate with her, though? She had stolen my engagement ring. Yet Joe had forgiven me for losing it. Maybe forgiveness was the right road to walk on. I quietly prayed, asking for strength to forgive her. Gabriel darted across my mind. In last night's dream, he'd said our family needed me. Was it because I was thinking of them before I went to bed or was God trying to get my attention? Maybe God had given me the dreams about Dakota. She obviously was in some kind of trouble, but she had shut me out—slammed an invisible door in my face. If my dreams were right though, if there was a chance that God was talking to me about finding my family, I had to keep trying.

Hey, Dakota, this is Tamara. I hope you're okay. I just want you to know that I love you and I forgive you for taking my stuff. I meant what I said the night we hung out. I love you, and I still want you in my life. For now, you can reach me on this phone.

My finger hovered over the send button.

Did I mean these words? I imagined Dakota as a child—a helpless, hurting child. That's what she was underneath the rough exterior and that's who she'd always be in my mind. I hit send and anxiously stared at the phone as I ate the rest of my cereal. It was too much to hope she would text me back, but I couldn't help it. I put my empty bowl into the sink and then poured myself a cup of coffee. Joe should be here any minute.

I walked across the room and opened my top dresser drawer. Might as well get in the shower now. Joe could let himself in. I found some clothes and headed to the bathroom.

By the time I dressed, I expected Joe to already be here. Most of the time he was at least fifteen minutes early, but it was already twelve minutes after ten, and he was late. I blew my hair dry, put on makeup, and tried not to worry. I couldn't help but think of every bad scenario that could have befallen him while driving home exhausted. What if he fell asleep at the wheel? What if he hit someone? Or ran into a ditch with no phone? Why hadn't I let him stay with me?

I walked out of my bathroom and snagged Joe's phone. Who would I even call? The hospital maybe? Or Caleb? I scrolled through Joe's contacts with shaky hands. Right before I clicked on Caleb's name, my front door opened, and Joe walked through, freshly showered.

I ran to him and threw my arms around his waist.

He embraced me back, his strong arms crushing me to him. "Good morning to you too."

"You're late." The words came out harsher than I intended. "You're never late."

"Uh, sorry. I couldn't find my phone last night to set an alarm. Slept over ten hours."

"It was in my couch." I withdrew and walked toward the table. "Its ringing woke me." I grabbed the phone and handed it to him. "Whoever it was left a message. I also used your phone to text my sister."

A look of concern flitted over his features. "Your sister?"

"Well, I texted my phone. I'm not even sure she still has it."

"We need to get you a new phone today and have that other one shut off."

Absolutely not. "That's the only way I can get ahold of her."

"Yeah, but if you get another line attached to that one, she can track you."

"She wouldn't do that." She clearly couldn't stand the sight of me. "Besides that, it means I can find her, right?"

"I thought we both agreed that finding your family wasn't safe." The firmness in his voice scared me.

"I never said I was going to stop looking for them."

He let out a frustrated sigh before lifting the phone again. He tapped on the screen and held the phone to his ear.

You have to find them, Gabriel's voice rang in my ears. My pulse quickened. I wanted to cry. It was clear Joe wanted me to stop my search, but how could I let this go?

"Oh, wow," Joe said, holding the phone closer to his ear.

"What is it?" It was hard to tell from his expression if it was good news or not.

"Trudy is awake."

Awake? That sounded positive. "Is she okay?"

He held his finger in the air, listening for a few more seconds and then put the phone down. "We need to go."

CHAPTER 35

December 6, 10:40 a.m.

JOE

The pungent smell of rubber gloves and disinfectant circled my nose as the doors to the ICU swung open. Once again, I was brought back to age seventeen after receiving the phone call about Mom. Nothing could have prepared me for seeing her, swollen and bloody, tubes hanging everywhere. I hadn't been ready for the devastating loss that lay in front of me, and in the end, I had been powerless to save her.

Tamara squeezed my hand, grounding me back to the here and now. Soon we stood in front of Trudy's room. The door was slightly cracked. I tapped on the door and pushed it open.

Roger sat beside her bed, holding her hand, expression strained. He stood and waved us in.

Trudy noticed us and struggled to move, pulling at a tube in her arm.

"Hey now, you just relax," I said.

Trudy's skin was so pale it seemed translucent, and dark shadows encircled her eyes.

"Joe," she croaked out. "Tamara."

Tamara put her hand on Trudy's. "You don't need to talk. You just focus on getting better."

Trudy nodded, through a strained smile. "Joe, can we speak alone?" she said, voice weak.

"Sure." I glanced at Tamara. Confusion lined her brow.

Roger walked around the bed, head down, voice low. "Tamara, would you like to go grab some coffee?"

She gave a slight shrug and turned toward the door. Roger followed after her.

I scooted a chair next to Trudy's bed and took hold of her hand. "I'm so glad you're awake. I was scared you were going to leave us." I swallowed back the emotions that threatened to come. "I'm not ready for that."

Trudy placed her other hand on top of mine. "It's going to take more—" she coughed mid-sentence "—than a bullet to take me out." A wry smirk appeared on her sullen face.

At least her sense of humor was intact.

"We need to talk, Joe." Her eyelids seemed heavy, as if she was having a hard time keeping them open.

"I'm right here."

"How's the diner doing?"

The diner? Really? The diner should be the last thing on her mind. "It's been closed since the shooting, the police have it under investigation."

Across the hall, it sounded as if someone was coding. My adrenaline spiked.

What was that look in Trudy's tired features? Fear? Concern?

"That's not going to work," she croaked out, then took a sip of the water from the plastic hospital cup. "The place needs to be open."

"Okay..." This didn't make any sense. She'd been unconscious for over forty-eight hours, fighting for her life, and she was concerned about the diner? She'd barely been there for the last three months, ever since she'd move to Salem to be closer to Roger. "I'm sorry, but I'm having trouble with this.

There's nothing we can do right now, plus everyone needed a break for a few days after the shooting. They're scared."

She nodded slightly, and her eyelids fluttered again. "I understand, but I've been through this before. Once I recover a bit more, a social worker will explain my medical benefits. They're not good. I have a high deductible and high coinsurance." Her features sagged with exhaustion.

I squeezed her hand. "You can't worry about that now, Trudy. You just need to concentrate on getting better. Let me take care of the rest."

"The books need to be in good order. I'm still paying the hospital bill from when I was here before."

"You know the books are good. And the diner's been turning a great profit. We'll be fine."

"You don't understand." She took in a long-labored breath. "I'm going to need to sell the place. I need every dime I can get from it."

Sell the diner? Trudy was right. I did *not* see where she was going with this. I wasn't ready to think about that now. There were so many people who would be affected. "That's definitely a lot to consider—"

She held up a frail hand. "Selling it is my only option."

I chewed the inside of my lip, fighting the emotion that threatened to come. My whole world was off balance, and this added one more thing to the tilt. "Okay, if that's what you want to do, I'll make sure everything is in order."

"Thank you, Joe." Trudy leaned back in her bed and closed her eyes.

Suddenly that's all I wanted to do. Find a quiet place, curl into a ball, and sleep for days.

CHAPTER 36
December 6, 11:10 a.m.

TAMARA

As soon as we left Trudy's room, Roger's phone rang. He answered the call and then excused himself, which was somewhat of a relief. Trudy loved Roger, but I didn't know him that well and now, in the midst of this tragedy, didn't seem like the best time to acquaint ourselves.

I took a left, then a right and walked down a long corridor toward the cafeteria, a familiar sadness weighing down every step.

I should have been thankful. Trudy was awake. She was alive. Though it would be a long recovery, she looked as if she was going to pull through. Why was my heart so heavy, then? Why couldn't I shake this foreboding feeling that something was drastically wrong? This feeling that said the proverbial hammer was about to come crashing down. My whole life felt out of place and out of sorts, and I didn't know how to put it back together. Should I dig deeper into this thing with Gabriel? If I did, would it hurt my relationship with Joe? How could I convince him that I couldn't give up on my family now? Not after what Dakota and Maddie had told me. Sure, things with Dakota had ended badly, but what if things could be different with the rest of them? Then again, where would I start? Dakota had been my only lead.

Ahead, I spotted a little shop and then the cafeteria.

"Tamara?" From down the hall, Claire hurried toward me. "So good to see you! I didn't know when you were coming back. Joe said you found your sister."

"Yeah." I *so* wasn't ready to recount that story. "How are you doing?"

"It's been a rough few days, to say the least."

"Tell me about it..." An awkward silence hung in the air for a moment. "Do you want to grab some coffee with me? Trudy asked to speak with Joe alone."

"Trudy's awake?" Claire's pitch rose an octave.

"Yeah, she looks pretty rough, but the fact that she's awake is a good sign."

"I'm so relieved." She placed her hand on her chest. "I've been down on myself for days. If she had died, I would've blamed myself forever, no matter what I said to Joe."

What had she said to Joe? Had she blamed him for it somehow? "It's nobody's fault, Claire." We started walking toward the cafeteria. A long, drawn-out silence followed us to the door. "Claire, I owe you an apology."

She gave me a sideways glance. "Huh?"

"Joe told me you got served at the restaurant the day we left. I'm sorry we didn't make sure you were all right before we left."

"Oh, that was stupid." She waved it off. We turned the corner into the cafeteria and stopped in front of the coffee urns.

"Come on, you don't have to put up a brave front. Whatever is going on, you can trust me."

There was a struggle inside Claire's soft brown eyes. "It's seriously not a big deal."

"Listen, Claire, you were such a good friend to me during the pregnancy. If you're going through a hard time, I don't want you to go through it alone. Let me be here for you."

She looked down at the floor and was quiet for a while

before she spoke. "If I tell you, you can't tell a soul. Not even Joe."

That would be hard. I didn't like keeping things from him, but this sounded serious. "I promise."

Claire scanned the room before pouring herself a coffee. "Let's sit over there." She nodded at the empty left corner of the room.

I poured my own cup and added cream and sugar before following her to a table. I sat down.

She scooted in close and brought the coffee to her mouth. Steam drifted around her face as she drank. "This is surprisingly good for a hospital."

I took a sip of mine and agreed with her.

She set down her cup and messed with the edges.

I waited silently for her to speak, giving her the space she needed to gather courage.

"Do you remember when I first came to work at the diner, I told you I needed to get out of the bar scene?"

I nodded, vaguely remembering her saying something like that.

"Well, I made some pretty big mistakes. It cost me my marriage at the time. Not that my ex was an angel either, but I was worse. Kenneth has never forgiven me for what I did to him. Unfortunately, Samuel has always paid the price for it."

Claire sighed and swirled her coffee around. "The papers are part of his latest stunt. He's trying to get full custody by making me sound like an unfit mother." Her voice quavered on the last part.

How awful for Claire and Samuel. He was only three years old and being used as a pawn to hurt his own mother. "But Claire, you're a great mom."

"You think so?" Her lips trembled and a single tear rolled down her cheek. "You should see the lies throughout that horrific document. It's so twisted. And he's got this big shot lawyer too." She paused as more tears fell. "I don't know what to do. I don't have money for a lawyer. If I don't figure it out, I could lose custody of my baby."

"I'm so sorry, Claire." I grabbed a few napkins from the dispenser on the table next to me and handed them to her. "I guess I don't understand what brought it on. Didn't you and Kenneth agree on split custody from the beginning?"

Claire dabbed her face and blew her nose. "Yes, but Kenneth has a semi-new girlfriend. They got serious and, get this, she's pregnant."

I choked on the coffee. "Was it planned?"

She batted at the air. "Who knows? They've only been together for a few months."

"That's quick."

"Yeah, maybe she's the replacement wife ... and mom."

"Don't say that. You're not going to lose Samuel."

"But how do you know?"

"It's called faith." Is this how Joe felt most of the time? Me constantly bringing him my problems and him having enough faith for the both of us.

"Well, I hope you're right."

I placed my hand on her arm. "You saw what I've gone through over the last six months, and I'm still standing, right? You're going to get through this. And I'll be praying."

"Thanks, Tamara. I think God might answer your prayers more than mine."

"I highly doubt that."

"Hey, T." Joe's voice came from behind me, then I felt his hand on my shoulder. "We need to talk."

A wave of anxiety rushed through me. It sounded ominous. I nodded, then he walked away without saying a word to Claire. Strange. That wasn't like Joe.

I refocused on Claire. "Looks like Joe's done with Trudy." I hurried to my feet and grabbed my coffee. "Everything is going to work out. I'm sure of it."

"I hope you're right." She stood and gave me a hug.

I squeezed her back. "If you ever need to talk, I'm here."

Claire's phone rang, and worry overshadowed her features. She answered it and then stepped a few feet away for privacy. I said a quick prayer for her as I walked across the room and pushed through the double doors.

It took me a few moments to find Joe. He was at the end of the hall, talking on his phone, pacing back and forth. His expression was serious, as if he was on a mission and no one would stand in his way.

I took a few steps forward and pushed down the anxiety buzzing around in my guts.

"No, that's not going to work. We need someone over there immediately." Joe's tone was more intense than I expected. "Okay, yes." He ran a hand through his dark hair and blew out a breath. "We'll pay the extra." Joe ended the call and turned toward me. "Oh, hey." He flashed me a sad smile.

"What's going on?

His brows creased and worry lines appeared on his forehead. "Things did *not* go well with Trudy."

"Is she all right?"

"Yeah, she's doing fine. I mean, she will be." Joe slid his phone in his back pocket. "But right now, she's really stressed out about finances. She wants us to get ready to sell the diner."

His words slammed into my already fragile heart like a freight train running off its tracks. "That doesn't make sense. She's not in any place to do that."

"I know, but she trusts me to handle the details."

My mind swirled around this new knowledge. If Trudy sold the place, everybody's jobs were on the line. "What are we going to tell everyone?"

"For now, we keep it under wraps. The diner needs to run as smoothly as possible. We can't have people quitting because of fear. I'm going to work on beefing up security too. It's top priority that everyone feels safe."

I nodded. That didn't seem fair, but I understood his point.

"I guess we need to head to the diner and call an employee meeting. We need to reopen tomorrow."

After the chaos, I needed life to slow down so I could process and figure out my next move, but it looked as if we were going full speed ahead. "But what about the police investigation?"

"I just finished talking to the officer in charge. He said they were done processing the scene last night. That means we're in the clear to reopen."

That was quick. "Wow. Okay... I was hoping for a bit more time. I still need to get a new phone."

"You *definitely* need a phone." Joe heaved out a sigh. "Let's just figure it out on the way." He weaved his fingers through mine, and we headed out to his Jeep.

CHAPTER 37

December 6, 1:00 p.m.

JOE

Tamara dropped me off at the diner and then drove to the mall to buy a new phone. The place felt cold as I stepped through the door. I flipped on the light and checked the heater. Seventy-three degrees. Perhaps it was my insides that were cold. How was I going to keep this news from everyone? How was I going to look them in the eye and act like this was a normal day at work? Like they would definitely have their jobs in a month. Tomorrow we had to start business as usual, and I wasn't sure I was ready for that. Everyone, including me, needed at least a week's paid vacation to sort through the wreckage of the past few days. Too bad this was the real world. There was no way to escape it.

On the drive to the diner, Tamara had called the employees. Most of them would be here within the hour. Hopefully, Tamara would make it back by then. I walked into the dining room and turned on the light. An eerie feeling crept over me, and goosebumps rose on my arms. The scene of the crime.

The cleaning company had done a good job. The room looked as it usually did. All thirteen tables in perfect order, everything in its proper place, as if it were any other day. I stood in silence, the heaviness of the situation settling in my stomach.

In a matter of a few days, our whole lives were knocked off kilter because of Tam—

I killed the thought immediately. I wouldn't blame Tamara. She had dragged me on that wild goose chase to find her sister, but it wasn't as if she'd put the gun in the guy's hand. This was just a bunch of bad luck hitting at once.

I went into the kitchen and started two pots of coffee for the employees when they arrived. Then I went back to my office and busied myself for the next forty-five minutes with paperwork and other menial tasks. The sound of the backdoor banging against the frame startled me. I poked my head out of the office.

Frank was near the employee time clock, about to punch in.

"Hey, Frank, there's fresh coffee on."

He threw a wry grin, a quick wave, and headed straight for the coffeepot. I sat back down at my desk and braced myself for the meeting. I wasn't ready to look at each one of them and lie, but what choice did I have? The door slammed again, and I headed out to greet people. This time it was Claire, then Trisha and Betty trailed in after her. I check my phone. It was time for the meeting, and Tamara wasn't back. A few more employees arrived, so I started without her.

"Thank you for coming. I know this has been a scary experience for all of you. The good news is, if you haven't heard, Trudy is awake and has requested us to resume the diner's schedule as if nothing has happened."

"But something *has* happened." Trisha's voice quavered. "How are we supposed to feel safe coming to work every day after this?"

"Trisha, thank you for the question. I want to validate your fear, but I spoke to the police and they told me thieves rarely return to the same spot. Even so, tomorrow a new security system is being installed. On top of that, we'll be going over new safety standards that everyone will abide by."

"That seems flimsy, Joe. I don't want to risk my life for this job. I don't make near enough money for that." Trisha said.

Betty snorted out a sarcastic chuckle. "I agree with Trisha. We don't get paid enough for this."

Where was Tamara? I could use her support right now.

"Listen, I've worked here for over three years now and this is the first incident that I'm aware of."

"Incident?" Trisha scoffed. "Trudy was shot, Joe. She could have been killed." I'd never seen Trisha so confrontational.

"All I am saying is that this was more of a freak act of violence. With the proper precautions, we will make sure everyone is safe."

"What kind of precautions?" Betty asked in a huff.

"Like when working at night, no one walks to their car alone. Always make sure the door is locked when you turn the *open* sign off. And a really big one is if someone says they have a gun, give them the money in the till. Nobody needs to be a hero."

Trisha crossed her arms in front of her but remained silent. Sounds came through the back door, opening and closing. Footsteps down the hall. A guilty look hung on Tamara's beautiful face as she walked in the door. She mouthed a *sorry* and held up her new cellphone.

I gave her a weak smile and turned my attention back to the meeting. The next thirty minutes were filled with questions about safety protocol and how they should be implemented. Trisha and Betty both gave me the most trouble, and I guess I couldn't blame them. They were scared, and rightfully so.

"All right, everyone. We will start tomorrow with everyone on their normal shift except for me and Tamara. We will be working extra hours to make sure the safety protocols are properly in place. Unless there are any more questions, this meeting is over."

I glanced around the room. Everyone stayed silent, for

which I was grateful. I made eye contact with Tamara again, and she gave me a sympathetic look.

The room filled with noise as people stood and began to exit. Betty made a few snide comments to Trisha about the safety meeting on the way out.

I ambled to the end of the table. "Let's go into the office," I whispered in her ear. She nodded and slid her hand in mine. We left the break room and walked to the small room.

I let out a deep sigh. "Well, that was about as fun as getting punched in the throat."

"I'm sorry, babe." Tamara ran her hand around my shoulders.

"Just think what they'll be like when we break the news that we're selling the diner. With Trisha's attitude, she might stage a walkout."

"Yeah... Hopefully it won't come to that. Maybe we could figure out a way to talk Trudy into keeping the place."

"I can't see that happening. She was pretty adamant about needing money." There had to be a way to make our world stop spinning.

"In lighter news, I upgraded my phone." Tamara drew away and brought out her new iPhone. "The line at the store was horrendous, but this thing was worth the wait. I'll text you my new number." She tapped on the screen a few times and then hit the send icon.

My phone chirped, and I looked at it. A heart emoji and a kissy face had come through. I smiled. At least we still had each other.

CHAPTER 38

December 16, 7:40 p.m.

DAKOTA

I stumbled out of my room and into the kitchen, head pounding. Ten days of camping out at a cop's house. Ten days with no drugs. Ten days in hell. It had been a constant rotation of night sweats, insomnia, and sleeping most of the day. Rinse and repeat. This morning, I put myself out with a couple of sleeping pills and a six pack of Tim's beer. Oh, and when I was awake, all I did was eat Tim's cop food. The kind that makes you pack on the l-beeze. I'd probably gained at least five pounds since being here.

I opened the fridge. There wasn't much to choose from—three tallboys, some Chinese takeout that wasn't that good the first time around, and half a pepperoni pizza from last night's dinner. I grabbed the Kung Pao chicken and tallboy Budweiser. A bit of the hair of the dog. It would help with the headache, but vodka would be better. I pulled out my phone and found Tim's number.

The beer is almost gone, please get some vodka.

If I hadn't been so careless, betting the whole stack of

money I stole from Tamara, I could have bought some from the liquor store myself. My phone beeped.

Copy that. On my way.

I stared at the message. He'd almost been too nice since that night with Lisa. He'd given me as much space as I needed as long as I stayed put.

I took a long chug of the beer and clicked on the TV. At least Tim had cable television with On Demand, but for the love of all that was unholy, I was bored with a capital B. He had every channel you could possibly think of, and I could record as many shows as I wanted. Tim didn't even seem to mind when I accidentally erased some of his.

I took a large bite of Kung Pao chicken, washed it down with beer, and settled back into Tim's recliner, smelling his sweet musky scent. Why was he still single? He was probably the most attractive guy in this one-horse town, with his olive skin, dark eyes, and defined muscles, but he was terminally available. Maybe he was in the closet. He hadn't made a pass at me since I've been here, but then again, I doubt he would. We were *so* not on that level.

I shoveled in another bite of Chinese food. The door swung open behind me. Tim in full uniform stepped inside, a twelve-pack of Budweiser in one hand and a fifth of Grey Goose vodka in the other. I raised an eyebrow. He walked across the room, set the liquor on the kitchen counter, and went into his room.

I hurried into the kitchen and took two glasses out of the cupboard, filled them with ice, and poured each of us a double. I quickly drank one and re-poured it. Minutes later, Tim exited his room wearing sweats and a white tank. I eyed his sculpted shoulders and an unfamiliar feeling swirled in my abdomen. I took a large drink of the vodka and handed him the other glass.

"I rarely drink hard liquor anymore."

I pushed the glass into his hand. "Come on, Timmy, for old time's sake."

He sighed and ran his hand through his dark hair. "There's something I need to tell you, Dakota."

"What? You're kicking me out? But I've been on my best behavior." I stuck out my bottom lip in a mock pout.

He shook his head and took a large swallow of his drink. "No. I want to find a way to keep you safe forever. I just don't know how."

Was that fear radiating from him? I almost knew what he was going to say before he said it.

"Ryan's out. He made bail today."

The room tilted a bit. My reprieve was over.

"I'm not going to let him hurt you." His hand rested on my shoulder. He was so warm.

Or was I cold? For the briefest moment, I let myself imagine falling into him, letting him hold me as I broke down. That wasn't me though. I wasn't some damsel in distress. I could take care of myself. I'd *always* taken care of myself. I jerked away from his touch.

"Listen, Dakota." He stepped toward me. "I can help you. Really help you. I know you know things about Ryan. If you testify against him, I can get you immunity and put into protective custody. We can have him put away for a long time."

I glared at him. "That's it, huh? That's why you kept me here? So you could get ahead in your career?"

"What? No!" Tim grabbed my wrist. "I'm trying to figure out a way to keep you safe. I can't keep hiding you forever."

"Whatever." I shook away from him, ran to my room and threw some clothes in my bag.

Tim followed after me. He grabbed hold of my elbow, turning me toward him. "Dakota, stop, you can't leave."

"What? Am I your prisoner? You going to handcuff me to the bed?"

"Come on, Dakota. Do you hear yourself? You're twisting

my words. I'm only trying to help." His voice had a desperate edge to it. "You're in the safest place right here."

He was right. There was no place to go that Ryan couldn't find me. I sunk down on the bed.

Tim sat next to me, his arm on mine, as if somehow, he was afraid to let go.

"I don't understand why you even care to help me. I've been awful to you since we were fourteen years old."

Tim slid his hand around mine. "I know more than anyone what you've been through. I know what he did to you."

Thoughts of Gabriel filled my head and how he had touched me. Tim was the only person I'd ever told.

"I should have done something then, but I didn't know what to do. You made me promise never to tell anyone, and I didn't." His hand was shaking around mine. "I promise you I never told a soul."

I looked up.

His expression was tortured as he spoke. "When you started doing drugs, I felt responsible."

"We were both kids. There was nothing you could have done."

He tucked a lock of hair behind my ear. "Someone should have been there to protect you. You deserved that much."

I searched his rich-chocolate eyes, so full of tenderness and caring. Regret weighed down every cell of my being. If only I could go back in time and take a different path. My gaze landed on his full lips. What would it feel like to be touched by someone who actually cared for me? Would it fill this gaping hole in my soul that drugs and partying couldn't? How would it feel to taste that kind of love? Didn't matter. I'd never be worthy of it.

His lips touched mine. So soft. So gentle. Heat pulsed through my core. For the briefest moment, I saw what my life could have been like if I'd chosen a different path. Timothy Moore would have been the center of my whole world. I stiffened as tears stung my eyes. But I *did* choose this life and the insanity that came with it. Tim didn't know who I was. I jerked away from his touch.

"I'm sorry. That was out of line." He stood, head down and then bolted out of the room.

I wanted to yell. To scream, *Come back. I want more.* So. Much. More. But then everything hit like a landslide, covering me, stealing my breath. Whatever had just happened between Tim and me disappeared under the weight of the frigid truth. Ryan was out of jail, and it was only a matter of time until he found me.

CHAPTER 39

December 16, 10:15 p.m.

TAMARA

I set the box of Christmas lights on the diner counter and let out an exhausted sigh. The final customer had left, and now I had the *privilege* of hanging holiday decorations. It should have been done weeks ago, but there had been no time.

For the past ten days, it'd been pretty much nonstop work upgrading the security and getting the diner ready to sell while conducting business as usual. Neither Joe nor I had had a single day off work since the diner reopened. Between Trisha and Betty's reluctance about coming to work, I'd had to cover four serving shifts in the first week. The hard thing was that Joe and I, though we'd seen each other every day, had barely had a chance to talk. Besides that, I hadn't had time to process the emotions of the losses that happened in Quilcene or my quickly changing life.

When I was being honest with myself, I wasn't doing well. For the most part the busyness kept the depression cloud at bay, but I wondered how long the reprieve would last. It didn't help that I wasn't sleeping well. Every night seemed to be filled with night visions of Gabriel imploring me to find my family. Why did finding them have to be so hard? Why did going back there have to hold such sorrow? I yawned and shoved the thoughts of my family away. I couldn't focus on that now. Otherwise, I might go insane.

Claire came through the double doors that separated the kitchen from the dining room. "Did you lock the door?"

"Yup. And set the alarm too. All systems are affirmative," I said in a silly robotic voice.

She snorted and gave me a knowing glance. Joe had been over the top about the safety protocol for the last few weeks. Claire looked down at the box. "Sorry I can't stay and help out. It's my night with Sammy."

I took a tangled strand from the box and worked on unwinding it. "No worries. Joe will be out in a bit to help. How are things going with that stuff with your ex?"

"Awful." She grabbed her purse from behind the counter and slung it over her shoulder. "I'm continuously walking on eggshells with my interactions with him. I feel like I'm under a microscope."

"I'm so sorry." I wished there were better words to say, but nothing came to mind.

"Yeah, so am I, but what can you do?"

I untwisted another strand of lights, hoping they actually worked. "You could kill him. I'd help you hide the body," I said to lighten the mood.

She laughed out loud. "How 'bout next Thursday?"

"It's a date." I threw her a cheesy grin.

"You're the best."

I followed her to the back and locked the door behind her, then I walked down the hallway to check on Joe. He sat behind the desk, counting out the day's earnings, preparing to make the drop. I watched him in silence, sadness creeping over me. This was all he did anymore. Work, work, and more work.

He finished counting the stack of ones before looking at me. "Hey, there." He smiled, but there was an exhaustion behind his eyes. The kind that was so much deeper than physical. "How's it going out there?"

"Everyone's gone. The lights are partially untangled. I'm about to brew a fresh pot of coffee."

"Sounds great. I'll be out in a few."

I nodded and made my way back to the dining room and started the coffee. We had at least a few hours of work ahead of us, and Joe had already been here for eleven hours. Another long day for him. Darkness descended over my soul at the thought. A part of me hoped the restaurant would sell quickly, and I'd get my fiancé back.

I plugged in a light strand, and it actually lit up. Success. I laid the strand aside and worked on another one. It would take a lot to cover the six-foot Douglas fir Joe had purchased along with the windows.

The coffee finished brewing, and I poured myself a cup. Thoughts of Dakota invaded my mind as I grabbed the cream out of the fridge. I'd texted her on my new phone as soon as I got it, but she never replied. Who knew if she even had the phone still? She had probably sold it for drugs. I leaned back against the counter and took a long sip of coffee.

A minute later, Joe pushed through the double doors, carrying another box of Christmas decorations. He set them down next to the lights and turned to me.

"Coffee?" I asked and took a drink.

"Yes, please."

I grabbed a cup, filled it, and added cream and sugar. I taunted him with it and playfully demanded a kiss before handing it over.

He took a seat next to me and quietly sipped his coffee for a couple minutes. "I need to talk to you."

Fear slithered through my belly, churning with the coffee. "Oh yeah?"

"Well, I've been working on an idea that could save this place. I didn't want to say anything until I was sure, but there's a good possibility that I could purchase the diner."

I choked on the liquid in my mouth. "Are you serious? How? You don't have that kind of money."

He set down his cup. "I have great credit, and my house is completely paid off. I could mortgage the house for the down payment."

Anger smoldered underneath the shock. How long had he been working on this thing behind my back? "I don't know, Joe. That's a lot to take on. Especially right now."

"You know I've dreamt about owning my own restaurant forever. And nothing would change. We'd get to keep our jobs, and so would everyone else. It's a win-win situation."

"Okay..." Then why did I feel so unsettled by the idea? And why was he just now telling me?

"You know, it's not set in stone. There's still a lot to figure out. Just think about it."

I glanced down at the floor, unable to look him in the eye.

Joe folded his arms around me. "I know it's been a rough few weeks. I'll make it up to you tomorrow."

"Tomorrow?"

"Yeah. I have a special evening planned for us," he said.

I shoved away my frustration and focused on the feeling of his closeness instead. I'd deal with this new set of emotions another day. For now, I'd let his familiar embrace comfort me the way I so desperately needed. Taking in a long steadying breath, I wished time would freeze, and we could stay here, lost in each other. A place where nothing else mattered but us.

CHAPTER 40

December 17, 1:00 a.m.

TAMARA

When I finally returned home from the late night at the diner, I was exhausted but wired from the coffee. For a while I lay in bed, staring at the ceiling, wishing that Joe was there with me to hold and comfort me like he had earlier. His arms around me inoculated me from the fear and made me feel more sure. But here in the darkness, the only thing I felt was the broken edges of my heart with a new intensity.

I thought I was past this grief, but it had never left me. A three-hour drive and a night with my sister was all it had taken to uncover this deep chasm that had been buried inside of me. I pressed my head against the pillow and begged God to help me sleep, but I couldn't feel his presence as I used to, only an empty sadness that created a deeper void.

For the next hour, I tossed and turned as dark thoughts pestered me like angry hornets, each one leaving a welt. Dakota, Gabriel, my mom, Joe's frustration with me wanting to continue the search, Trudy's health, the sale of the diner. And now Joe wanted to purchase it. What was he thinking?

We couldn't handle that right now. Or maybe *I* couldn't. I rolled over and punched a pillow. I just needed to fall into peaceful slumber and forget. I threw off my blankets, ran to the bathroom, and opened the medicine cabinet. My antidepressants taunted me. In the midst of the chaos, I'd forgotten to take them. I guess I'd just start again tomorrow. I grabbed the bottle of sleeping pills and poured two in my hand. I popped them in my mouth and washed them down with water, using my hand as a cup.

Settling back into bed, I waited for the pills to pull me under.

At first darkness blanketed me, the peaceful kind where everything was muted, but then an old familiar nightmare began. Railing accusations poured through my mind as I ran down a dimly lit corridor being chased by an ominous force. Every failure of my life slammed against me as I pushed forward. My lungs burned as they fought for air. A light at the end of the hallway pulled me toward it. Then he was there—the man cloaked in black. I screamed and fell to the ground. He was all around me, sucking the life out of my soul. There was no escape.

I woke with a start, gasping for breath, sweat beading on my forehead. The air in the room was thick with tangible fear. An invisible weight sat on my sternum, and my heart pounded against my ribcage.

It was just a dream. It wasn't real. I took in three slow inhales to calm my racing pulse. Why did it feel so real? Maybe I was going insane. The stress had finally caught up with me. I tried to pray, but the more I did, the heavier I felt. They say that God will never leave you, but I didn't think he could feel any farther away. I glanced at the clock. It was only 6:30 am. Joe wouldn't be awake yet, and even if he was, he'd probably be too busy with the diner. He'd been distant lately. Just like God.

I stumbled out of bed and started a pot of coffee. Maybe I needed some fresh air. Or a cigarette. I shook away the thought, grabbed my old journal, and found the page about the nightmare I'd had last January. I scanned the page and then flipped to the previous one with the poem I'd written during that time.

A man stands in front of me but all around me at the same time.

My pulse thudded loud in my ears. I thought I had conquered the darkness. Now it seemed as if it were engulfing me whole. I ran to the bathroom and grabbed the antidepressants. Was this because I had forgotten to take them? It had to be more than that. I shook a pill into my hand, popped it in my mouth and swallowed it down, praying it would kick in soon. Too bad these things could take three or four weeks to start working.

I cursed, frustrated with myself. How in the world had I gotten here again? I looked around my gloomy apartment, a desperate feeling gathering in my guts. I couldn't stay here today. I had to clear my head. After brushing my teeth and throwing on some fresh clothes, I threw on a hoodie, grabbed my keys and bolted out the door.

For hours, I busied myself outside of the house. Though it was cold and drizzly out, I took a walk down to the pier, then went grocery shopping. The mundane tasks didn't help. Depression and anxiety burrowed deeper into my soul with each step. Before heading to check out, I grabbed a deli sandwich for Joe. Lunch with him might help snap me out of my funk.

I loaded the groceries into the car and drove to the diner. When I pulled up, Joe's Jeep wasn't in the parking lot. A cold sensation settled in my chest. Where was he? I shot him a quick text and fiddled with the radio while waiting for a reply. I could go inside, but I wasn't in the mood to interact with anyone else. A few minutes later, my phone dinged.

I'm out running errands. Looking forward to our date tonight.
Love you.

Tonight? I needed him now. I had needed him all week. I blinked back tears as I focused on the message. Becoming emotional wouldn't help. A reminder notification rattled my phone. *Appointment with David at two o'clock.* Crud. I'd completely spaced it. I turned the car around and sped out of the parking lot.

When I got home, I quickly unpacked the groceries and scarfed down the sandwich I'd bought for Joe. Pastrami on whole wheat. It was a bit dry, but it filled the void. I threw on my coat and rushed out the door.

I was only a few minutes late arriving at Hope Chapel, I hurried up the steps, through the double doors, and down the hall to David's office. I paused before entering his workspace. Was I ready for this? No matter. I was here now. I tapped on the door, turned the handle and went inside.

"Good afternoon, Tamara." David stood from behind his oak desk.

I beelined it to the leather chair and slumped down. "Hey, David," I said with a sigh. "Sorry I'm late."

"No worries." He sat back down. "How have you been?"

"Not great." What an understatement. More like flat terrible. I twisted the ring on my left hand, keeping my gaze on my lap, my chest aching.

"Yeah, I'm sorry to hear that. I know it's been a hard season for you. How are things with Joe?"

"I don't know..." My throat felt thick. I swallowed hard, pushing back the emotions. "He seems to be doing great. As soon as we got home, he threw himself into work. He's been so busy making sure the diner's safe and ready to sell, he hasn't noticed how down I've been."

"That must be really lonely." His soft words comforted me.

My eyes welled, and I bit the inside of my cheek. "It has been, and now he's talking about buying the diner himself."

"That's a big decision. How do you feel about that?"

"Honestly, I don't feel good about anything right now. I'm beginning to think I really screwed up."

David's eyebrows furrowed, and the lines in his forehead deepened. "What do you mean exactly?"

I wrung my hands as I searched for the right words. How could I explain this pervasive darkness I didn't understand? Ever since Dakota, things had felt hopeless. And God ... there seemed to be a dense wall of blackness separating us. Maybe after my mistakes, he was done with me. With that thought, the emotional dam burst, and a torrent of tears came with it. I buried my head in my hands.

David moved over to the chair next to me and put his hand on my shoulder. "It's okay, Tamara. You don't have to be strong." He handed me a tissue with his other hand.

I blotted my face but continued to cry. "I just feel like I failed somehow," I forced out.

"We've all failed. It's part of the human condition," he said softly. "But that's what grace is for. The Bible says, where sin abounds, grace abounds even more."

"Then why is the darkness back? Why does God feel so far away? It's like he's punishing me."

"Tamara, please look at me."

I hesitantly brought my gaze to his.

Compassion shone in his features. "I promise you, God's not punishing you."

"Then why do I feel so cut off? Why is everything going wrong?"

He tilted his head slightly and spoke, his voice tender. "Have you ever considered the possibility that it's because you were on the right path? That because you were going in the way God had led you, you came under attack?"

"That doesn't make sense. I got drunk in Quilcene with my sister. Then I slept with Joe. It's been awful ever since."

"But Trudy was shot before that. Things were beginning to unravel before either of those things."

I blinked rapidly. I couldn't make sense of David's words. "Then why do I feel so guilty and cut off?"

"From what I know from our past sessions, perhaps it's related to the abandonment you felt from your own father." He spoke slowly, seeming to choose his words wisely.

"My father?"

He gave me a sympathetic nod. "We often relate to God the same way we relate to our own earthly father. The trauma you experienced from him could be affecting how you see God."

"How is that fair? Because my dad abused and abandoned me, it's keeping me from God?" I bit my lip, my insides burning like a bed of hot coals. "Wouldn't God be able to cut through my trauma instead of abandoning me too?"

"It's not like that exactly." David shut his eyes for a moment.

What was he doing? Was I too much for him?

He opened his eyes, and a fresh peace radiated from them. "I don't think we can simply talk through this. If it's okay with you, I would like to do things a little different and lead you through some guided prayer. What do you think?"

"At this point, I'd try whatever it takes."

David nodded and placed his hand on my shoulder again. "Holy Spirit, come," he said, then was quiet for a long time. It felt ... awkward. Was I supposed to say something or just sit there in silence?

Eventually, David spoke again. "Tamara, I want you to ask Father God what he wants to show you."

Father God? Did I even want to pray? I wasn't sure, but I did want freedom. I ignored the pain, and I prayed silently, asking the question.

"What do you see?" David asked after a moment.

The only thing I saw was the black emptiness of my mind. "Nothing."

"That's okay. Let's just wait a few more minutes."

Anxiety and anger took turns bombarding my stomach. What if we waited and God didn't say anything, or I didn't know how to hear him? What if this darkness was who I truly was? A part of me wanted to bolt out of the room. This whole thing seemed pointless and frustrating. David was like some sort of Jedi master when it came to listening to God, and I was a deep void.

"What do you see in your mind's eye?"

I wanted to lie so I wouldn't disappoint him. "Just black." I confessed.

"It's okay. Relax. What do you sense?"

I waited another few minutes, throat tight, claustrophobia constricting my airway. "It feels like I'm trapped behind a wall."

"That may be it. An emotional barrier you constructed to protect yourself." David paused for a few beats. "Holy Spirit, show us where this wall started and if it's safe to take it down."

The atmosphere in the room slowly changed as the air felt denser, more peaceful.

"Do you feel that?" David's voice was warm and thick like honey.

"Yes," I whispered, overwhelmed and relieved.

"Do you see anything now?"

It was still black as before, but I felt lighter, and it was easier to breathe. "No."

"I'm seeing a picture," David said. "Let me know if it makes sense to you."

"What is it?" I was excited and sad at the same time. I needed to hear from God for myself.

"It's you as a little girl, possibly six or seven, and you're hiding under a church pew."

My throat constricted. Levi had gotten that same image about me months ago. In my mind's eye, I could see it too. "I see it. I'm by myself and crying, feeling like no one would keep me safe from the violence at my house." The feeling of God's love seemed to grow thicker in the room. "That was the moment when I realized I was utterly alone in this world, and I would have to take care of myself." Tears fell from my cheeks in big drops. "That was when I first learned my only escape was to run and hide."

I allowed my whole heart to reach out to myself as this little girl. The last time I'd experienced this memory, I'd felt exposed, but this time it was different. I wanted to tell this younger part of myself that things were going to get better for her, and she didn't deserve the hurt she was going through.

Sadness engulfed me, pressing hard on my lungs. *I* didn't deserve the pain. Why *did* I have to go through all that trauma? Why *did* I have to run to protect myself?

The scene dimmed, and the atmosphere shifted. In an instant, the ominous force from my nightmare was back, taking with it every ounce of peace. Coldness and fear gripped me, along with a foreboding sensation deep inside me.

"What's going on?" David shifted in his chair.

"The darkness is back. I feel so alone." In the vision I, the little girl, began to run.

"Tamara, ask where God is in this picture."

I didn't want to, but he was right. I had to face it. "God, where are you?" It was like I was transported back to my nightmare, running away, with the darkness surrounding me, engulfing me. "God, where are you?" I cried out in a desperate scream.

Almost immediately, a light pierced through, bringing with it a feeling of warmth. The little girl was hunched over on the floor. Jesus walked through the light, knelt down, and put his arms around her. "I feel him," I whispered as stillness filled my being.

"What is he doing?"

"He's picking me up and holding me close. I feel light."

"Good, good. Focus on that place inside of him. You're safe there, Tamara. He's never left you."

I nodded as the tears flowed. I wished every moment could feel like this. Secure and loved. For a long time, I soaked in the moment, letting myself drown in it.

"How are you feeling?" David's soft voice brought me back to the present.

"Peaceful."

David nodded. "God's always right there with you, closer than you think, even if you don't feel it. I have one last thought for you."

I nodded, still basking in the peace I felt. "What is it?"

"Remember when I mentioned how God gives you promises to get through the battle?"

"Yeah." I nodded again, thinking back to the page in my journal where I started to do just that but scratched them out because of fear.

"I think now it is more important than ever to write down your promises and speak them out loud. The Bible tells us in Isaiah to remind God of his word. It's not that God forgets what he said, but I believe he wants to make sure that we remember.

His words were both hopeful and ominous. Could I really trust God to fulfill the promises he gave me? They seemed so far away and unattainable. I didn't know if I could bring myself to hope, only to be crushed again. Praying once more, I asked God to give me strength to believe.

CHAPTER 41

December 17, 3:10 p.m.

TAMARA

On the drive home, I blasted David Crowder and sang at the top of my lungs. The sweet peaceful warmth lingered with me until I reached my apartment. For the first time since this whole ordeal started, I felt hope.

As soon as I stepped into my apartment, my inner peace faded. I flipped on the lights, but even then, the room held this dull eerie feeling. Another familiar wave of sadness brushed over me, bringing with it the sense of impending doom that I'd had this morning. This time, though, instead of fear, anger welled inside of me.

I wouldn't be a victim of this any longer.

"Whatever you are, I'm not afraid of you anymore," I said firmly. "You can no longer torment my life." I ran across the room and flung open the window. Leave in the name of Jesus!" As the words left my mouth, the same peace I felt in David's office returned. The image of Jesus entering with a burst of light flashed in my mind, and with it my apartment grew lighter.

I took my old journal, flipped to the poem, and read the last few lines.

There must be more to this lonely life

The garbage I eat will not satisfy
I scream for more, but my call is unheard
My love is lost, and my end is near
So I fall.

No. That was not the end of this poem. This was not the end to my life. I picked up a pen and added to it.

Suddenly, the light cuts the darkness like a sword its foe
Warmth enters me, and the cold retreats
You are here, I feel you.

I stared at the last line, focusing on God and the wonderful things he'd done for me, comfort wrapping around my soul. Dakota and the rest of my family filled my mind, and, in that moment, I was sure I'd been on the right path. I may have made some big mistakes along the way, but finding my family was the right thing to do.

I grabbed my phone out of my back pocket and scrolled to my old number. Dakota hadn't responded yet, but I had to keep trying.

Dakota, I want you to know that I am praying for you and that I love you so much. I know I abandoned you when you needed me the most, and I really want to make it up to you. I don't know where you are or why you pushed me away, but I want us to be a family again. I can help you get out of the life you're stuck in. You can come live with me in East Vancouver while you get your life back on track. I can even get you a job at the Highway 99 Diner. Just think about it. I love you.

I hit send and prayed the message would reach through the barrier she had placed around herself. She may not even have the phone, but if she did... Joe said that if we kept the phone line connected, she could easily track me. If she still had it, I could track her as well.

I swiped my phone, clicked the Find My iPhone app, and pressed on my old number. The phone was detected as online, and the map above showed where my old phone was. That meant it wasn't dead. But had Dakota sold it? Why would she have kept it? She had her own phone.

Just then, I noticed the time. Joe would be here in under an hour. I tossed the phone aside and undressed on my way to the bathroom. After a quick shower, I dried off and dressed in a fitted black dress. I blew out my hair and applied a light amount of makeup.

There was a knock at the door. Joe wasn't using his key again? I ran to the door and swung it open.

Joe stood in front of me, wearing dark slacks and a blue button-up, a long-stemmed rose in one hand, and a small gift bag in the other.

My insides melted.

"You look stunning." Joe leaned in, kissed me lightly, and I caught a whiff of his cologne. "You gonna invite me in?" He gave a cheesy grin.

I mirrored his expression and stepped aside while making an exaggerated sweeping gesture.

He handed me the rose and gift bag before stealing another kiss. "Open it," he whispered as he pulled away.

Butterflies swirled in my stomach as I reached for the bag. I took out the black velvet box, popped it open, and gasped. A ruby in the shape of a heart hung on a gold chain. The ruby was set in 14k rose gold on the end of a twisted bale. The other side of the bale held a twinkling diamond studded at the end. "This is too much."

"No such thing. It's going to go great with that dress." He took the necklace out of the box and fastened it around my neck.

The necklace felt heavy. Could he afford such extravagance when we might both be out of jobs soon?

He must have sensed what I was feeling, because he drew me close and spoke softly. "No matter what, I will always find a way to spoil you, T. We are going to be okay, trust me."

I nodded and forced a smile. He was right. I was being overly dramatic.

"Come on, let's get to the restaurant so we can make our reservation." He untwined from me and walked to the door.

"Sounds good." I donned my jacket, grabbed my phone off the table, and followed Joe out to his Jeep. Once inside the vehicle, my phone beeped, and I checked it. Dakota? Nope. Claire asking me to pray. She'd had a rough day with her ex and his shenanigans.

Joe started the vehicle and The Cars' "Just What I Needed" bellowed from the speakers.

I let my mind wander as we drove to the restaurant. Should I tell Joe about trying to text Dakota again and what I'd discovered on Find My iPhone? What would I even say? Um... babe, I know you don't like my sister much, especially after she stole my engagement ring you spent thousands of dollars on, but I kind of offered her a job at the diner.

What was I thinking? Joe would never go for that. Besides, we didn't even know what the future of the diner looked like. Before I could find the right words, we turned into the restaurant parking lot. We both climbed out of the car and walked to the front. Joe opened the door for me and smells of sautéed garlic and oregano wafted around us. The host gave a welcoming smile and led us to a table toward the back of the restaurant.

The table was elegantly set with a white cloth, wine glasses, and a candle in the middle. Joe pulled out a chair for me, then sat across from me.

The candle flickered in the middle of the table as the server came over, filled our water glasses, and told us about the chef's choice for tonight—tuna tartare with avocado, capers, and sesame seeds. My stomach recoiled at the suggestion.

When the server walked away, I leaned in. "Have you ever eaten here?" I scanned the menu. "I don't see prices."

"That's because everything's free." Joe winked with an adorable smile.

"You're hilarious. It's because they don't want to scare us off."

He chuckled. "Order whatever you want."

Why was he throwing money around as if it was unlimited? "Think I'll just have a side salad." I closed the menu.

"I brought you here because I want to spoil you. It's been way too long since we've had a night out. Trust me."

I took in the softness in his expression. He was right. It *had* been a while. I shouldn't let fear of the future invade this lovely evening Joe had planned for us. I reopened the menu and scanned it. All the items on the menu looked delicious, but I decided on the risotto. When the waitress came back, I ordered it, and Joe ordered the Fiorentina steak.

After the waitress left, Joe reached for my hand. "Are you okay? You seem distant."

"I'm sorry. This is wonderful, and I appreciate the effort, but it's hard to enjoy such elegance when our future is in flux."

"We are going to be fine. I figured out a way to keep everyone's jobs."

"Without buying the diner? Joe, that's great! Did you talk Trudy into not selling?" I took a sip of water.

"I didn't."

Confusion made my head ache. "I thought you said... am I missing something?"

"When you texted me earlier, I was at the bank." He placed his hand over mine. "The numbers were perfect. I'm going to do it, T. I'm buying the diner. The paperwork will be ready within the week."

What? So that was it? He was going forward without even

giving me a voice in the decision? I took another drink of my water, suddenly wishing it was something stronger. "But, Joe, we haven't talked this through yet."

"I know, I know, but everyone will keep their jobs, and Trudy's medical bills will be taken care of. It's an all-around win."

I pressed my fingers against my skull. "I just don't understand. I thought we were going to talk about this tonight, but it's as if you've already decided."

"We *are* talking about it! Yes, the ball is rolling, but if you really are so much against it, I can still back out. I was just so excited."

Something felt seriously off about this decision, and I couldn't quite put my finger on it. Sure, I was frustrated that he was making such a big move without my input. It could also throw a monkey wrench into plans of finding my family, but it was more than that—a niggling in my guts that said run in the opposite direction. "I know, Joe, and I want you to have your dream, but this feels like a lot to take on right now. Have you thought it through?"

"I have. You and I already run the place, but now it will be ours. It's what I've always wanted. *We* always wanted."

"I know it is, babe." My face flushed. Maybe under different circumstances buying the diner could even be perfect, but now, it didn't feel right.

The waitress returned with our food and set the plates in front of us.

Joe eyed the food. Smells of garlic and basil wafted in the air.

I took a few bites in silence, trying to sort through my thoughts. "I don't feel good about it, Joe. I don't think you should do it."

He finished chewing before speaking. "Care to expound on that."

I averted my gaze, focusing on my plate, afraid to say how I truly felt. "It just seems like you might be trying to control the situation."

Joe cut into his steak, an injured look overtaking his expression. "I'm not trying to control anything."

"Okay, because you don't have to save everybody all the time. People can take care of themselves."

Joe swallowed his food and took a drink of water. "Believe me, Tamara, this is so much more than that. I really want this."

I smiled with a heavy heart, searching for the words that could help him understand why this was the wrong move. Truth was, Joe had done such a great job with the diner that he deserved the place. I'm sure there were plenty of good reasons he didn't want to let it go. I took a bite of risotto, praying silently for help.

"How was your meeting with David this afternoon?"

My head snapped up mid-chew, surprised by the sudden subject change. Did that mean his mind was made? "It was amazing." How could I even explain an experience so powerful and intimate without cheapening it? For now, it would have to stay between me and God, but I did need to tell him what my breakthrough had led me to. "I actually have some things I need to talk to you about."

"Okay..."

"It's about Dakota."

His eyes narrowed. "What about her?"

"I tried texting her again today."

"What? Tamara. I thought we decided you were going to drop this."

My fist clenched around the napkin on my lap. "We decided? Oh, I guess the same way *we* decided to buy the diner."

"That's so not fair. I'm doing that for us."

"It doesn't feel like it."

"What's that supposed to mean?"

"Never mind." I shoved another bite in my mouth.

"No. I want to know."

"It means we've barely talked all week. I've been falling apart, and you didn't even notice."

Joe exhaled sharply. "You are right. I've been preoccupied. I'm sorry."

"I forgive you, but I need you to understand. I think it's time for me to look for my family again."

"What?" His eyebrows flickered as if he was trying to put the words in the right order. "Tamara, seriously? Now? After what happened with Dakota? It doesn't seem right, and the timing is terrible."

"The timing is always going to be terrible, but I have to do this now or I may never do it."

Joe set down his fork. "I just don't feel good about it."

"That's it? Well, I don't 'feel good' about you buying the diner."

"You can't compare the two. Buying the diner helps everyone involved. Finding your family could lead to disaster. They're toxic, Tamara. Look what happened last time."

I threw my napkin on my barely touched food and stood, tears burning the back of my eyes. "Last I checked, I came from that family, so I guess that makes me toxic too."

"Tamara, wait. I'm sorry."

I grabbed my purse from the back of the chair and hurried toward the door. The cold air stung my face as I stepped outside and opened the Uber app.

"Tamara, Tamara, please stop." Joe's voice and footsteps came from behind me.

I walked faster. Thirty seconds later, he grabbed a hold of my arm, spinning me around.

I jerked away from his grip.

"I'm sorry, T. I shouldn't have said that in there."

I kept my gaze on the ground. "I just feel like there's no way to make you understand my need to find them. I feel like God's leading me to it, and you're standing in the way."

"I just don't want you to get hurt. It kills me to see you in pain." He slid his arms around me. "I hate what they've done to you."

"I'm sorry, Joe. I truly am. I know this is hard on you, but if I don't deal with what's back there and the grief they caused me, I'll never be whole. I want every one of your dreams to come true. I just know, though, that if I don't fix the brokenness inside of me, I'll never be worthy of you."

He placed his hand on my shoulders. "Look at me, T."

I finally met his gaze.

"You are already worthy. There's nothing you can do to make me love you any more than I already do. But if this is what you need, then we'll do it. We'll find them. I'll do whatever it takes." He said the words with conviction, but I could tell how much it cost him.

I leaned into him, suddenly exhausted. I may have won this battle, but with so much of my past still to uncover, who knew if we'd win the war?

CHAPTER 42

December 18, 8:45 a.m.

JOE

Yawning, I sat back in the office chair, my eyes stinging from the sleepless night. For hours, I'd sifted through the documents the banker had sent, my mind preoccupied with Tamara and our fight. I took in another long breath, trying to shake away the heavy knot in the center of my chest. We'd never fought like that before. I hated that I hurt her, but a part of me hoped that she'd never find her family—this guttural need to protect her from anything that would cause her pain. But she wasn't letting it go, which meant I needed to find a way to minimize the collateral damage. I couldn't see how, though. Why couldn't she give them up? They had already hurt her so much. I stood, coffee cup in hand, and walked out to the dining room.

Claire bustled from table to table, filling coffee and water cups. The restaurant had been surprisingly busy since reopening. Buying the place was the right move. It was the only move that made sense. I wished Tamara could see that.

Claire spotted me on her way to the register. "Hey, boss man."

"Hey." An idea rushed into my mind. "Come talk to me in my office when you have a minute."

"Am I in trouble?" She grinned.

I chuckled half-heartedly and held out my coffee mug. "I need your help."

"Whatever you need, boss," she said with a fake New York accent as she filled my cup.

"Thanks." I stepped behind the counter and took the cream out of the mini fridge. After mixing my coffee the way I liked it, I headed back to the office to sort out my thoughts. Tamara was dead set on finding her family. I was dead set on buying the diner. There *was* a way to make this work. I opened Google and typed "private investigator" into the search engine.

The things we did for love.

I scrolled through the list of names. The cheapest one was forty dollars an hour with a three-star rating. The next guy was a hundred dollars an hour, but had thirty five-star reviews. Sighing, I rested my head on my hand. This could get expensive fast.

Claire peeped her head in the door.

I shut my laptop and motioned for her to come in.

"What's up?" She entered and settled into the chair across from me.

Where to even start? "There's a secret I have to tell you, but it needs to be in the strictest confidence."

"Sure, yeah, of course." Claire leaned forward in the seat and rested her chin on her fist, positioning herself to listen.

I took a moment to gather my thoughts. "Trudy is planning on selling the diner."

"Are you serious?"

"As a heart attack. Tamara and I haven't told anyone because we didn't want to cause a panic, but I think I've found a solution."

My phone rang. It was the hospital, probably Trudy. She'd been improving every day. A week ago, they had moved her to a room in the recovery unit. "Hold on. I need to get this." I hit the green icon and brought the phone to my ear.

"Hey, Joe, I was just checking in to see how things went with Tamara last night?"

"It went great." I lied with false enthusiasm. "Just continuing to work out the details. If things go well, we'll have this deal closed by the end of the week."

She was silent for a moment. "So Tamara is on board with it?"

Not exactly, but she would be. I'd make sure of it. "Yeah, of course."

"Okay, because you don't have to do this."

I made eye contact with Claire and noticed a question mark in her expression.

"I know, Trudy, but I really want this."

"All right, you still coming by this afternoon?"

"Yup. See you after a bit." I hung up the phone and turned my attention back to Claire.

"You're going to buy the diner?" she asked.

"Yes. And this is where you come in. But first, I need to ask you a personal question."

Claire fidgeted in her seat, seeming uncomfortable.

"How's your sobriety going?"

"Umm, good. Why?"

"There are some things going on with Tamara. Both of us may have to leave for a week or so in the near future." If the private investigator found her family, there was no way I'd let her face them alone. "I was hoping you'd be willing to take over again while we're gone."

"I don't know, Joe. Last time was pretty rough."

I bit the inside of my lip. Rough was an understatement. "I know, but this time it will be different. We have the new safety protocols, and I can enlist Frank to help."

She hesitated for a long moment, an inner battle showing in her eyes. "I appreciate the opportunity, and I'd love to help, but there are some big things going on in my life."

"What kind of things?"

Claire glanced down at her hands, which were now folded in her lap. "Tamara hasn't told you?"

I shook my head, throat tightening. More things Tamara had been keeping from me.

"I asked her not to, but I guess I assumed she would. You two don't seem like the kind of couple that keep things from each other."

We usually didn't. "Can you tell me?"

She was silent for a few moments, gaze still down. "When I was served those papers, it was my ex suing me for full custody of Samuel. It's his way of making me pay for the awful things I did to him when we were married. It doesn't matter to him that I've completely turned my life around."

"I'm sorry, Claire. I wish you would have told me then."

She looked at me, expression pained. "I seriously don't know what to do. He's fabricated a bunch of lies and hired this hotshot attorney. How can I stand against that?"

"That *is* scary but know that I'm in your corner. I'll be a character witness if you need, and I'm sure Tamara will too."

"Thanks, Joe that means a lot. And I do want to help you and Tamara with this transition. I'm just scared."

"Understandable." I glanced at my watch and stood. In twenty minutes, I was supposed to be at the bank to work out more details of the diner sale. "I need to go for now, but can I pray for you about this situation?"

She threw me an awkward glance and looked around the room. "You mean, like, right now?"

"Yes. I believe that God can work this out for you."

She stood and nodded.

I took hold of her hand and prayed. "God, you know the truth. Expose the lies for what they are, and let Claire know that you are walking beside her through this trial, that you are on her side. In the name of Jesus, amen."

A tear rolled down Claire's cheek, and she wiped it away. "Do you really think God is on my side?"

"I know he is."

"Thanks, Joe."

"You're welcome." I hugged her, then picked up the stack of paperwork my banker had requested for the loan underwriters off my desk. As I left the room, I whispered a prayer that Tamara would find a way to get on board with this. I also prayed for wisdom and strength as I went forward with this huge transition. Excitement welled in me as I climbed in the Jeep. Purchasing the diner was one huge step toward my dreams coming true, and in less than a week it was happening.

CHAPTER 43
December 21, 9:15 a.m.
DAKOTA

I lay in bed, staring at Tamara's phone. Five days ago, she'd sent me a message, and I must have read it close to a hundred times. *She* wanted *me* to come down to Vancouver and work for her after stealing from her. The girl was certifiably nuts. Besides, I didn't need a handout.

I rolled over, reached for the half-empty beer off the nightstand and downed the stale contents. The withdrawals were getting a little easier. My headaches were lessening, and I had finally been able to get a solid five hours of continuous sleep last night, with the help of sleeping pills, of course.

I grabbed a T-shirt from the floor, smell checked it and threw it on before stumbling out of the bedroom into the kitchen. The aroma of pancakes and sausage hung in the air. The way Tim ate, you'd think he'd be morbidly obese. He was already in full uniform, sitting at the table scanning the daily news. He was the oldest twenty-two-year-old I'd ever met.

Setting aside the paper, he looked at me and reached for his coffee. "Hey. I'm glad you're up. I thought I was going to have to come wake you. I wanted to talk to you before leaving."

We hadn't talked much since our unexpected kiss last week. For the most part, I stayed in the room while he was home, only venturing out for meals. I walked across the room and poured myself a cup of coffee. "What's up?"

"I'm heading to Sacramento for a mandatory police training for a few days." Next to the door was a navy-blue duffel bag.

I was going to be here alone? I didn't like that idea. I grabbed my coffee and took a spot next to him at the table. "California?"

"Yeah, I fought to get out of it, but I couldn't. That means you'll be here... unprotected." He placed a nine-millimeter gun on the table and slid it toward me. "Klassen will be running patrols of the house, but it still makes me nervous."

I stared at the gun for a few beats and then waved off his concern. "Ryan would never think to look for me here."

"That's not true. It's a small town, and we both know what Ryan's capable of."

"I still don't understand why you care."

A deep brooding expression crossed his features. "Do I need to spell this out for you? Come on, Dakota. I'm surprised you haven't figured it out."

"What's that supposed to mean?

He averted his gaze. "Why do you think I am the way I am? Why do you think I became a cop?"

"Because you like donuts?"

His lips twitched as if he was trying to fight back a smile. Then he looked up, his eyes piercing into what was left of my soul.

My heart thudded against my ribcage. What was he doing to me?

"It was because of you." He let out the smallest laugh that felt more like it should be a cry. "I was powerless to stop the evil that hurt you." He was quiet for a long while, his gaze holding mine. "If I couldn't help you, maybe I could help someone else. But it always came back to you..." More silence. "You didn't deserve what Gabriel did to you. Or what your dad did."

I swallowed back the lump swelling in my throat as his words wrapped around me.

"You deserved to be protected. If you were, I know you would have made better choices. You would have a better life. But here we both are, and I *still* can't guarantee your safety."

My thoughts flashed to the jar of ashes in my duffel bag where I'd stashed them away. Tim didn't have a clue who I was. He didn't know what I was capable of. "It's not your job to protect me, Tim. I've been doing okay so far without you."

Another sad laugh flew out of his perfect lips. "Do you hear yourself, Dakota? Do you actually believe that?"

"I'm still here, aren't I?"

"That's the thing—you don't have to be. There's gotta be a place for you to go while I'm gone. What about Tamara?"

I shot him a scowl. "What about her?"

"Wasn't she here looking for you about a month ago? I'm sure she'd take you in while you figured things out."

I rose to my feet. I didn't want to think about Tamara. "She hates me."

"How could you say that? I saw her the day Ryan lied about you being dead. She was devastated. She could barely speak."

That familiar sting of guilt collided against the lining of my stomach. "Look, Tim, it's none of your business, so back off!"

Tim stood. "I'm not trying to upset you. I'm just trying to think of the best solution. As much as I like having you here, you can't hide out here forever. Your sister might be the best thing for you right now."

Tamara *had* been so eager to rebuild our relationship, but I'd pushed her away. I had stolen her ring to save my butt and sent her a message to stay the hell out of my life.

"Just think about it." He walked to the door and slung the duffel bag over his shoulder.

Our gazes connected for a long moment. I thought about the kiss we had shared. How ironic. I'd been running from him since we were kids, but now I wanted to run after him. To

243

believe him when he said that I'd have been a better person if things had been different.

"And hey, I was planning on being in Redding for Christmas this year, but if you are still here, I can come back right after the conference ends."

"Seriously? I haven't celebrated Christmas for years. Don't worry about me."

Tim opened the door, then turned back to me, eyes shaded with sadness. "Take care of yourself, Dakota."

He closed the door, and I secured the deadbolt before turning off the lights. This was it. I grabbed some food and turned on the television. A nervous feeling gathered in my core as I shoved in the first bite of pancakes. I was alone in a city where Ryan was looking for me. *Don't think about that now.*

I scrolled through the DVR, hit the next episode of *The Walking Dead* and barked out a sick laugh. *The walking dead.* Pretty much what I was. I could run from Ryan, but I certainly couldn't hide. I took another mouthful of pancakes and tried to focus on the show. It was no use. Tim's words kept spinning around in my head. He'd said Tamara had been devastated when she'd thought Ryan had killed me.

I paused the television and dug through my purse to find Tamara's ring. As I stared at it, what Tim had told me mixed with the message from Tamara twisted around my brain. Could I be a different person? Could I make things right? I stepped into my bedroom and pulled out the jar of ashes, a wave of dread crashing against me. It would mean coming clean. It would mean, for once in my screwed-up life, I'd have to tell the truth. I didn't know what was worse—facing Ryan or facing reality. Facing the truth was the only real option.

On the way back to the kitchen, I placed the ring back in my purse. I grabbed the vodka out of the cupboard, took a large chug, gaze landing on the gun. Acid burned my stomach as I eyed the weapon. I picked it up, imagining taking Ryan out with a single shot, ending the torment he'd put me through over the years. Seemed like too easy of a way out for a lowlife like Ryan. He deserved a life in prison, tormented by the creeps that were bigger and badder than he was.

With the bottle in one hand and the gun in the other, I went back to my room, weighed down by the dark thoughts. If Ryan came here, would I have the guts to pull the trigger? Knowing my luck, I'd miss him completely, and he would wrestle the gun from my hands and kill me with my own weapon. I set the gun down on the dresser next to my bed and chugged the vodka. Chances were he would never come here. I just needed to pack and get the heck out of dodge before I could worry about any of that.

I snagged a few of the scattered shirts laying on the floor and folded them, setting them in the bag next to the jar of ashes, thinking of Tamara. What would I even say to her when I showed up on her doorstep? *I stole your ring because I was trying to protect you?*

That was only half of the story.

I guzzled more vodka, then arranged the clothes neatly in the bag. By the time I finished packing, I'd practically polished off the bottle. I sat down on the bed, emotionally exhausted. If I was going to find a way down to Tamara tomorrow, I would need to be well rested. I grabbed the bottle of sleeping pills that was beside my bed. I opened the container, downed three pills, and washed them down with the rest of the vodka. Hopefully, they would do the trick.

CHAPTER 44
December 21, 6:40 p.m.

JOE

I placed the paperwork in a file in the top drawer and rattled the keys through my fingers. This morning I'd signed on the dotted line and now The Highway 99 Diner was officially mine. For years I'd dreamed about owning my own place, and now here I was.

I wanted to smile, but something was amiss inside of me. I'd asked Tamara to be there for the signing, but she'd refused. She'd been distant since our fight, and I hadn't found a way to bridge the gap. And though I'd spoken to several private investigators, I couldn't bring myself to tell her about my plans. Not yet. I kept hoping that she'd let it go and I wouldn't have to pull the trigger. I stood and grabbed my jacket.

Claire popped her head around the doorframe. "You got a minute?"

I checked my watch. 6:45. I was supposed to be meeting Tamara at her apartment at 7:30. "I have a few. What can I do for you?

She walked into the room and took a seat on the wooden chair. "I have some big news."

"Okay..."

"You know a few days ago when you prayed for me?"

"Yeah?"

She twisted a lock of hair around her finger. "You're never going to believe this."

"Try me." At this point in my life, I was pretty sure I'd heard it all.

"Last night, I got a call from Gabi, Kenneth's girlfriend." She paused dramatically. "I know I shouldn't be happy about this because it's so twisted."

"What happened?"

"She was hysterical. She asked if Kenneth had ever laid hands on me."

"Has he?"

She was quiet for a beat too long. "Yeah, I guess he did. But he always made me feel like it was my fault. After a while, I started to believe it."

"I'm so sorry, Claire."

"But that's the thing. He hit her too, and she had the guts to stand up to him. He went to jail last night. And Gabi told me she'd testify against him in the custody case if he tried to go forward with it."

I didn't know what to say. I'd never realized the hardships Claire had walked through. This whole time of knowing her, and I'd never seen that part of her.

"I believe what you said the other day is true." Claire said.

"What was that exactly?" I could barely remember what I said last night, let alone a few days ago.

Her chin tilted and a smile crept up her face. "That God is on my side. It's like He fought this battle for me."

"I love that. I'm so happy for you." I stood and slid the diner keys into my pocket.

"I'm happy for me too." She beamed. "You heading to Tamara's?"

"Yeah." I fiddled with the keys in my pocket. "Maybe you could pray for us."

Lines appeared in her forehead. "You guys all right?"

"Yeah, sure. I just have something big to talk to her about tonight."

Claire raised an eyebrow. "Like what?"

"I can't say now, but please keep us in your prayers."

With a slight smile, she tilted her head to the side. "Until last night I wasn't sure prayer would help, but you might make a believer out of me yet, Phillips."

"I have no doubt about that." I slid on my jacket and headed out the door, unsure if I was ready to face Tamara.

CHAPTER 45

December 21, 7:25 p.m.

DAKOTA

My eyes snapped open to a loud crash. I gasped and rolled over in bed, head pounding.

"Wakey, wakey." A slimy yet eerily dry voice filled my room, followed by a sick, menacing laugh.

No. This couldn't be happening. It had to be a nightmare.

The light clicked on, and I squinted. Ryan stood at the end of the bed, greasy dark hair slicked back, my purse in hand. Behind him the curtain blew in the breeze.

My whole body tensed and my heart jackhammered. I held back the scream that was climbing in my throat. No one would hear it anyway. I sat up as the room spun. Why did I have to take so many sleeping pills?

"Where is it, Dakota?" He dumped the contents of my purse over my feet. "Where is my merchandise?" He picked through the contents of my purse like a bum picking through garbage. "Or my money. I'll take either one."

What could I say? It was gone. Every bit of it. Up in smoke on the other end of a glass pipe. I was so dead. "How'd you find me?"

Another round of laughter. "You have terrible friends. She sold you out for another hit."

Lisa? Acid turned in my guts. Of course, she would.

"What's this?" He took Tamara's ring and lifted it toward the light.

"It's nothing." A shot of adrenaline spiked through my veins.

The ring sparkled under the light as he inspected it. "It doesn't look like nothing to me." He slid it into his pocket.

No!

He picked up Tamara's cell phone, his dead eyes flickering with curiosity.

I scanned the room for the gun and spotted it on the dresser where I left it. It was too far away. He could reach it before I could.

He began to laugh again. "Dakota, you're heartless. I thought I was bad, but stealing from your own family?" He held the phone in the air like a prized possession, a mocking grin twisting his lips. "That was Tamara's ring, wasn't it?"

Both of my hands curled into fists. He was toying with me.

"This could come in handy later." He slipped the phone in his back pocket and tilted his head. "But now, I need my money." He reached for my wallet and opened it. Still completely empty. He threw it at me and grabbed me by my shirt, pulling me out of bed. "What the hell, Dakota?"

Barf. His breath reeked as if he had licked a rotten garbage can. I cringed.

He slammed me against the wall. "I'm going to ask you one more time. Where. Is. My. Money?"

My pulse thundered, blood pounding in my ears. "It's gone."

His fist connected with my jaw, and pain radiated through me. I twisted and fought against his grasp, refusing to go down without a fight. Still delirious from the sleeping pills, I pushed my weight against Ryan, and we fell on the bed. "You know that turns me on, baby." He grabbed hold of my wrist and pressed them hard against the mattress. "There are ways you can work off that money." He slowly licked the side of my cheek.

I gagged as I squirmed and fought underneath him. "I'd rather die!" I screamed. "I'd rather effing die!"

His fist came hard and unmercifully across the bridge of my nose.

I kicked and rocked back and forth, fighting against his weight. Then his hands were around my neck, squeezing the air out of me. I clawed at his face as his fingers dug into my throat. I flailed and kicked, but it was no use, his hands were too strong. The light faded as I lost consciousness.

CHAPTER 46

December 21, 7:40 p.m.

TAMARA

Anxiety swirled in my stomach as I stared at my phone, reading the message I'd sent my old cell almost a week ago. The phone said the message had been read, but had it been read by Dakota or someone she pawned it off to? I paced my living room and prayed for the thousandth time that day. Dakota had been on my mind since I woke this morning along with this foreboding that felt impossible to shake. I lifted the phone to draft another text. I typed out her name and then deleted it.

Texting was a dead end. Even if she still had my phone, things hadn't changed on her part.

My phone beeped, and my heart jumped. Dakota? No. A text from Joe.

Be there soon :)

Another onslaught of emotion assaulted me, and I sucked in a sharp breath. Today was the day that the deal was final with the diner, and he'd said he was taking me out to celebrate. I wasn't so enthusiastic. I hadn't even dressed for our date yet. I threw the phone aside and berated myself for not being more supportive of his dream. I wanted to be happy for him, I really did, but I was still so ticked at him for making this big of a decision without me and going through with it despite my reservations. As the week progressed, the restless feeling in my gut, that buying the diner was a bad idea, grew. Joe, on the other hand, was on cloud nine as if he believed his dreams were suddenly coming true.

I opened my dresser and found an outfit. A floral royal-blue baby doll shirt and leggings. I dressed and threw my hair into a high ponytail. Then I brushed on mascara and applied some lip gloss.

A few minutes later the deadbolt rattled, and Joe opened the door, carrying a brown paper bag teeming with groceries. He walked across the room, set the bag on the table and turned to me.

"What's this?"

He came over, placed his hand on my back and kissed me gently. "You've seemed tired lately, so I thought I'd cook you dinner tonight instead of going out."

I smiled with relief. He was the sweetest ever. "Great. Whatcha making?"

"New York strip steak with wasabi mashed potatoes and sautéed veggies." He withdrew, went back into the kitchen, and began unloading the bag.

"Sounds delicious." I hadn't eaten much today with the anxiety. I glanced at my phone resting on my bed. Would this be a good time to tell him about Dakota? Probably not. Things hadn't been quite the same between me and Joe since the fight about my family. "Can I help you cook?"

He shot a look of mock horror. "I don't know, babe. Last time—"

"Whatever." I stepped into the kitchen and washed my hands in the sink.

"All right. If you insist." He handed me a bag of potatoes with a playful grin. "I need these washed and peeled. Do you think you can handle it?"

"You're hilarious." I glared at him, grabbed a potato out of the bag, and rinsed it.

His smile widened. "Come on, T. I'm teasing you."

I flicked water at him and took another potato out of the bag.

"Watch yourself, girl. You mess with the bull."

"Oh, I'm so scared." I giggled, my mood lightening. The playful banter was exactly what I needed, and I silently let the moment comfort me.

Joe found a cutting board and began dicing veggies. "So, I saw Claire on the way out of the office. She said things are turning around with her ex. He got arrested last night for domestic violence."

I gasped, feeling the emotional whiplash. Her ex-husband was abusive? How could I not know? Why wouldn't she have told me?

Joe pulled a head of broccoli out of the bag and lopped off the stalks. "It looks like he'll have to drop the custody thing altogether."

That was good news, but sadness still hovered in the air. What other pain had she carried alone? "That's good, I guess."

"Tamara, it's great news. A few days ago, I had prayed for her that God would show her that he's on her side, and then this happens. You should have seen her today. It was as if she understood that God loved her."

I nodded and tried to smile, but an unfamiliar feeling swirled in my stomach. Jealousy? What was wrong with me? I rinsed another potato and pushed away the ugly emotion.

"There's something else I've been meaning to tell you." He set down the knife and turned toward me. "Last week I asked her if she'd be willing to train for your position."

"What? Why?"

He wiped his hands on his jeans and stepped in closer. "I've been thinking about this thing with you and your family."

"My family?" I turned off the faucet and wiped my hands on a kitchen towel before turning to him.

"Yes. I know how important this is to you, so I did some digging. I talked to a few private investigators—"

"Wow, Joe, really?" I couldn't believe he made time for this in the middle of his busy week. Guilt pounded me in the guts. I'd been such a jerk about him buying the diner and now he was doing this for me. I would truly never deserve him.

"Yes, really. But I want to do it my way this time. We need to go in slow, make sure the diner is stable, that everyone is trained well enough, just in case we need to leave for a week or two."

"Okay, yes." He was probably right. After last time, we needed a solid plan.

He wrapped me in an embrace. "I love you, T. We're going to make it through this."

Across the room, my phone rang.

Joe hesitantly stepped away from me and walked over to pick it up. He froze, a puzzled look flitting over his face.

"What is it?"

"It's a number with a 360-area code."

That was from the peninsula. Dakota. "Answer it!"

"Hello." Joe was silent for a few moments and darkness descended over his features. "She's not available right now."

"Joe!"

He put his finger over his lips, his expression hardening. "You will never touch her!"

Terror pulsed through my whole body like a lightning bolt ripping through me. *Ryan, not Dakota.*

Joe dropped the phone, and it bounced across the linoleum. Our eyes met.

"What's happening, Joe?"

I knew what he was going to say before he said it. "That was Ryan. He said he had Dakota. He says he wants five thousand dollars, or he'll kill her."

I doubled over, pulse racing.

Joe was at my side. "Tamara, what's going on?"

"I—I don't know," I gasped out. "My heart's racing. My chest is tingly."

"You're okay, just have a seat."

I sat on my daybed, fighting for air. So much for Joe's slow plan. If we didn't act now, Dakota could die.

CHAPTER 47

December 21, 9:10 p.m.

DAKOTA

It was dark. So dark. My whole head throbbed, starting from my neck and reaching to my hair. A cold band held my wrist suspended against something hard. Where was I? I blinked a few times trying to make sense of my surroundings. My eyes adjusted. I was lying in a bed. I moved my right arm and metal clinked against metal. Ryan had handcuffed me to a bedpost. To *his* bedpost. Thoughts of him hovering over me, propositioning me for sex, bombarded my thoughts. Bile rose in my throat, and I swallowed it down. Was I his prisoner now? What a depraved lowlife. What else did he have planned for me? Why didn't he just kill me when he had the chance? He was capable. I had to get out of here.

I listened for a few minutes. The house was eerily quiet.

I flipped around so my legs were facing the metal bars. I kicked at the top bar with all my might. A sharp ache radiated down my arm, but I ignored the stabbing discomfort and kicked again and again. After seven painful blows, it came loose. I rolled off the bed, ran across the room, and flicked on the light.

This *was* his bedroom, and it was fairly clean, as it had been every other time I'd been here. Ryan's curtains were thick and black, allowing no light in or out, whether day or night. I ran to his dresser and rifled through his things. Escaping would do me no good if I didn't have cash to travel with. In his second drawer, I found Tamara's ring and a stash of twenties, which I pocketed. Stealing more from Ryan was dangerous, but if he found me, I was dead anyway. At least this way I would have enough for a bus ticket.

But what about Tamara's phone? I searched through the dresser and around the room. It could be anywhere. It didn't matter. It was just a phone, right? Tamara had a new one already. Confusion niggled at the edge of my brain. Why would he leave her ring in the drawer, but keep her phone on him?

Sounds of wheels on gravel spiked adrenaline in my veins. Was I too late? I turned off the light, slipped out of the room and down the hallway toward the backdoor.

I wished I had a match. I'd light this place on fire and watch it go up in flames. This whole town could burn, for that matter. I should have left years ago, the way Tamara had. She'd always been the smart one. I ran around the house and looked to see if it was Ryan's car. The driveway was empty. Pausing for a moment, I took inventory of my body. I was hurting, but nothing was broken. I started back to Tim's house, staying in the shadows. Every time I'd see car lights, I'd duck out of view. Ryan had thugs everywhere. And who knew how long it would be before he discovered I was gone.

Thirty-five minutes later, I climbed through the shattered bedroom window. I went to Tim's landline, found his pad of important numbers, and dialed his cell. He answered after three rings, his voice sharp. "Dakota?"

"Yeah, it's me."

"I just got a call from Woodleaf. He said Ryan contacted Tamara, telling her he had you." His voice spiked with each word.

The side of my face ached. He must have gotten Tamara's number by using her phone. Broken shards swam in my stomach. "He did have me. I escaped, but I need to get out of here. I need a ride to the bus station."

A string of expletives poured from his mouth. "You're right. You *have* to get out of there." He was quiet for a long moment. "I'll have someone there in less than five minutes. Do you still have the gun I gave you?"

I peeked inside the bedroom at the dresser. The gun was gone. "Ryan took it. Whoever you send can't be a cop. They'll take one look at me and take me in for a report. Or worse, they'll take me to a hospital."

More foul language. "I swear to you, Dakota. I will kill Ryan Cooke if it's the last thing I do."

"Can I have the privilege of watching?"

A humorless laugh came through the line. "Nope. Can't risk witnesses."

"I can keep a secret."

Another chuckle. "You just sit tight. Someone will be there soon. And Dakota, there is a gun underneath the left side of my bed. If Ryan shows up before your ride gets there, don't hesitate to use it."

My hand trembled around the phone. "Thank you, Tim. Please know whatever happens, what you did for me means everything."

"I love you, Dakota." His voice cracked on the words. "I always have."

"I know." A single tear streamed down my face. If I got out of this mess alive, I'd spend the rest of my life trying to be the person Tim thought I truly was. I set the phone on the receiver, went to his bedroom, and found his gun. Now all I could do was wait.

CHAPTER 48
December 22, 6:45 a.m.

JOE

The diner was too quiet. Last night, I stayed with Tamara through the night, holding her, feeling entirely helpless. We contacted the local authorities within minutes of Ryan's call, but hadn't heard a thing since. I walked down the hall to the kitchen in a haze and poured another cup of coffee. If we didn't hear from Officer Woodleaf soon, Tamara would no doubt want to take matters into her own hands. Truth was we *did* have money if we needed to pay Ryan off... I cringed at the thought. What was I thinking? To what lengths would I go for this woman? I was literally insane. The intensity of the last month had pushed me over the edge.

Get it together, man. I just needed to focus on the here and now. Claire and Frank would be here any moment to open the place. I started another pot of coffee, turned on the grill and checked the mini fridges to make sure they were stocked.

The back door opened and closed. I looked around the wall. Claire. Great. I was hoping to make it back to the office before she arrived so I wouldn't have to talk to her or anyone. I needed time to sort this out. To figure out a game plan that didn't involve me surrendering my money to a psychopath.

"Hey, J—" She stopped, demeanor shifting. "You don't look so good."

I observed the coffee mug in my hand. I didn't feel so good. "Yeah, I'm fine."

"Fine? You know what that stands for, right?"

A chuckle came out of my mouth, more of a reflex than anything. One of my sponsors' favorite sayings. "Freaked out, insecure, neurotic and emotional." Claire didn't know the half of it.

"That's one way to put it." Silence for a few beats. "Whatever it is, I'm here if you want to talk about it."

"Talking is a waste of breath at this point." I started down the hall toward the office.

Claire put a hand on my shoulder. "Or we could *pray* about it."

I wasn't ready to do that either. "I'll be okay, Claire. But yes, please keep us in your prayers."

She gave a tentative smile and dropped her hand. "Whatever is going on, I'm sure things will turn out okay."

There was no way she could possibly know that. She didn't know the ax hanging over our heads, ready to drop at any moment. I gave a polite nod and averted my gazed. "I'll be in my office if anyone needs me."

I walked down the hall and sat down in front of my desk. Setting down my coffee, I buried my head in my hands. I tried to pray, but no words came. After sitting in silence for five minutes, I stood and went to the safe. I put in the combination and withdrew the deposit bag bills. Three thousand two hundred thirty-six dollars. Luckily, we didn't have a chance to make any drops this weekend, but it wouldn't be enough for Ryan. I'd have to stop by the bank for the rest, if it came to that.

Across the room, my cell phone rang. I shoved the money back in the bag and secured it in the safe before retrieving my phone.

Officer Woodleaf.

My pulse spiked and I grabbed my phone from the desk and hit the green icon. "Please tell me you found Dakota."

"She's safe."

I breathed a sigh of relief.

"We have an APB out for Ryan."

"Thank you for letting me know." At least I'd have good news to report to Tamara when I went to check on her.

"We finally have enough on Ryan to put him away for a long time."

Couldn't they just put a bullet in his head? It would be the only way Tamara would truly be free.

Claire popped her head in the room. "Someone's out here asking for Tamara. I told her she wasn't here, then she asked for you."

I lifted my pointer finger in the air. "Please keep me updated with the Ryan situation. Everyone will breathe easier when he's behind bars again."

"Will do."

I ended the call. "Did you get a name?"

"Dakota, I think. She's ah ... pretty beat up."

I rushed down the hall and through the double doors. Dakota was the only one in the restaurant besides Claire and Frank. She sat at a table, facing away from me, the hood of her sweatshirt up, and a duffel bag next to her feet.

"Dakota?" I had no idea how to react to her being here. What if it was a set up?

She turned toward me, and my heart dropped. Around her right eye was a deep purple bruise. She had a gash on her nose, and her upper lip was swollen.

"Tamara told me where she worked. I need to speak with her."

"You can't be serious. How do I know you're safe? Last time I left her with you, you stole her ring, her money, and her phone."

She grimaced and winced. "Let's just say I've had a change of heart."

I crossed my arms in front of me. "That's not good enough. How do I know that you're not in league with Ryan?"

She snorted. "I hate Ryan. He can burn in hell as far as I'm concerned. But right now, I need to see my sister. I have to talk to her." She reached into her pocket. "I stole this back from Ryan for her." Tamara's engagement ring sparkled under the fluorescent light. "Just take me to her, Joe. Let me make this right."

Nothing in me trusted her, but Tamara would kill me if she knew Dakota was begging to see her and I refused.

"Please, Joe. I need to do this."

I gave her a slow, unsteady nod. "Give me a minute." I turned to head back to my office. Claire stood behind the counter, gaze down, filling salt shakers. She'd witnessed the whole exchange and probably thought I was crazy. I was pretty sure she was right.

The bell clanged as I pushed through the double doors. Frank gave me a weary nod. He'd seen it too. I threw him a wave and ignored the heat that climbed my neck. Once in the office, I grabbed my jacket, keys, and phone.

As much as I hated this, I had to take her to Tamara.

CHAPTER 49

December 22, 7:20 a.m.

JOE

For a few minutes I hesitated, fighting the inner battle, my phone clinched in my hand. Taking a deep breath, I clicked the icon next to Tamara's name. I doubted she'd be awake, but there was nothing else to do. After a few rings, it went to voicemail. I hit end and made my way back to the dining room, avoiding eye contact with Frank and Claire. As I walked past Dakota, she rose and followed me.

When we got to my Jeep, she put her duffel in the back seat. The car ride was painfully quiet. Dakota chewed her fingernails as she stared out the window while I fiddled with the radio. As we drew closer, I wondered if I should have blindfolded her so she wouldn't be able to find Tamara's house. Freaking ridiculous. I stomped on the gas.

Fifteen minutes later, I turned into Tamara's apartment complex and parked into a guest spot. I killed the engine and climbed out.

Dakota grabbed her stuff and followed me up the sidewalk. "This is where Tamara lives?"

I stuck my key into the deadbolt and turned. "Yeah."

"And you live with her?"

"I live across town. Why?"

She shook her head. "I just imagined her place would be ... nicer."

I sneered and opened the door. Why did her assumption bother me so much?

Tamara was sound asleep, curled into a ball on her daybed, her hair covering her face like a curtain. I walked over and sat beside her. After the night she'd had, I didn't want to wake her. Behind me, Dakota scanned the pictures on the opposite wall.

I gently swept Tamara's hair away from her face. "Tamara, sweetie, someone's here to see you."

She stirred a bit under my hand.

I wished so badly that I could just curl myself around her and pretend the last month had never happened—to forget the loss and heartbreak. "Come on, baby." I kissed the side of her cheek.

Her eyes fluttered open, and then they grew wide. "Dakota?" Her gaze darted from Dakota to me and then back to her. She threw off the blanket and sat up. "Dakota?" she said again, disbelief lacing her tone. She jumped out of bed and threw her arms around her sister.

Dakota gasped. "Easy, sis."

Tamara stepped away and searched her face, taking in the damage Ryan had done. "What did he do to you? How did you get away?"

"That's not important right now. There's so many things that need to be said." Dakota glanced over at me.

Was she wanting me to leave? She couldn't be serious.

"Can I have a few minutes with my sister?" Dakota said.

"Absolutely not. Last time I left you with her—"

"Joe, please." Tamara interrupted, imploring me with her gaze. "Let's not go there. Dakota's here and she's alive. That's what matters right now."

Déjà vu. Exactly what she said last time.

I inhaled deeply to hold back the anger that ached to come out. "Dakota, how about you give me and Tamara a minute?"

"Yeah, sure. I'll be outside." She stepped toward the door, leaving her bag in the middle of the room.

"Dakota, no." Tamara looked as though she was afraid Dakota might disappear. "Joe, please."

"I'll be fine. I need a cigarette anyway." Dakota walked outside and shut the door behind her.

Tamara regarded me, eyes tired. "What was that about?"

"Do you really have to ask me that? Last time, she stole a whole lot from you!"

She flinched. "That doesn't matter. I've already forgiven her for that."

I gaped. How could she say that? "It doesn't matter that she stole your engagement ring?"

"Of course it does. I didn't mean that." She reached for my hand.

I jerked away from her touch. "Do you know what I did this morning?" I paused for dramatic effect, anger building. "I counted the money in the safe to make sure we'd have enough to pay Ryan, just in case the cops didn't come through for us. Do you know how insane that is?"

"Joe—"

"No, Tamara, let me say this." My hands curled into fists. "I need to say this. I would have put us in harm's way because that's what you would've wanted me to do."

"But that didn't happen, and she's here now."

"That's not the point." I raised a hand in the air, exasperated. "The point is that I was willing to follow you into Crazyland because I didn't want to lose you. Do you realize how awful that is? I'm pretty sure I'd follow you to hell if you asked me too. It's not right. I can't keep doing this."

"What are you saying, Joe?"

"I'm saying I love you too much. It's literally killing me."

"What does that mean?" she asked, sounding scared.

"I don't know. Every time you've needed me, I've been here. I've held you as you mourned over another man's child. And I would have taken all that pain within myself so you wouldn't have to bear it. All I wanted to do was give you a new life. One that was happy and full of the joy both of us lost. But you were so determined to find them, and now our lives are a disaster. When we went back there, it was like stepping into a minefield that neither of us were ready for."

Tamara came close and put a cautious hand on mine. "Joe, please hear me right now. I haven't meant to hurt you. I'm so thankful for every moment you've been there for me, but they're my family. They're a part of me. I would never keep you back from your mom if she were alive."

I looked down at her hand, a war raging inside of me. "It's not the same thing. You don't see me trying to track down my abusive father, do you?"

"You never knew him! You never felt responsible for him. I left Dakota! I abandoned her! And what about my mom? She never hit me."

"She never protected you either." There was no reasoning with this madness. Why did I have to love her so much?

"What do you want me to do?"

"I want you to choose what's safe for you. And sometimes I want you to be there for me when I need you. I'm strong, Tamara, but this is breaking me."

"I'm so sorry, Joe. I don't want to lose you. You've been the absolute best thing in my life."

I slid my arms around her, my heart breaking. I didn't want to lose her either, but sometimes I felt like I was holding on to her so tightly that I was losing myself. "I'm going back to the diner, I guess. I'll check in with you later." I pulled away. I wished so badly that she'd tell me not to go, beg me to stay, tell me she chose me over her family, but that was an empty wish. Even though I had been the one to love her through her deepest sorrow, I was sure she'd always choose them.

CHAPTER 50

December 22, 8:20 a.m.

TAMARA

For a long moment, I stared at the door after Joe left, doubts overwhelming me, images of his pained expression battering my soul. Were we going to make it through this? The thought crushed me. I hated that I was doing this to him, but there was no other choice. Dakota was here. Not only had she escaped from Ryan, she'd come looking for me. I wasn't exactly sure why she was here, but I'd been praying for this for weeks. Exhaustion blanketed me as I fervently prayed that God would strengthen Joe and that somehow we'd survive this.

I walked into the kitchen and started a pot of coffee.

Behind me, the door closed. "I'm pretty sure he hates me."

I turned to Dakota. "He's just having a tough time."

"He has every right to, and so do you." She took a few steps to her duffel bag.

"I could never hate you." The coffee dropped into the pot, releasing its rich aroma. I couldn't wait for it to finish. I was in desperate need of a cup and about twelve more hours of sleep.

"The morning is young, sis, and there's lots of truth to catch up on." Dakota reached into the pocket on the side of her bag.

A dart of anxiety hit my stomach. That sounded ominous.

She drug out my engagement ring. She still had it? That was a good sign, right?

She seemed to struggle with her words. "I told myself the reason I took this from you was that I was protecting you." She held the ring toward me. "But really I was trying to protect myself. I've been running from the truth for a long time, and it's cost me way too much. I'm so sorry for taking this and for everything else I took from you."

"I've already forgiven you, Dakota." Before taking it from her, I removed Joe's mom's ring to make room for my engagement ring, then slid it on my finger where it belonged. Joe and I would be okay. After the dust settled, we'd find we loved each other more than ever. It was the testing of love that made it stronger, wasn't it? "Thank you for bringing this back. It means so much to me."

"I never should have stolen it." The shame in her voice made me sad.

"You're here now, and that's what matters."

"See, I don't understand that. Do you not love Joe? How could you be so nonchalant about me taking your ring?"

"This isn't about how much I love him. He is the best thing that has ever happened to me. My forgiveness has to do with how much I love you. There's nothing you can do or say that would make me stop loving you."

Dakota let out a half-laugh, half-cry. "You have no idea what else I've stolen from you. What I've stolen from our family."

I eyed Dakota, probing her damaged features. "I've taken things from our family too. I abandoned you and the rest of our family for six years because of lies and fears, but it's time to let the past go. I have, six months ago, when I gave my life to God. When I did, He made me new." A long almost eerie silence. "I believe he can make our family new."

Tears welled in Dakota's eyes. "That's a nice sentiment, sis, but even if it were true, there are some things even God himself can't put back together."

In my mind, I prayed for the right words to say. I, more than anyone, understood her doubts, but her sitting in front of me now seemed like a sign of God's goodness—that he was able to restore our family even through the worst circumstances. He was trustworthy. She was living proof of that.

CHAPTER 51

December 22, 8:35 a.m.

DAKOTA

Tamara's face was so pale, it was almost as if I could see right through her, but an unexpected hope still shone in her features. It was astounding. She had been through so much, but she still believed that things would be okay. The idea was beautiful, even in its naïveté. I hated that I was going to be the one who would snuff out that hope.

"God can put anything together." Tamara gave me a weak smile. "He's that big."

This was a mistake coming here. I should have continued south as far as I could go and never looked back. "I have a lot to tell you." Uneasiness prickled at my core, around the lies and secrets, I'd kept for years. "But you look tired. Maybe you should rest, and we could talk another time."

"Just tell me. Whatever it is, we'll work through it together."

How had she become so optimistic? She should be scared. I ran a hand through my hair and exhaled. I had no idea where to begin this horror story. "Can I get some coffee?"

"Yeah. Of course." Tamara hurried into the kitchenette and grabbed two mugs from the cupboard. "How do you take it?"

"Black." Like my soul. I looked down at the duffel bag and

then at the door. What was I doing here? I could just bolt now. Tamara had her ring back. She knew I was sorry. That was enough, wasn't it? I wasn't strong enough to do this.

"Here you go." Tamara handed me the cup. The writing on the side of the mug said, *difficult roads often lead to beautiful destinations.* I rolled my eyes and took a sip of the steaming coffee. Beautiful destinations? What a load of crap.

"Let's sit down." Coffee in hand, Tamara ambled to the couch.

Reluctantly, I followed and sat next to her. I stared at the contents on the wooden chest in front of us. Specifically, the half burnt vanilla candle in the middle of it. Tamara's apartment was clean but kind of dumpy. She may have left the trailer park years ago, but in so many ways she was still there.

"What's on your mind, Dakota?"

I sat back in the loveseat and sipped the coffee. What I wouldn't give for some whiskey in this cup. "Did Gabriel ever touch you when we were kids?"

"Like, what do you mean touch? Like *touch*, touch?"

"Of course, that's what I mean. I'm not talking about a high-five, Tamara."

"What?" So much disbelief in that one word. "No, never."

"I guess I was the one who drew the short straw."

"Dakota, what are you saying?"

I tried to focus on the heat of the mug in my hand instead of the relentless images bombarding my mind. "Do you really want me to tell you that when he said he was taking me to the park, he was actually taking me behind the house to touch me in a way a brother never should? Then at night, when everyone was asleep, he'd sneak into our room and do it again?"

"But I was right there. How could I have not known? I'm so sorry."

"It is what it is, sis. It all ended when I was thirteen, and I began to fight back." My gaze met hers.

Guilt and sorrow painted her features. There was no way she could have known.

Why was I even telling her this? Was it to make myself look better once the truth emerged? "The thing that really twisted me on the inside was that I never told anyone, because I was afraid of what Dad would do to him. How screwed up is that?" For a moment I saw it so clearly. I had sacrificed my own safety for the safety of my perpetrator. "Please tell me, sis, how does God help in this situation? Where was he in this?"

Tamara's already pale face turned an ashen gray color. "I don't know." Her voice quaked. "I just know what he did for me. I didn't tell you before, but last year's pregnancy was a result of date rape. I was so broken after it that I wanted to die, but it was in that place of desperation that I met God. If he can heal my heart, He can surely heal you."

"That's only half the story."

The night was so sharp in my mind, as if it had happened just the day before. The night that sealed my fate like the final nail in the proverbial coffin. "After you left home, everything changed. Mom took more hours at work, and when she was home, she'd lock herself in her room, but everyone in the house could hear her crying. Dad drank a lot more and stayed on the road as much as possible. Gabriel became a recluse for a bit, and then he had some sort of religious awakening. He started sounding a lot like you do right now. God this. Jesus that." I focused on Tamara again. Her gaze fell to the floor, focusing on the cracked linoleum. "I hated it. Gabriel would talk about the forgiveness of Jesus, and all I could think about was what he had done to me when I was a child."

Tamara flinched. Oh, how I wished it was the end of the story.

"One night about a year after you left, I was out at the power lines at a party with Ryan and his crew. Gabriel somehow heard about it and found us." That night was still sharper than something that had happened five minutes ago—sharp enough to make me bleed from the inside out. "Gabriel had knelt in front of me, begging me to come with him. 'I'm so sorry, Dakota, for what I've done. What I did to you was wrong. I don't want to lose you like we lost Tamara. Our family can't take any more losses.'"

I could still see the tears falling down his face, so honest in their sincerity. But it didn't matter to me. I was already too numb and pushed him away. Then Ryan stepped in and started a fight. Gabriel dodged several punches and then landed a few good ones, knocking Ryan to the ground. Gabriel turned toward me once more, pleading with me to go with him. Behind him, Ryan regained his composure and then came at him hard. A part of me relished in the beating. Gabriel was getting what he had coming to him. He was being punished for what he did to me. But then, Gabriel's head hit the bumper of Ryan's truck as he fell to the ground. Ryan continued to kick him in the abdomen and beat his lifeless body. Minutes went by before he realized Gabriel wasn't breathing.

Tears streamed down Tamara's cheeks as I recounted the night I had lost my soul. "I ran over to his body. I tried giving him CPR, but I didn't have a clue what I was doing. I screamed and begged for Ryan to help him, but he refused. Nobody else did anything either. Ryan told them everyone would go down if anyone went to the cops. Then he built a huge bonfire and threw Gabriel's body on it." Coldness crept over me as I watched my brother—my abuser, my own blood—fade to ash. A guttural sob climbed my throat. "I didn't want him to die, Tamara. I promise. I didn't want him to die." The anguish I'd suppressed through the years erupted like an angry volcano.

Tamara's arms came around me. She was weeping too. "It's not your fault," she said emphatically. "Do you hear me, it's *not* your fault."

"If I would've just left with him." I said through sobs. "If I would've forgiven him—"

"You didn't do this, Dakota. Ryan did. You were just a

child. A hurting, abandoned, neglected child. Do you hear me?" For a moment, I was a child again, being comforted by my big sister. The sister who had always been there for me. Why couldn't we just go back there and do everything different?

For a long time, we held each other, sobbing. Tamara whispered the name of Jesus again and again—as if she was trying to release her sorrow by chanting his name. Eventually, I pulled away, reached for my duffel bag and took out the jar of ashes—the evidence that this story was true. The next day I'd walked back to the spot and filled this mason jar with Gabriel's ashes.

"This is what's left of him." As I handed Tamara the ashes, she broke. I saw it as clear as a lightning bolt flashing across the darkened sky. She doubled over and let out the kind of wail that made my blood run cold. I wanted to comfort her, but I didn't know how. All I could do was sit there and watch her implode and know I was the one responsible for this.

CHAPTER 52

December 22, 10:10 a.m.

TAMARA

My soul split wide open, ripped apart from top to bottom with the force of a hurricane. I hated what Gabriel had done to Dakota, but now he was gone—gone forever. I'd never see him again. I gripped the jar of ashes like a buoy in a turbulent ocean. This was all that was left of my brother—my sister's abuser.

Another sob erupted from my throat. "Jesus," I cried again. How could this be happening? "Jesus." It hurt too much. My heart was burning flesh, the pain all-consuming and relentless.

"I'm so sorry, Tamara. I'm so sorry." Dakota's voice splintered as she said the words.

Only more fuel to the raging fire. This was more my fault than hers. I should have never left town without her. I should have been there to protect her. She should have never had to walk through this alone. "Jesus."

Would I make it through this? How did Dakota do it this whole time? How could she hold onto this secret without it killing her too? Tears fell off my face like waterfalls, dripping down onto my hand that gripped the mason jar. "Jesus, please. Please help me." If this pain—this fire didn't stop, I wasn't sure what would be left of me. Suddenly, yet somehow subtly, I felt warmth rest on my shoulders, just like in David's office, but stronger. A tingling sensation crept down my spine and my limbs.

And then the faintest whisper inside of my being. *Give them to me.*

I sobbed harder, tightening my grip around the jar. "I can't." The tingling warmth reached my fingers and then circled around my back again. The strangest sense of something being poured over my head. It felt like peace, the most beautiful, perfect peace that only God himself could bring. The whole room was filled with this presence. Could Dakota feel it too?

Give me the ashes.

That voice was so sweet, so tender, so kind. And still my heart refused. This was the only thing I had left of my brother. "I can't, Jesus." That wonderful peace swirled around me, pressing against me, holding me together, dampening the burn.

Trust me, the whisper repeated. *Give them to me.*

I couldn't fight against it this time. I had to let go. The darkness faded around me into light, and the fire in my soul no longer stung. A man with love blazing in his eyes walked toward me. Jesus? A new kind of fire kindled inside my being, so warm, but one that would never burn me. Liquid love crashed through me.

He reached toward the jar in my hands. I handed the ashes to him. In that moment, I would have given him anything. I knew then that He was worthy of my whole life, and he wanted it, even if it had been reduced to ashes.

Jesus twisted the lid off the jar. My entire family appeared before my vision then—everyone except for Gabriel. We were standing in the place where my childhood home had stood, now nothing but ash, dirt, and trash. Something gleamed in Jesus' expression as he removed the lid and let Gabriel's ashes scatter around us. Under our feet the gray ground turned green. Where there had been death sprouted the most beautiful garden.

Jesus' gold-flecked eyes pierced through my being with fire and love. Though he didn't say anything aloud, a thousand words passed between us in that moment. Strength poured through my soul. I didn't know what battles lay ahead, but whatever was on the other side of this had to be beautiful. I would receive beauty for these ashes. Words poured through my head. *Be strong and courageous for I am with you. Even until the end.* Then as suddenly as it came, the vision was gone, and the light faded.

The jar was still in my hands, and I could feel Dakota next to me on the couch. A part of me didn't want to open my eyes, because once I did, I'd have to face it again and a fresh wave of grief would overtake me. I couldn't get lost in another wave. Dakota needed me to be strong. Though parts of me were still fracturing, I had God to hold me together. She didn't.

I forced myself to open my eyes. Grief did come then as I stared into my baby sister's battered face. What else had she endured? "I'm so sorry you've had to carry this alone for so long." I placed the jar on the wooden chest. "That must have been absolute hell."

"That's it? I tell you Gabriel's dead because of me, and you're concerned about my feelings?"

I took hold of her hand. "Dakota, it's not your fault. You can't blame yourself for what Ryan did to our brother. Gabriel was right. Our family has lost enough. It's time to let the healing begin."

Dakota jerked her hand away and crossed her arms in front of her waist as if she was holding herself together. "After what I just told you, you actually believe there can be healing for our family?"

For a second, the vision I'd just seen came before me. "I do. But Dakota ..." I paused for a moment and braced myself for her reaction before saying the words. "I need to know if you know where our parents are."

Instantly, she stood. "I need a cigarette." She started to the door.

"Dakota, please." I grabbed her hand and rose. "I deserve to know if they're all right, and they need to know the truth. That is the only way we might be made whole."

Dakota trembled under the weight of a thousand lies being exposed. "I can't go back there. They're not like you, Tamara. They already hate me. This will only make it worse."

"You don't know that. Whatever happens, we'll face together."

She bit her bottom lip as tears pooled in her eyes. "They're in Aberdeen, Washington. They've been there since the fire."

"Aberdeen?" That was so close to where I'd been in Ocean Shores years ago. Only a thirty-minute drive away.

Dakota jerked away from my grasp. "I'm going to smoke."

This time I didn't try to stop her. She needed the moment's reprieve, and so did I. How could my family have been so near and I hadn't even known? I looked down at my brother's ashes. How could I have not felt that he was gone? I had let myself get so cut off from my family, and now all I wanted was to have them back. To restore the lost years. That almost felt like too big of a dream. But Jesus himself had just shown up in my living room to show me it was possible.

What about Joe? Would he believe me? Would he stand with me as I set out on this journey? Or would I have to go forward alone?

CHAPTER 53

December 22, 9:55 p.m.

TAMARA

Dakota sat across from me in my kitchen, eating a bowl of Cinnamon Toast Crunch. After finishing her last bite, she slurped the sweetened milk from the bowl—just like when we were kids. After her confession we had spent most of the day sleeping and then vegging out on reruns of the Golden Girls to give each other an emotional reprieve.

I set my bowl in the sink. "Sorry for the lame dinner. If Joe were here, he'd make you a proper meal." My heart hurt at the mention of his name. With the way he left this morning, I wasn't sure where we stood and for the moment, I was too scared to find out.

"Are you kidding me, sis?" Dakota said cracking a grin. "This is the best meal I've had in weeks. Tim only eats steak, potatoes, pancakes, and an occasional donut."

"Sounds like a keeper."

Sadness flickered over Dakota's features, and she looked away.

"Hey, I was thinking that after we talk to the cops about this, we should take a road trip to Aberdeen to talk to Mom and Dad."

Her neck snapped, head turning toward me. "I thought you understood. I can't face them."

"Just hear me out. Like I said before, we'll do it together."

"Do you know how much it took for me to come here?" Dakota scooted away from the table, frowning as she stood. "And that's only because you're the one person in our family who has ever shown they cared."

"They deserve to know."

"Yeah, well, we deserved a lot of things and never got them."

"Dakota, come on."

She bolted to the door. "I'm going to walk to the store. I'm out of smokes."

Before I could say another word, the door slammed behind her. My heart went cold. What if she didn't come back? My phone dinged, and I ran across the room to pick it up, hoping it was Joe.

Just a stupid ad for a new health shake I'd been looking into. I couldn't remember giving them my number. I clicked on Joe's name and stared at the last message I had sent him, fear turning in my guts. Had I somehow lost the one person who I cared about the most? The one good thing in my life? I typed out a message. *Your silence is scaring me.*

My finger hovered over the send button, but I deleted it instead. There were so many things that had happened today, and he wasn't here. I had lost my brother, and he didn't have a clue that his silence only added to my grief. It wasn't like him.

A light tapping sounded from the door. I looked at the knob, fear quickening my pulse. Every other time Dakota had left today, she had come right back in without knocking. Maybe it was Joe, but he would have just come in too.

Were those scratches at the door? Adrenaline shot through my veins. Something was off. I crept over to the door.

It swung open. Dakota's face was stricken with horror. Behind her, Ryan held a gun to her back with one hand and my old phone in his other. "Looky what we have here. Alas, both

Jensen sisters in one place at one time. Merry effing Christmas to me." He shoved Dakota forward, and she slammed into me.

My cell phone fell to the floor and bounced across the linoleum.

"I hope you both have money, or this is going to turn into a bloodbath."

I pushed Dakota behind me. "This isn't about her, Ryan."

He let out a hair-raising laugh. "What? She didn't tell you? She owes me almost as much as you do."

"No, she was too busy telling me how you murdered our brother."

"Well, I guess now you know what I'm capable off." Ryan step forward and pointed the gun at my head.

What was I doing? I was going to get both of us killed.

"I need ten grand in less than, I don't know..." He glanced at the ceiling, his hand stroking his chin. "Forty-five minutes, or you're both dead."

"We don't have that kind of money," Dakota said.

Ryan grabbed Dakota by her hair. She yelped. My stomach twisted.

He pulled her to him. "Then figure it out!"

"Fine!" I shouted.

Dakota shot me a terrified glance.

There was only one option, and I wasn't sure there'd be enough. "I'll get you your money."

Ryan let Dakota go. "Now that's what I wanted to hear."

"We have to go to the diner."

Ryan glared at me. "The diner?"

"My fiancé owns a diner." Joe would never forgive me for this, but what choice did I have? "We have a safe there." Hopefully, he hadn't made the drop.

Ryan looked back and forth between Dakota and me. "If you're lying to me, I'm going to kill Dakota slowly and make you watch."

Fear slithered down my spine. "I'm not lying."

"Well, then, here's the deal. My car is parked in the visitor's section. We're going to act like we're old friends on the way out there. Got it?"

I nodded slowly.

"Awesome. Dakota can be my girlfriend." He grabbed her around the waist, bringing her close.

Her face shone with fear and disgust. I wanted to throw myself at him, to wrestle the gun from his hand and shoot him myself. For years he'd stolen my life, and now I find out he'd been tormenting my sister and killed my brother. Inwardly, I prayed that justice would finally be served.

I followed them out to an old blue Monte Carlo. He shoved Dakota in the front seat, and I climbed in the back. The stench of old beer, cigarettes, and dirty socks mingled together in the air. Repulsive.

The car started and the hard beats of Rob Zombie's "Dragula" boomed through the speakers. Some things never changed. Ryan put the car in reverse and pulled out of the parking lot.

God, please help. I numbly gave Ryan directions to the diner and prayed again for a miracle. Everyone should be gone by now, except maybe Joe.

The thought of his name crushed what was left of my heart. If there was hope for us when he left this morning, after this it would be gone. Taking money from the diner to pay off Ryan was crossing every line left in our relationship. It was like throwing a grenade into a burning building. I stared out the window, watching the cars go by. Was there some way to signal one of them without Ryan noticing?

"Jesus," I whispered under my breath. I thought of this morning and how He had showed up when I thought I needed him the most. I needed him more now. *God, please help,* I repeated desperately in my mind.

Twenty minutes later, we drove into the diner parking lot. In so many ways, my journey had started here when I met Joe and then Levi. Would it end here, too? Even if I did give Ryan the money, there was no guarantee that he wouldn't kill us. Ryan exited the car and came around to the passenger side. He opened my door first, and then Dakota's. She kept her head down as we both followed him to the back of the car. He opened the trunk and pulled out a red gas bottle and loop of rope. Nausea tore through me.

Why had I brought him here? He had planned to kill us all along.

We walked to the back door. With shaky hands, I opened it with my key and said another prayer as I punched in the security code. If Joe had his phone on him, he'd get a notification that the restaurant was being unlocked. Surely, that would alert him that something was wrong. I turned on the light, and we walked down the hall to the office. I flicked on the light and went straight to the safe. I glanced at Ryan and then Dakota. Her gaze was still on the floor, as if looking at me was too much.

Ryan nudged me with the gun.

I put the code in the safe and opened it. Empty. My heart plummeted into my guts, and my focus landed at the red gas can on the floor next to Ryan's feet. We were so dead. "It's gone. Joe must have made the deposit."

Ryan spat out a string of curse words. "Wrong answer." The base of his gun smacked hard against my forehead. Pain shot through my skull, and blood trickled down my face.

Ryan brought out my old phone, scrolled through the numbers and hit send.

CHAPTER 54
December 22, 10:25 p.m.

JOE

The moonlight reflected off the rippling water in broken beautiful shards. I breathed in deep, inhaling the night air, wishing it would take away the ache in the back of my throat. The whole day I'd struggled to hold on to sobriety as I continuously batted away images of heading to the liquor store and downing a whole bottle of tequila. Even now my muscles were tight with craving and my stomach was twisted, longing for a drink. *God, grant me the serenity to accept the things I cannot change.* I could've gone to a late meeting after work, but I was pretty sure it wouldn't help. Problem was I couldn't figure out what would.

My phone buzzed from my back pocket, but I ignored it and took in another inhale through my nose. The pier and its surrounding beauty made me think of Tamara and all the good that we were, which saddened me even more. She was my whole world. If it wasn't for her unwavering desire to reconnect with her family, our relationship would have been exactly on track. We'd be that perfect couple everyone was jealous of because we were so happy.

I picked up a rock and threw it into the water.

I guess it wasn't her fault that she was born into that crazy dysfunctional family. The way that she loved them unconditionally after what they had put her through was part of what made me care for her like I did. She was still willing to love them and do the hard work of restoration, even if they stole from her.

I snagged another rock and chucked it into the bay. Why couldn't she just leave them behind like she had for so many years?

Because she'd never truly be whole.

I didn't like that answer, but I knew it was true.

My phone played Tamara's ringtone, and I dug my phone from my back pocket. As I went to press the answer icon, I noticed it was a different number with an old picture. Tamara's old phone.

Anger and fear, with their jagged sharp edges, impaled me in an instant.

"Hello." My voice came out in a whisper.

"I'm going to cut to the chase. I'm here at your establishment with your fiancé and her worthless sister. They're both going to go up in flames in T-minus thirty minutes and counting if you don't have ten grand cash pronto. Comprende?"

Panic tore through me. How in the hell was this happening? He had Tamara at the diner? Had Dakota coming here been a setup? No. He had Tamara's old phone. He'd used it to track her. I knew she should have disconnected that line.

"Do you understand?"

"Yes."

"No cops or they both die." The line went dead.

I ran to my Jeep, climbed in, and tore out of the parking lot. *God, please, please help. Please keep her safe. I can't lose her.* Overhead, the full moon hung bright in the sky, peeking through clouds. When the smoke cleared and life settled, she was the one thing that mattered.

I pressed on the accelerator, pushing the engine past ninety.

Who cared if I saw flashing lights at this point? I had to get to her. At 99ᵗʰ Street I slowed to turn and then gunned the engine again. My pulse raced the entire way there as different scenarios flew through my mind. I wanted to pray more, but I couldn't get the words out. When I turned into the parking lot of the diner, my Jeep lights lit up the windows.

Behind the glass, Tamara and Dakota were in the middle of the dining room, tied to chairs back to back.

Fear clawed at my throat. The only car in the parking lot was an old blue Monte Carlo. I parked next to the building and grabbed the bank bag from my glove box. There wasn't quite five grand in there. I'd taken it out of the safe but never made it to the bank. My phone rang again. I answered it.

The back door opened, and Ryan's head popped out. "You got my money?"

I held the bank bag in the air. "Right here."

"Go put it inside my car."

"Give me Tamara first."

He pointed a nine-millimeter at me. "You don't make the rules here."

I crossed the parking lot and threw the money bag inside his car. "There. Now give me Tamara."

He cracked a menacing smile and then raised a lit Zippo lighter over his head. "She's all yours." He threw the burning lighter into the restaurant. Behind him, the flames rose quickly. Murder flashed in my thoughts—taking him to the ground and making him pay for what he'd put Tamara through.

Instead, I ran to the front door, rushing to stay ahead of the flames. From the corner of my eye, I saw Ryan bolting to his car.

I unlocked the front door and yanked it open. Flames quickly spread through the restaurant. I ran to Tamara. Her eyes were wide with fear as she struggled against the ropes that held her and Dakota to the chairs. Smoke swirled around us, and the fire licked the side of the counter as I worked on the knot. One final twist and the ropes were loose. Flames danced along the counter, consuming the till. Heat surrounded us like an inferno. I helped both of them out of the chairs, and we sprinted out of the building.

Outside the fresh air cleansed our lungs, and I pulled Tamara into me. She sobbed into my chest. Ryan's car was gone.

Sirens pierced the night air as flames spread through the front of the diner. Maybe they'd make it in time to save the place, but in light of this, it didn't matter. The one thing I cared most about was safe in my arms.

CHAPTER 55

December 22, 11:35 p.m.

JOE

It was hard to focus on the officer's questions. I told him what I knew, but I had no idea where Ryan had gone or what he'd used to burn down the diner. As the man talked, I kept glancing over at the ambulance. When they had arrived, the paramedics took Tamara into the back to tend to her head wound. They'd urged me to stay away and give them space. I hated the space. I wanted to be near her. To never let her out of my sight again. I ached everywhere. I was a huge bundle of agony, and the only thing that would comfort me now was Tamara. I hoped she felt the same way after our fight earlier and then my abandoning her to this.

Three questions later, the officer finished and left to talk to his partner. I sat down on a concrete parking block next to the police car with a sigh. The glow of the now almost fully burnt-down diner flickered across my face. The firefighters had done what they could, but it wasn't enough. The one thing I thought would secure Tamara's and my future, gone.

I glanced over at Dakota, who was pacing, smoking a cigarette with intensity, as if it was the last one on the planet. Anger rose within me. I knew the minute she arrived something terrible would happen, but I hadn't imagined this. She'd led

Ryan right to us. Now he knew where Tamara lived. Why didn't I take his gun from him and shoot him when I had the chance?

The ache flared in the back of my throat, along with the thoughts of whiskey to dampen it. I pressed back the desire. Drinking wouldn't help a thing. Perhaps I could start smoking instead. Prayer surely was supposed to be the answer, but I was too exhausted. I stood and brushed myself off.

A muffled voice came over the police radio. "Suspect driving a blue Monte Carlo located on I-5 south entering Portland. A57 in pursuit."

My ears perked up. That was Ryan. I looked over at the officers. They were still off to the side of the lot, talking and taking notes, oblivious to the radio's squawk exiting their open door.

"Copy that, A57." Another voice came over the line. Should I be listening in? Probably not, but this was too important.

"Suspect exiting onto 99 east."

My pulse raced. That wasn't far from here. I scanned the parking lot and stopped at the ambulance Tamara was in. If Ryan was circling back for us, I had to get her out of here.

"Shots fired, requesting backup."

"Copy, A57, C62 in route." A third voice came over the line.

This couldn't be real. I was stuck inside some bad adrenaline packed cop movie. Was Ryan actually shooting at them while driving? I kept glancing over at the two officers, who still seemed oblivious to what was going on.

The next few things coming through were cryptic police talk, but I could decipher that a few more cars had joined the chase. Maybe they would finally take him to jail. I tried to find joy in the thought of justice being served, but jail, even a life sentence, didn't seem like enough for Ryan. Not to mention the inevitable court trial Tamara and I would have to go through.

"Vehicle disabled at Northeast Fremont Street." The voice left the radio. "Suspect is fleeing on foot into Irving Park. Pursuing." The radio was silent for a few minutes, then the voice returned. "Officer down, returning fire."

Ryan shot an officer? He was legitimately insane. Maybe they would just lock him away in a mental ward without a trial.

The two officers ran toward me and jumped in the car. "Suspect down." The door slammed, and they sped away, sirens blaring, lights flashing.

I couldn't breathe. I stood, partially in shock and partially relieved. *Suspect down?* From what I knew, officers were trained to shoot to kill—especially if they were being shot at. Did that mean Ryan was dead? I hurried to the ambulance just as Tamara stepped out of it, her forehead patched with a butterfly bandage. I drew her to me and stood in shock for a few moments.

"What happened out here? Why the sirens?"

"Ryan's been shot, Tamara. I think he might be dead."

CHAPTER 56

December 22, 11:55 p.m.

TAMARA

I pressed my head into Joe's shoulder. Ryan was shot? Possibly dead? I didn't even know how to feel about that.

Joe drew away. "I'm going to give Officer Woodleaf a call to see if I can get any more information."

I nodded and scanned the parking lot. On the other side, Dakota stood shivering, a Red Cross blanket wrapped around her shoulders. "Yeah, I'll go tell Dakota."

Darkness descended over Joe's features, then he looked at his phone and scrolled through the contacts. Did he blame Dakota for what had happened tonight? He found the number, hit the green icon, and stepped a few feet away.

I crossed the parking lot to Dakota. "How are you doing over here?"

She took a long drag of her cigarette and blew the smoke away from me, gaze down. "I'm not sure."

Man, a cigarette sounded good right now. I glanced over at Joe.

He paced a ten feet radius, holding his phone to his ear, expression distant.

"I have some news. Ryan's been shot."

Dakota's head jerked up.

"Joe thinks he might be dead. He's trying to track down the information."

Dakota's face held a look that I didn't understand. I was expecting relief. Possibly even jubilation. But she wore a sad, vulnerable demeanor that didn't make sense.

A hand rested on my shoulder, and I jumped.

Joe stood beside me. "I'm sorry. I didn't mean to startle you."

"At this point, I'd probably jump at my own shadow. What did you find out?"

"Woodleaf said he would call as soon as he heard anything. You ready to get out of here?"

I glanced at Dakota. Her battered face was pale in the moonlight, causing the bruising to be more prominent.

"Yeah. I'm exhausted, and I need to take Dakota back to the apartment."

A pained expression washed over Joe. "Can I talk to you for a minute?"

"Sure." We took a few steps away.

"Please stay with me tonight. After this, I want you close."

The angry words he'd spoken this morning rushed over me, battering my fragile heart. Then not hearing from him the whole day? I thought he'd given up on us, but he'd been there when I needed him most. He'd saved both of our lives, and even though his restaurant was destroyed, he wanted me close.

Why wasn't he yelling at me? Why wasn't he cursing the day we met? It didn't make sense but, in that moment, it didn't matter. I needed him and somehow, he still needed me too. "What about Dakota?"

"She can sleep on my couch."

That meant I'd be in his bed...

"I'll sleep on the floor. I just need you close."

"Okay." I needed him near too.

He wove his fingers through mine and led me to his Jeep. I signaled for Dakota to follow us. Joe opened the door for me and then walked around the vehicle. Dakota climbed in the back seat, shivering beneath the blanket.

I cranked the heat and rubbed my hands together. "We're going to stay at Joe's tonight. Is there stuff you need at my apartment?"

"Um, yeah. My bag."

"We'll stop by Tamara's on the way home." Joe started the Jeep and backed up, pausing for a final look at the diner. The firefighters were still working hard to put out the fire, but at this point, I didn't think there'd be much to recover.

The ride back to my apartment was awkwardly quiet. A thousand questions poured through my mind as I thought back over the day's discoveries. What was going on with Dakota? Her reaction to Ryan's demise unearthed a question that I hadn't thought of earlier when she had told me about Gabriel. Why had she stuck around? Why, after all Ryan had put her through, did she stay in Quilcene when my parents moved? Was it the drugs? There had to be other places she could get drugs. It just didn't make sense. The question burned inside of me as we drove. I needed to talk to her, and it needed to be alone.

CHAPTER 57

December 23, 12:15 a.m.

TAMARA

At my apartment, Joe parked next to my car, and we exited the vehicle. I hoped Joe would wait outside so I could have a few minutes alone with Dakota, but he hovered like a guardian angel on assignment.

I shoved some clothes into an overnight bag and asked Joe to speak with me privately. Dakota gave me a strange look, but I ignored it and stepped out the front door.

Joe followed me, concern lining his handsome features. "What is it?"

I locked my gaze with his. There were still so many unresolved issues between us. We needed our own time alone to work through everything that had happened today, but I needed to sort through the things that felt off about Dakota's story before bringing her into his house.

"I need to talk to my sister for a few minutes. Alone. Why don't you go ahead, and we'll be right behind you?"

He opened his mouth to say something, but seemed to think better of it.

"I'm sorry. I know this is hard. I just feel like she won't open up in front of you."

Silence. A battle raged behind his deep hazel eyes. "I could

305

have lost you tonight." The hurt in his words impaled my heart, but I had to do this.

"I understand your hesitation. How about I'll drive to your house and you follow us in the Jeep? That way you can make sure we're safe."

"I hate this. I honestly don't want you anywhere near her unless I'm there."

"You'll be right behind us."

Joe drew in a breath and nodded with hesitation.

"Thank you, Joe. I know we have a lot to talk about."

"Yeah... we do."

I opened the door. "You ready, Dakota?"

She slung the duffel bag over her shoulder and walked outside. While she waited, she had changed into a pair of my yoga pants and a blue hoodie.

"We're taking my car."

She and Joe exchanged a frigid glance.

We walked to our vehicles and loaded our bags in the back.

Meat Loaf's "I Would Do Anything for Love" blared out of the speakers when I started the engine. Images of me and Dakota, dancing around our living room, singing into hairbrushes, our hair and make-up punked-out like 90s divas, filled my mind. Those days, when our parents were gone working and the boys were off doing their own thing, were probably the happiest of our childhood.

I reached to turn down the volume, but Dakota's hand came over mine. "Let it play."

Our eyes met. From the look in them, she was having the same memories I was. I gave her a weak smile, backed out of the parking spot, and pulled away from the apartment complex. Joe's headlights appeared in my rearview mirror.

The song ended and a guy with a sexy radio voice purred that the music would continue after a brief note from their sponsors.

I turned down the volume. "How are you doing over there?"

Dakota brought out her pack of cigarettes. "Not sure. I'm a bit numb, I guess. Do you mind if I smoke?"

"Go ahead." She'd probably need a cigarette for this conversation. "Dakota, I have a question for you."

She lit up, took a long drag and blew it out the window.

"Why did you still hang out with Ryan after what he did? Why didn't you leave town with Mom and Dad?"

"That's two questions, sis," she said, her sarcastic tone back in full swing.

"Kinda. Why didn't you leave with them? Why didn't you turn Ryan in?"

She barked out a sick laugh. "You make it sound easy. But I guess you would. Leaving has always been easy for you."

"So, we're back to this?" After this afternoon, I thought I'd reached through her walls.

"What do you want from me? There is only so much one person can take for one day."

"I want the truth. Ryan might be dead. You could be finally free, and you seem almost sad that he's gone." I flipped on the turn signal and made a left onto Sycamore Street.

"The truth? Sometimes the truth doesn't matter. Because whether Ryan lives or dies, it doesn't change a damn thing. Knowing Ryan, it was probably a flesh wound, and he'll be back on the street within a month." She flicked her cigarette in the ashtray.

That couldn't be. He'd crossed way too many lines. "I just need to know."

"Fine." She was quiet for a few minutes as if gathering her thoughts. "About three months after Gabriel died, I couldn't take it anymore. I wanted to go to the police, but was afraid to do it myself. I went to Logan, one of the guys who was there that night, and begged him to go with me. He said he would, but he must have narked me off to Ryan. That night Ryan snuck through my window and pulled me outside. He said that if I told anyone, he'd kill my whole family. He said he'd watch them burn just like Gabriel. He told me from that moment on, he owned me. Three days later, I was off in the woods by myself getting high when the fire started in the trailer park. It was ours that burnt first. After that, someone left an anonymous tip to the police department that they saw me light the fire."

"Ryan." His name sounded like a curse word as it flew out of my mouth.

"Yup. They brought me in, but there was no real evidence that it was me. Dad was furious. Mom was sullen. Both seemed to believe I did it. I couldn't leave with them after that. I stayed with some older friends and tried to avoid Ryan, but he was always there. And he always made it clear that he would own me forever."

"Jesus." I prayed quietly. I wanted to scream and cry for all the pain she had carried over the years. "I'm so sorry, Dakota." The words felt hollow, empty. Nowhere close to touching the devastation that her life had been. My phone rang, and I jumped. I looked down at the screen.

Joe.

I answered it.

"I just got off the phone with Officer Woodleaf. Ryan's dead."

I trembled and breathed in the relief that filled my lungs.

"It's over, Tamara," he said.

I took in his words and glanced over at Dakota. Hopefully, this meant that the healing could finally begin for her. "I'll see you at the house."

I ended the call and set down the phone. "Ryan's dead."

She hung her head, and her hand curled around the pack of smokes. A sob came up her throat and then another.

I parked in front of Joe's house and put my hand on her shoulder. "You're free, Dakota. He can't hurt you anymore."

Her body trembled as a lifetime of grief slid down her face.

I shut the car off and drew her into an embrace. We sat like that for a long time as she cried into my shoulder. I cried too, as all that she described to me played before me like a movie reel. One excruciating scene after the next. "It's over, sis."

She pulled away and wiped at her tears. "This doesn't change the damage he's done. Gabriel's still dead and our family is still broken."

"But you're not under Ryan's power anymore. As for our family, the healing started with us today. We can be the change, Dakota."

She let out a twisted laugh. "Did you just quote Gandhi?"

"I guess. But it's the truth, right? We can be the change in our family?"

"Maybe you can, but I'm not sure I can be that strong." She wiped her face with her sleeve.

"You're stronger than you think." I couldn't have lived through half of what she had. I looked at Joe's house and thought about everything we had been through. He had believed in me before I did. Maybe I could do the same for Dakota. "And now you have me. We'll get there together."

She gave me a weak, teary smile. "For now, I just need sleep."

"Me too." We climbed out of the car and made our way to Joe's door. Sleep was what I needed, but one more conversation had to happen before I could. I opened the door and walked down the hall.

Joe quietly greeted us with blankets and a pillow for Dakota. I thanked him with a hug and told him I would be up in a minute. He nodded and left the room, looking as weary as I felt.

After the stories Dakota had told me today, I didn't want to leave her, but I had to face Joe. If I didn't, I might lose him forever. I hugged Dakota and then ascended the stairs slowly, feet heavy. I didn't know how he still wanted me here, but I guess I was about to find out.

I rounded the corner and paused in the door. Joe sat on the bed, somewhat disheveled, an empty, vacant look in his eye. For a moment I was paralyzed, struck by the utter brokenness in his countenance. What had changed in the short car ride with Dakota?

Our gazes met, and there were a million words communicated in that single look. Love, compassion, even understanding, but there was pain too. So much loss and disappointment, tangled into one big, bloody mess.

"Come here." He patted the bed next to him.

I wanted to run to him—to hold him until the rest of forever—to hear his kind faith-filled words whispering in my ear, telling me we were going to be okay. That we were going to make it through this. Instead, I slowly walked across the room, doubt weighing down each step. Tears spilled down my face as soon as I reached the bed.

"I'm so sorry, Joe. I'm so, so sorry," I said through a sob. I expected his arms to come around me then, to comfort me like he always did, but they didn't. Fear left my insides cold. I wanted to look at him. To see the expression on his face, but I was terrified that I had pushed him too far this time.

"I didn't mean for any of this to happen." Words began to gush out of my mouth as I told him the whole horrific story that Dakota had told me. If he knew the gruesome details of the story maybe, somehow, he would forgive me.

After a long silence, he turned to me, looking tired. So tired. "I am not mad at you, Tamara, I just want you to understand how crazy this whole thing got. I could have lost you tonight."

"I know. I am so sorry. I shouldn't have brought Ryan to the diner. I just couldn't see any other way. He was going to kill us." Graciously, Joe's arms engulfed me then, and I lost myself in another round of tears, crushing my head into his shoulder. "I'm so sorry," I said again through a muffled sob.

"I was so scared." His grip around me tightened, and then he also broke. "I love you so much, Tamara," he said through cracked, fragile breaths. "If you had died, I would have died in the bottle."

We held each other and cried. We were two lovers caught in the eye of the storm, holding on for dear life. There was still so much to say between us, but we were both too emotionally spent to talk anymore, and that was okay. After what seemed like a waterfall of tears spilled from both of us, we eventually lay back and let a merciful slumber take us under.

CHAPTER 58

December 23, 11:00 a.m.

TAMARA

Joe's arms were locked around me like vice grips when I woke the next morning, or was it afternoon? So much for him sleeping on the floor. At this point, what did it matter? After the turmoil, we needed the security of each other's arms. I looked over at the clock. Eleven. We'd slept for over ten hours.

Was Dakota still sleeping? I listened for a minute.

The house was silent.

Gently, I worked my way out of Joe's embrace, careful not to wake him, and tiptoed into the bathroom. It would be good to have some time with Dakota before he woke. I went to the toilet, washed my hands then headed downstairs to the living room. The comforter that Dakota slept under was in a wrinkled mess at the end of the couch, but she wasn't there.

I scanned the room, an eerie feeling opening in my stomach. The jar of my brother's ashes sat on Joe's coffee table next to a folded piece of paper. Head spinning, I crept toward the table, then picked up the note and unfolded it.

Hey, sis,

I'm so sorry, but I can't stick around. I hope you realize your love and forgiveness means the world to me. You said you wanted to be the change in our family. With the kind of love you have inside of you, I think maybe you can pull it off. I wish I were strong like you, but I can't face the rest of our family after what I've taken from them. I'm going to go somewhere to get the help I've needed for a long time. Please forgive me for leaving like this and for what I've taken from you. This will be the last time.

Love always, Dakota

At the bottom of the page was our parents' address.

Sucker punch right in the sternum. Tears stung my eyes as I looked down at the jar of ashes and back at the note. These were the only things I had left of my brother and my sister.

"Tamara?" I was vaguely aware of Joe calling my name.

I stumbled down the hall to the front door, out onto the porch, and took in a large gulp of air, scanning the driveway. Where was my car?

Another blow to my abdomen. *Please forgive me for leaving like this and for what I've taken from you. This will be the last time.*

Unbelievable. Un-freaking-believable. She took my car.

"Tamara?" Joe's voice again.

He couldn't know this. He'd hate Dakota forever. His footsteps came toward me. I needed a moment to assimilate this, but I was out of time.

"What's going on?"

I turned toward him.

Joe walked to me, rubbing the sleep from his eyes, hair disarrayed.

"Dakota's gone," I whispered.

He glanced at me and then around the driveway, confusion settling over his features. "Where's your car?"

"She took it."

Shock and anger rushed over his face. "You mean she stole it?" He walked into the driveway barefoot and looked down the road. "That's it. I'm not going to let her get away with this. Not this time," he said through gritted teeth.

"What is that supposed to mean?"

"I'm calling the cops." He came back to the porch.

"Joe, no!" I grabbed hold of his arm. "You can't."

He narrowed his eyes, pulling away from my grip. "She stole your ring and now your car, and you're just going to let her get away with it?"

"She's confused. I pushed her too hard. I should have never pressured her to go to our parents together."

"How can you be defending that—" He clenched his jaw shut and composed himself before speaking again. "Tamara, this is textbook enabling behavior. If you don't send her a clear message, the cycle will continue forever."

"I don't care what you say. We are not calling the cops. She'd never forgive me."

Joe gaped. "Do you hear yourself? She's the one who needs forgiveness. You don't deserve what she's doing to you."

"She didn't deserve me abandoning her either!" I pushed past him and back into the living room.

Joe followed. "You can't always save people, Tamara. Sometimes you just have to let them go."

"So, that's it, just let her go?" My voice elevated as I turned around. "That's your answer? Do you expect me to forget about my family as if they never existed?"

"That is not what I am saying." Joe threw his hands in the air, his tone harsh. "But this insanity has to stop."

"Or what? You going to leave me like you did all day yesterday."

Joe flinched, hurt overshadowing his features. "No, T. That's not what I'm saying. I don't want to lose you."

I took in a deep breath as the anger drained from my body. I didn't want to lose him either. "I shouldn't have said that. I'm reeling right now, Joe. I just found out yesterday my brother died, and now I have to go tell my family without Dakota."

"I'm more than sorry about that, but you can't keep chasing someone who is continually hurting us. You're better off without her."

The bitter words injured my soul. "This isn't like you, Joe!"

"What? To actually show that I have feelings? Well, I do, and they hurt just as bad as yours! You lost your brother yesterday, and I am so sorry for that. But Tamara, I lost something yesterday too and it was because of her."

"Dakota's the victim!" I yelled. "I abandoned her. If you're going to blame anyone, blame me."

"Oh, come on, Tamara. You can't possibly believe that. She was doing drugs before you left her. She chose this life. You didn't. It's insane to think you can save her."

"Now you are calling me insane?"

"This whole thing is insane."

"How can you have such little compassion? What Gabriel did to her could have been me. I could have turned out just like her."

"You're nothing like her! She's poison. She'll consume your whole life if you keep letting her."

"How can you say that?"

"Damn it, Tamara. She stole everything from us." Joe swung his hands in the air, hit a lamp, and it went crashing to the ground.

I looked at the shards of glass scattered across the wooden floor in shock. What was happening?

He stared dejectedly at the broken lamp for a beat, sighed, and sat down on the couch.

"What in the hell was that?"

"I don't know, Tamara. I'm just angry and, honestly, so very tired." Joe stared at the floor, dejected. "I feel like you're more concerned about your family than you are me at the moment. They've only ever given you grief. I've held you through your deepest pain, and now when I need you, I'm getting nothing in return." A storm waged in his tired eyes. "I can't keep doing this anymore. The fight is gone, and I can't keep going."

His expression unnerved me. I was losing him. I had pushed him too far. "What are you saying, Joe?"

"I don't know." He blew out a breath, gaze down.

In so many ways, Joe *was* right. I wished so badly I could let my family go. I wished I could forget the past and move forward with this incredible man in front of me. I gently placed my hand on his arm. As I did, the vision I had the day before played through my mind in a split second. Jesus gathering my family together, Gabriel's ashes blowing around us and the beautiful garden springing up beneath our feet.

It's time, beloved.

The familiar rush of the Holy Spirit flooded through me and I knew beyond reason, I had to go. Joe may have been done, but I was just getting started with this journey.

"Joe, please look at me." We made eye contact, and a dam burst inside of me. I had to go forward with my family and as much as it hurt, I'd be doing it alone. "Joe, I love you more than life itself, but I have their address now, and it's time for me to face them. I feel God leading me in this."

Hurt flickered across his features. "That's it, huh? I guess I can't argue with God." His tone was flat. Distant.

A tear fell down my cheek, and I brushed it away. "I'm sorry, Joe. I *have* to do this."

"So that's it, you're going to leave me two days before Christmas to deal with this mess by myself?"

I looked down at the ashes, my soul coming apart at its seams. "Please, Joe, I'm begging you to understand. My brother died five years ago, and my parents and the rest of my family don't even know. Just come with me, and we can deal with it later." Even as I said the words, I felt him pull away.

"I can't go down this road with you any longer."

"And I can't stop now." Standing, I pushed back the flood

of emotions and grabbed Gabriel's ashes along with Dakota's note off the coffee table.

Joe grabbed a hold of my wrist.

I exhaled and met his gaze. His eyes held a deep, beseeching expression that caused my heart to fumble. I didn't want to leave him, but I had to go. "I'm sorry, Joe. I have to do this."

"How, Tamara? You don't even have a car."

"I'll figure it out." My heart shattered as I walked out the door. A part of me wanted Joe to run after me, to beg me to stay. A part of me wanted to turn around and beg for his forgiveness. Instead, I stepped forward with fresh resolve. Though it may have just cost me everything, I pushed forward. My vision blurred as tears rolled down my cheeks. I pulled out my phone and clicked on the Uber app. It was time to face my past, and this time I'd have to do it alone.

CHAPTER 59

December 23, 4:17 p.m.

TAMARA

"Landslide" by Fleetwood Mac played through my ear buds as I stared out the bus window. Outside the sky was gray, and most of the trees had lost their leaves. It was winter in my soul as much as it was outside.

I rested my head against the window and thought of everything that had transpired over the last month. So. Much. Loss.

A tear slid down my face. At least I had the whole back row to myself. It had only been an hour since we'd left Vancouver, three more hours until we passed through Aberdeen. I thought about the look in Joe's eyes as I walked out the door, and my heart sunk even farther, deepening the anguish. I prayed that somehow, someway, Joe would forgive me for leaving—for running straight into the eye of the storm. At this moment, I questioned my own sanity.

Be strong and courageous, for I am with you. Even until the end. The words Jesus had spoken to me in the vision with the ashes ran through my mind and chills ran down my spine. What else would lay ahead of me that I would need to be courageous for? It already felt like I'd lost everything I cared about, but I couldn't deny I felt God's presence pushing me forward. It didn't make sense. Why would he lead me away from Joe when he needed me the most? Joe deserved so much better than I had given him. He'd loved me so well over the months, and now he was hurting, and I had left him to fend for himself? It didn't seem right. Maybe I was going insane.

I pulled out my journal to try to write down my thoughts in an attempt to make sense of it all. The future seemed bleak no matter which way I turned. Things could go well with my family, but I may have lost Joe forever. Then there was the possibility that my family would reject me.

The page opened to the short list of promises I had begun in my journal.

Beauty for ashes.
Dad will walk me down the aisle.

The last one was scratched out. At this point, that was the one that was hardest to believe. It would mean not one relationship restored, but two. I closed my eyes again and remembered back to David's office and the miracle God had done inside of me. That wonderful moment helped me fight the pain and the doubt that any good could come out of my future. I pushed away the fear and darkness.

With the remaining strength I had inside of me, I rewrote the last promise. *Dad will walk me down the aisle to Joe.* I had to believe my dad would walk me down the aisle. I had to believe my family would be restored. I had to believe Joe and I would find our way back to each other.

A single flame of hope settled deep down inside my heart. One day my winter would turn to spring. The sun would rise. Flowers would grow. Warmth would fill me once again. It was a faint hope—a whisper so quiet I could barely hear it.

The last day I had attended Hope Chapel, while I was still

pregnant, David had preached a sermon on Romans and used a scripture that said all things work together for good for those who love God. I had hung on every word as he spoke, resting my hand on my basketball sized belly. I knew then that the day was coming when I would say goodbye to the precious life I was carrying, and I believed God was giving me a promise that would bring me through. In many ways it strengthened me through those first few dark weeks. Could the same promise carry me through this?

I wasn't sure how God could bring good from any of this heartbreak. My brother dying, my sister disappearing yet again, Joe's dreams burning down, and now our relationship gone. It did not seem possible, but I had to believe my story wasn't over. Things were far from good, which had to mean this was not the end. I closed my eyes once again and hoped it was true.

This was not the end.

Dear Reader

You may be wondering why we decided to end the book the way we did. Why bring Joe and Tamara through so much? Why not give them a happy ending in this book? Because the truth is, Jesus does not promise us an easy life. In fact, following him often makes life more challenging as he leads us into battle.

A few years ago, I felt God leading me in a clear direction that would require me to change my whole life. I set out on this beautiful walk of faith with fresh excitement because I believed he would honor my sacrifice and dedication, and great things would happen. Instead, the winds of adversity began to blow, beating against my naive expectations. God had not led me down an easy path but one that would teach me things that only trials can—perseverance.

I found myself in the fight of my life, and as I continued to move forward, there were great losses. During this time, my father passed away, my husband lost his job, and many of my expectations were shattered. Every blow I took, every disappointment and pain I received, I felt like Rocky Balboa being beaten down by Apollo Creed, unable to win. I wanted to run away, to surrender to depression and give up, but I fought daily to keep my hope alive.

Looking back, I don't believe that God caused any of the hardships, but he did lead me into the wilderness to face the enemy of my soul to reveal my true identity as an overcomer. Through it all, I learned that God is not afraid of the mess that comes out of our hearts, and he is there to comfort us in our pain. In fact, I realize now, much like a splinter, the lies in my heart had to be exposed to be healed and make room for the truth.

This journey of perseverance is one many of us are on. In the face of great adversity, we are forced to ask ourselves if following our dreams is still worth it. Is God still good in the midst of pain? Is love worth fighting for, even when your world feels like it is collapsing?

I want to respond to you right now with a resounding yes. To all of it.

I want to encourage you, dear reader, if you are walking through hell, keep walking, even if you have to crawl. Just like Joe and Tamara, this is not the end of your story. You will get through the pain, and you will receive your promises.

Blessings in Christ,
Elisheba Haxby & Jesse Vincent
ElishebaHaxby@gmail.com
AuthorJesseVincent@gmail.com

Next in Series

Thank you for reading Ninety-Nine Ashes!
If you enjoyed it, continue the series with:

Book 3: Ninety-Nine Promises

First chapter of Ninety-Nine Promises below:

December 23, 5:20 p.m. - Tamara

"When is your check out date?" The rail-thin man behind the counter asked.

Great question. My head throbbed behind my temples. I pulled out the debit card to Joe's and my joint account—the one we'd been adding to for months—the one meant for our wedding and honeymoon. A lump formed in the middle of my throat as I pushed the card toward the man. "I'm not sure."

He gave me a tentative smile and picked up the card. "The system needs a date. You can always change it if need be."

I looked down at the fake hardwood floors and swallowed hard. "How about a week?" Hopefully that would be long enough. Maybe my parents would invite me to stay with them for a while. Yeah, right. If they reacted anything like Dakota, they'd slam the door in my face and send me packing.

"Okay, perfect. We have you checking out the thirtieth then." He slid the card back to me, along with two room keycards. "You'll be in Room 206 for the week." He gave directions to the room and told me where the guest laundry was. "If you have any questions, just dial nine."

I gathered my things and drug them across the parking lot. Outside was frigid and damp with an arctic breeze rolling off the water from the harbor. Aberdeen Washington was on the southern tip of the Olympic Peninsula and had the constant smell of salt water in the air. It made me ache for the ocean. Somehow, I'd have to find a ride to Ocean Shores while I was here. Perhaps then I could find Charlie and finally thank him for his kindness years ago. *Two birds. One stone.*

Thoughts of me standing in front of the water, watching the waves roll on the shore and seagulls mining the beach for food comforted my heart. I *definitely* needed the ocean now. I walked up the stairs to the second floor, pulling my duffel bag behind me. My room was the sixth door down. The inside was basic and clean, but it had a musty old carpet smell, not too different from my apartment in Vancouver. I plopped down onto the bed and sighed. What now? My stomach growled, but I ignored it.

Lying back, my mind spun around the next possible move. When I had mapped it earlier, my parents' house was a mere four-minute walk from this hotel. Besides the affordability, this was the number one reason I had decided to stay here. But now that I was this close, my courage waned. What was I going to do anyway? Knock on the door with Gabriel's ashes, only to tell them their son was dead, and that Dakota had been his victim for years without them noticing. Bile stung my throat, and I closed my eyes. Taking in a large breath, I waited for the sick anxious feeling to pass. After a few minutes calming myself, I rolled off the bed and headed to the door, leaving the jar of ashes. The bad news could wait for now.

Before I could talk myself out of it, I marched toward my parents' house, determination in my steps. I hadn't walked away from everything that mattered in Vancouver to chicken out now. The sun dipped behind the horizon as I walked, and the sky glowed with an intense orange hue. Slowing, I took in the beauty. For a brief moment, peace washed over me, strengthening me to move forward. A few minutes later, I stood in front of the address Dakota had left me. The place was small and plain but taken care of. An older home with light brown siding, the windows trimmed with white. Definitely an upgrade from the trailer park.

On the street in front of the house was parked a burgundy log truck semi, its rear tires folded up over the front ones. I took a closer look. In the dim lighting, it was hard to read, so I pulled out my cell phone and switched on the flashlight. The logo on the side of the truck said Jensen's Trucking. Nice. After all those years of dreaming about it, my dad finally owned a business. I turned back to the house. It was fairly dark, but a light beamed from a window in the middle of the building.

A flurry of wind rushed through my hair, and I wrapped my jacket tighter around me. I glanced up and down the street. The neighborhood was quiet, everyone settled in for the winter night. I noticed then that the driveway was empty. I slowly crossed the manicured grass, feet unsteady as I crept to the lit window. My heart raced as I peered through the glass. My father sat in an old leather recliner, a beer in hand. He looked exactly how I thought he would, thick salt and pepper hair and a tad more weight around his midsection. Other than that, he looked the same as he always had. A ruggedly handsome face with a sturdy jawline set like the world had been hard on him. He focused on a boxing match on the fifty-inch flat screen television across the room from him. The new appliance didn't match the rest of the room. The floors were chipped hardwood with an ancient oriental rug in the center covering its flaws. The furniture was mismatched—an array of Goodwill specials, no doubt. The television, though, appeared almost brand new. Priorities. On the screen, the two men pounded each other. Head shot. Head shot. Abdomen. Dad winced a few times and made the occasional air jab along with the contenders.

Behind the television, the walls were lined with photographs of children I didn't recognize. At the end of the line of photos was a portrait of a family. Was that my brother Nathan? His arms were around a beautiful brunette with two small children in front of them. Emotions prickled in my throat. Nathan was married? From the picture, he looked quite happy. And I was an aunt? What else had I missed? Why did they only have pictures of them on the wall? Where was Josiah? Had he disappeared too?

Sounds of an engine coming around the corner startled me from my spying, and I ducked behind the house. The car stopped in the driveway and a door slammed.

"Paul!" the woman hollered. "I need help with these groceries."

My heart jumped at the sound of her voice. *Mom*. I hadn't heard that wonderful sound for six long years. My body screamed to run to her, but I stayed perfectly still. Frozen. A few moments later, I shook myself out of it and crept back to the window. Mom came through the door, two brown paper bags loaded with groceries in her arms.

"You gonna help me? The car's full."

"Not now. The fight's on." Dad took a swig of his half-finished beer.

Sadness and then frustration flickered in her tired eyes. *Oh Mom*. Longing made my stomach twist as I took in her appearance. The years hadn't treated her well. Her dark hair, once vibrant and thick, was now dull and stringy. She was thinner than I remembered, which made her face a bit sunken, but if I looked long enough, I could still see the beauty in her vacant features.

She sighed and set the bags on the table before heading back outside. My heart ached for her. In that one interaction, I saw the loneliness she had endured over the years at the selfishness of my father. Why couldn't he just pause the stupid fight and help her for five minutes? The door opened and closed four more times before the car was unloaded. Why so much food? Did other people live with them? Or was it Christmas dinner? That was probably it. Would Nathan and Josiah be in town for the holidays?

I ducked away from the window. This was the time to let them know I was here, but somehow, I couldn't. I was frozen. Literally and figuratively.

"Theresa!" Dad yelled as if she was far away. "Grab me another beer."

"Grab it yourself. I'm putting the groceries away."

My heart pounded against my chest, and for a split second I was a helpless little girl hiding under my bed, praying for the fighting to stop. I peeked into the window again and saw my father rising to his feet, face red. He stomped into the kitchen and took hold of my mom's arm, squeezing it hard. She winced, pain mangling her features.

"I don't work all week for this. When I say get me a beer, that means get me a beer. Got it?" he yelled in her face.

After all these years, nothing had changed. My entire childhood played before my eyes. The fighting. The abuse. The overwhelming sense of being alone. It all shattered inside of me at once. Why was I here? Why would God tell me to come? Why would God bring me back to the brokenness and pain? Before I could think of another agonizing question, I ran with all my might back to the hotel room.

I burst through the door, chest burning, gasping for air. My body ached for Joe. I wished desperately he was with me now, to have his strong arms around me, holding me together. Why would God lead me to face this alone? It seemed cruel. I paced the hotel room, wishing for answers, hoping for comfort, but nothing came. A thousand memories crashed over my mind at once, good mingling with the bad. My mom, when she was home with us, had been a great cook. On special occasions, the house would be riddled with pastries and cookies she'd made from scratch. When my dad was in a good mood, the house would be filled with his baritone voice, singing and being silly with us kids. Those moments were rare, though, and usually ended with someone being beat or my parents arguing. Sounds of my dad's angry voice berating my mother pounded in my ears. *How dumb are you, Theresa? It's like your paralyzed from the neck up.* Why hadn't she left him years ago? Why hadn't she protected us from him?

Maybe Joe had been right this whole time. Finding my family was a mistake. It wasn't like I could change the past, and I sure as hell couldn't change a thing here. I wasn't strong enough for this. I picked up my phone and scrolled to Joe's name. The injured look on his face right before I had left him sitting on his couch came before me. I'd hurt him deeply, and I wasn't sure there was a way to fix the damage between us. God had brought us back together before. I hoped beyond reason he would do it again.

Dejected, I sat down on the bed, with nothing to distract me from the sorrow and loss. Nobody here to hold me as the emotional turbulence came. My whole being longed for Joe. Guilt came with a massive torrent of grief as his last words played through my mind.

So that's it, you're leaving me two days before Christmas to clean up this mess by myself?

I didn't deserve his comfort. He needed mine, and I had left him for *this*. I scrolled to his name once more, finger hovering over the send button. Maybe it wasn't too late. Maybe I could plead insanity. Maybe if I begged hard enough, he'd forgive me and come rescue me from this hell. Tears rolled down my face, and I tossed the phone aside. As much as it hurt, I'd left this morning because I felt God leading me here. If I gave up now without giving him a chance to show me why, it would haunt me for the rest of my life. Besides, I couldn't go back to Vancouver yet, not without at least talking to my parents and telling them the truth.

Dread crashed over my soul. Facing my parents with the jar of Gabriel's ashes, telling them the secret Dakota had held all these years, suddenly felt like an impossible task.

God, I need your help, I'm sinking here. I buried my head in my hands, grief drowning me in its undertow.

Several times over the last few days, I'd heard God clearly, but now his voice felt a thousand miles away, and all I could think of was the way my dad clutched my mother's arms as he yelled at her. The act was mild in comparison to what he was capable of. Why had it set me off like it had? Angry tears fell down my face. That one act showed that nothing had changed. They may have been in a nicer house and owned their business, but underneath the rage was still alive and as active as it ever had been. I wiped my face and tried to shove down the memories that battered my insides like the boxers on my dad's big screen TV.

Snatching the remote, I flicked on the television to distract me from the unbearable torment in my chest. I flipped through the channels quickly, but nothing caught my interest. I needed to talk to someone. I needed to sort out this mess inside of my heart. I grabbed the phone again, scrolling through the names. Claire? No. Trudy? Definitely not. Joe? I stared at his name for a long time, praying that he'd call me. That he'd send me some sort of sign that we would be okay, but nothing came, and the agony in my heart increased. Finally, I swiped the contacts away and opened the safari app and googled Midways in Ocean Shores, hoping Charlie still worked there. I tapped on the phone number, and it dialed.

Three rings and someone answered. "Midways, this is Charlie."

For a moment, my voice was lost in shock. What would I even say after all this time?

"Hello. Anyone there?"

"Charlie?" It was all I could spit out.

"Yes? Can I help you?"

"Um... It's Tamara. I was just—"

"Tamara Jensen?" His voice changed from polite to surprised. "My goodness, how have you been? I can't believe it. I was seriously just thinking about you."

"Really?"

"Yes, really. You were on my heart when I woke up this morning. I said a prayer for you."

I smiled through the tears that had spilled over. The praying bartender. God had his soldiers in the most unlikely places. Back in Ocean Shores before I even had a thought of God, Charlie had been there, pointing the way toward him like a lighthouse in the midst of a storm. "Thank you for that. I could use all the prayers I can get right now."

"What's wrong?"

I pinched the bridge of my nose and sighed. "It's a really long story."

In the background, someone yelled out a drink order. "Hold on a sec." There was a muffled response from Charlie, and then he was back. "Sorry about that. What's going on with you?"

"This probably isn't the best time. You sound busy. What are you doing the next few days?"

He hesitated before answering. "I was actually heading out of town for Christmas. My family has a cabin rented up the McKenzie River in Oregon. It's the most central location for everyone."

Christmas. Of course, he wouldn't be available. I glanced around the dingy hotel room. This was what my Christmas would probably look like. "Okay, yeah. That makes sense. I was calling because I'm in Aberdeen. I'm not sure how long I'll be here. I thought it would be great to see you while I'm close."

"I would love that. I'll only be gone a few days. Why don't you give me your number, and I'll call you as soon as I get back into town?"

"Perfect." I said, but disappointment and loneliness weighed down my insides. I rattled off my number with the promise of connecting before leaving town and hung up.

I stood, went to my duffel and pulled out Gabriel's ashes. No matter what my childhood had been like, my parents deserved to know the truth. Then and only then could the healing actually begin. More tears came. Could there ever be true healing for us? Was God big enough to put the shattered parts of my family back together? Did I even want that? In every dark corner of my past, there had been brokenness and heartache. Anger welled up inside of me. All of the abuse and neglect had led to this. My sister molested and turned junkie. My brother—her abuser—dead. I hated him for what he did to Dakota, but my Lord, is this what he deserved? To die at the hands of a psychopath, burned to oblivion on a heap of ash? Stomach wrenching, sobs clawed up my throat. "God, why? It hurts too much. I can't do this alone!" I cried through a gasp. "I hate what Gabriel did. I hate what my parents did." I set the ashes aside and pounded the bed with my fist. "I'm angry, God! I'm so angry. Why did you let this happen to me? Why didn't you stop it?" For hours, I cried, the bitter sorrow crashing over me in turbulent waves, ebbing and flowing with the inner storm. As the tears subsided, a strange calm rested over my soul, and I heard the faintest whisper.

I'm angry too.

Was that God? He was also angry? That didn't make sense. I flipped over and more tears rolled down my cheeks. As I closed my eyes, a picture came into my mind, playing before my vision like a movie projector. I was five or six years old, waiting for my dad to come home. He'd been on the road an extra week, and last time I'd spoken to him, he'd promised he'd bring me home a surprise. After school that day, I'd put on my prettiest dress and had my mom braid my hair. Back then, I was Daddy's little girl, and he could do no wrong. Sure, he got angry sometimes, but it was never toward me, and in my underdeveloped mind, my siblings or Mom were at fault.

That day, when Dad came home in his semi, I ran to meet him. He had climbed from the truck, a huge smile on his handsome face. Then he'd lifted my tiny frame and twirled me around. "So good to see you, Cupcake. I missed you."

"Missed you too, Daddy." He set me on the ground, turned to his truck, and brought out a large stuffed blue dog with floppy ears and a curly tail. I squished the dog against me, joy lighting my mood. "Thank you, Daddy. I love it." He'd tousled my hair and regarded me with a fond expression. "Now you'll have something to snuggle with when I'm on the road."

Tears spilled over at the memory. There was more to my dad than the anger and abuse. Under the pain lived a man who loved his children. A man who loved me. Could we somehow return to the simple love we'd shared when I was a child? Could there be healing for him? For us? In the middle of the questions, another phrase played through my head. *I will restore to you the years that the swarming locust has eaten.*

Chills covered my body. Another promise ...? I crossed the room and fetched my journal from my purse. I flipped it open to the page of promises I had written.

Beauty for Ashes
Dad will walk me down the aisle to Joe.

I stared at the second line, a flurry of emotions overwhelming me. With the anger I held toward my dad, I wasn't sure if I wanted him in my life, let alone to be in my wedding. There would have to be a lot of changes inside of me and even more changes inside of him... *Lord, help me with this.*

Underneath the short list, I wrote down the words *The years of my life will be restored.*

I closed my journal and my eyes again and whispered a prayer asking God to help me believe these promises would be fulfilled. There was a chance I was completely losing my mind, but these new words breathed fresh life into my being. There was still a ton of hurt under the surface, but perhaps tomorrow, after a good night's sleep, I'd have the courage to face my parents.

Acknowledgments

To Aubrey from Elisheba, for all your love, support and sacrifice. Through this journey you've been my rock and my soft place to land. I love you.

To Mom and Dad from Jesse, thank you for supporting my dreams and for always providing a safe place to come home to.

To Maddy Buck, thank you for believing in my dream, sometimes more than myself. You have been more than a best friend; you've been my greatest support, cheering me on through the hardest moments.

To our financial backers: Maddie Buck, Melanie Campbell, Gail Perry, Rita Jane, Diane Rivas, Susan Christian, Michael Affronte Jr, Derek Woodruff, Rosanne Croft, Diane Larsen, Theresa Kreckma, Cindie and Leyman Tedford, Emily Tedford, Jody Smith, Lindy Jacobs, Martha Artyomenko, Jessie Johnson —thank you for investing in our dream. Your generosity means the world to us.

To our beta readers: Marra Watson, Jessie Johnson, Grace Rocca, Martha Artyomenko, Gary Klassen, Elizabeth Pfaff, Jody Smith, Charlene Finley, Cathi Kilian, and Catherine Madera. Your input into this project was invaluable. This story is much better because of the feedback you gave.

To Christiana Tarabochia, thank you for helping grow this book into what it is. As always, your edits helped form the characters and dialog into something special.

To Kit Duncan, thank you for your hard work. Because of

your speed and integrity of work we were able to release this book on time. You are a rock star!

To Marni MacRae, thank you for your encouragement on this project. Your thoughts and insight were extremely valuable while shaping the characters of this book.

To all of our other family and friends who also go through the ashes of life with us, your love and support is cherished and so very appreciated.

About The Authors

Elisheba and Jesse met in Youth With A Mission in 2001. Elisheba was impressed by Jesse's creative mind and his dedication to story crafting. Jesse was impressed by Elisheba's deep walk with Jesus and her commitment to emotional authenticity. They became friends and years later decided to start writing together through a set of supernatural circumstances.

Jesse carried the idea for their first book, Ninety-Nine, since 1999. At the time he knew it was a download from God, but struggled to write from an emotionally raw woman's point of view. Throughout the years when bringing this frustration to God, God simply responded with "this is not your story." Then in 2010 Elisheba heard from God to start writing and that her stories would lead people into an encounter with the love of God. She brought this word to Jesse and it clicked for both of them to work together on this project. The idea was conceived and nine months later the first book was birthed.

The journey of writing and publishing was quite challenging, filled with many hurdles and mistakes. But every step of the way God met them, helped them, and healed them. Over the many years of writing together, learning the craft, and pursuing inner healing, they decided to start a business to help other authors do the same. They wanted to combine their belief that God wants to create through His people with the need to help creatives be healed enough to partner with God and produce this creativity. To do this, they founded Above The Sun, LLC.

For more writing by Elisheba Haxby, Jesse Vincent, and Above The Sun, please visit:

ElishebaHaxby.com
AboveTheSun.org

What's Your Story?

Above The Sun is a community of hope-filled creators who believe the world can be transformed through authentic stories. Our mission is to develop authors who are committed to becoming whole in order to successfully bring their message to their unique areas of influence. If you have a book in you and you are willing to do the work to release it, we would love to connect.

Visit us at AboveTheSun.org